The Lost Dragon

Gracie Carter

ISBN (paperback): 978-1-9163660-0-8
ISBN (ebook): 978-1-9163660-1-5

Cover created with Photoshop.
Cover dragon image from Vexels.com
All fonts under the Open Font License.

For Cotton Socks, Trinity, Violet and Dougal,
who loved eating important pieces of paper.

Chapter 1

The moon shone bright and the wind felt anxious, like it was holding it's breath, waiting for something to happen. I was shivering but I didn't bother to shut my window, might as well get used to the cold since it's going to be home pretty soon, and I needed to hurry. I looked at the clock on my bedside table. 11:23pm. Another half an hour or so to go.

Are you sure? Asked that little, rational voice in my head. I ignored it. The tears that rolled their way down my cheeks were fast and came in huge quantities, but I had to keep moving. A few items of clothing, first aid supplies, as much food and water as could be carried that we'd taken from the kitchen, penknife, matches, all frantically packed into my rucksack.

11:27pm.

Don't stop, go, go, go.

If we wanted a decent head-start we had to get out soon. We had to speed up, ignore the urge to grieve. That had to wait. I could hear my brother moving quickly around in his room, packing stuff up and moving as fast as he could. I zipped up my pack and moved over to my desk where I switched on my laptop. As it loaded and I just had to wait, my mind replayed the phone call over and over again, going over every detail as if it were still happening.

A terrible accident.

Stop.

Among those who couldn't make it out.

No.

Deepest condolences.

STOP.

As you are both under eighteen, there are things to discuss and complications to sort out, a social worker and a member of our agency will be dispatched to you immediately to talk things over and figure out what to do with you. They should reach you in approximately forty-five minutes.

Nope.

I could feel my heart thumping faster, my throat welling up and I allowed myself to sob twice. No more, the internet finally loaded so I focused on quickly logging into the bank's website. All the money in my savings account, collected since my first birthday and gradually added to through the years, I moved it all into my current account. I cleared all history, removed all apps, deleted all documents, except my photos. It's not like they could give away what we were about to do - we didn't fully know ourselves - and if there was even the slightest chance we'd be able to return, I'd want these back. I changed my important passwords and wrote them down on a piece of paper which I stuffed into a pocket on the rucksack.

As an extra precaution I made a few quick internet searches to do with Scotland; train tickets, living costs, hotel rooms, anything to imply that we were heading there. Was it too much? Was I overthinking this? If someone were to go searching through my laptop, they would find almost everything blank, just a load of photos and some unexplained searches about Scotland, nothing else.

Yeah, that's suspicious. Best to leave it blank and keep them guessing; I re-wiped it all. Finally I changed the master password into the computer - it had to be something completely random, unsentimental so that it couldn't be guessed. I looked around the room for inspiration.

'L@mpsh@d3', that would do. I probably put too much effort into clearing everything, but I wanted to make sure they would have nothing on us. I shut the laptop down and quickly put it back on my desk.

Next I ran downstairs to the big cupboard and dug through our assorted coats. I quickly found our sleeping bags shoved messily into their storage sacks since neither of us could be bothered to put them away properly last time we went camping. I looked at the huge pack containing the tent, considering whether or not to pick it up. No, that would be too heavy to carry, we'd just have to sleep under the stars. I grabbed our warmest coats along with the sleeping bags, shut the cupboard door and rushed back up the stairs as time continued ticking away from us. *We should be gone.* I thought.

As I got to the top of the stairs I met my brother coming out of the bathroom clutching towels, tissues and other bathroom-y things. His eyes were red and streaming with

3

a panicked look in them. We didn't say anything, just locked eyes for a moment before both breaking out into a run towards our rooms.

Actually we both went into his, and dumped our loads onto the floor. I chucked his sleeping bag at him and grabbed my own, and we both took them out of their packs to fold them properly and make them as small as possible.

"Time?" I asked. Tripp looked up at his clock on the wall behind me.

"Eleven thirty-seven." He said. "We *have* to hurry." He clipped the sleeping bag onto the strap of his rucksack and started stuffing what he'd brought from the bathroom inside it.

I nodded, hurriedly stood up with all my stuff and went into my room to do the same.

"Iris," He called, his voice filled with fear. "Did you clear your laptop and sort your bank account?" I could hear him getting frustrated with himself for not being able to get the words out quick enough.

"Yep, all done. We're gonna have to leave our phones here too aren't we?"

"Yeah, but make sure to wipe it first."

That could take time that we didn't have. I grabbed my phone and unlocked it, going into settings and making it wipe everything. For good measure I removed the SIM card and put it in my pocket - I'd put that in a public bin somewhere once we were outside, then put the phone on my bed, leaving it to forget my identity.

My heart stopped at the sound of the doorbell. I looked to the clock - 11:39pm.

No. This couldn't be happening, not yet.

With a face like he'd seen a ghost, Tripp entered my room wearing his boots, coat and rucksack.

"They're e-early." He whispered in a panic. I nodded. The doorbell rang again, this time accompanied by insistant knocking on the door.

"W-what do we do?" I started hyperventilating slightly. Tripp thought for a moment, clearly trying to stay calm. The nervous stammer was coming out in both of us.

"They'll t-take us. They'll take us away and make us work for them if they g-get in." I pointed out.

"Or they'll just k-kill us." He countered.

"Don't say that!"

"We're gonna have to go out the b-back. Not the door, that's too visible from their point of view and we need to be high enough to get over the garage door, so we'll have to go out of my w-window, we can climb along the roof and onto the shed." He instructed, thinking quickly. I nodded and quickly followed him into his room.

The knocking downstairs got louder and harsher, and we heard loud voices.

"Open up!"

We both flinched and began moving faster at that.

"They're gonna get in." I panicked, trying to remain calm.

"No- no they won't." Tripp cried, his voice racked with nerves. He opened the window and looked down. We were on the second story, but the dining room roof jutted out to the left.

"This is fine." His voice quivered as he began helping me out onto the roof, my heart pounding from the height combined with the yelling and thumping from the front door. I got out onto the roof, where the wind taunted us for not getting out earlier.

I stabilised myself as much as I could by holding onto the drainpipe, making sure not to look down as I held out the other hand to help Tripp. I scooted over as he clambered out and together we crouched so that both our hands and feet were gripping onto to the guttering while making our way along the edge of the sloped roof, moving as quickly as we could without missing our footing and slipping to, well probably not our deaths but still injury. As I moved along I froze at the noise below.

Our back door opened and someone stepped out, this must be the social worker, or the member of the agency. I shuffled back and gripped onto Tripp tightly, hoping he would take this as the way of telling him to keep quiet that I intended. We leaned back, lying down on the roof as much as we could - though we had to lie on our sides because of our oversized rucksacks - to minimise our visibility.

How the hell had they gotten in? And how many were there? Whoever it was called our names in what was clearly a woman's voice, though she showed no sign that she had actually seen us. I tried to breathe as silently as I could when I had to give up holding my breath, fighting every instinct to run. I turned my head to look back at Tripp but he had his head turned up to his window, which he'd managed to shut behind him, though obviously couldn't lock it from out here. If someone went in there, they would know instantly that we'd used it to escape. I could hear people stomping around and shouting our names inside the house.

At least two people were in there, possibly three. Lights in neighbouring houses came on as the ruckus awoke the surrounding world.

The woman moved around the corner of our backyard that really shouldn't be dignified with the word 'garden', more of a pathetic little courtyard.

Tripp turned his head to me and flicked his eyes towards the garage door. I nodded and began inching back towards the shed, trying to negotiate my rucksack into moving without scraping against the roof loudly enough to give us away.

The woman walked right below us, slow and leisurely, like she was deciding which bag of apples to get from the supermarket, rather than hunting for two teenagers.

With one hand behind me, holding up the rucksack ever so slightly, I managed to get to the corner. If we could just move around here, we could leap onto the shed roof and be high enough to climb over the garage door.

I almost froze when I saw him.

A huge man who looked like he could easily rip a horse in half entered Tripp's room and started looking around.

Both of us tried to move quicker. I started to maneuver around the corner, but it was hard with the cold air seizing up my muscles and trying to immobilise me.

My eyes locked onto the burly guy in Tripp's room who's blindspot we were just in thanks to the curtains and how close we were to passing onto the other side of the roof. I managed to make it round and began wriggling over as Tripp moved along with me.

We were so close.

Not close enough. I heard a yell from the house as we must have been spotted and I'm fairly sure I would've just lay there and died from fear if Tripp hadn't grabbed my hand, jumped up pulling me with him and yelled "RUN!" as he shoved me from the roof of our house onto the shed. It wasn't a big gap, only about a foot or so which I was grateful for since that meant it wasn't overly hard for me to scramble to my feet as Tripp leaped over the gap and grabbed my hand again. I held on tightly, vaguely hearing people yelling but what, I couldn't tell. I'd gone into some kind of adrenaline-induced daze where I was no longer fully aware of one what was going on around me, I just knew I had to keep moving and not let go of the hand I gripped onto. I didn't even fully register the pain as I hit the road of the back alley behind our row of houses.

I was almost blinded as the bright, movement-activated lights from the backs of the shops opposite suddenly came to life. I heard more yelling, some of which I think came from Tripp, but I'd hit my head on the ground during the fall and was now even further from reality. Everything seemed to slow down and speed up at the same time, like a dream in which I half knew I was dreaming but still couldn't wake up. Noises became more distant and I saw black spots floating in front of me as Tripp pulled me up and my new lack of balance forced me to lean on him as we moved as quickly as we could towards the end of the road, lights still suddenly coming to life as we passed more shops.

Now that I was standing up I could feel my head throbbing and burning, about to explode, the tears on my face burning into my skin like little fiery snakes. I couldn't tell if I was still actually crying or if my eyes were just watering but whatever was happening, I was in a lot of pain. I could sort of hear Tripp saying things, encouraging things I think, like "Just a little further.", "We're gonna make it.", "Just hold on to me, you'll be fine." How the hell was he staying so calm? Maybe he wasn't, maybe my damaged head was messing with me more than I thought, and he was panicking and screaming and my brain was just calming everything down.

I suddenly felt dizzy, sickeningly dizzy, while my head felt like it was going to explode and my ears rang with the sound of someone screaming.

Was that me? Was I doing it out-loud, or was it just my brain going into a state beyond shock?

I realised I was on the ground, but I hadn't fallen, I was sure of that. Tripp was down too, and he was sort of dragging me under something - a car. It was less windy under here, but just as freezing. The screaming in my ears had stopped, but I still wasn't sure whether or not it had ever been real. The dizziness subsided a bit now that I was lying still, but the pain went nowhere.

Tripp and I held onto one another for both warmth and comfort as I'm pretty sure people calling our names ran up and down the street, splitting up and eventually moving out of audible range. Either that or I blacked out, I'm not sure which happened first.

Chapter 2

When I woke up, I didn't know where I was for a second.
But then I remembered; my parents were dead and their
company was after me and my twin brother because we
knew they existed, and that meant we knew too much.
We were now Iris and Tristan the orphans.
It was still dark outside which I took as a good sign - I'd
been unconscious for a few hours at most. I was
underneath a car on the cold, hard road, lying on my side
with a soft towel acting as a pillow. My head was in a
horrifying amount of pain, like I'd just been hit quite
badly.
Next to me, Tripp was lying on his back, staring up at the
mechanisms of the car and twiddling his thumbs. I poked
him in the neck to get his attention, so that I didn't make
any sounds, in case there was anyone unwanted around.
He quickly turned his head and, upon seeing me awake
pulled me into a tight hug. He breathed a heavy sigh of
relief before whispering, "Oh my god, you're awake. Are

you okay? You hit your head and it's my fault and I'm so, so sorry." He sounded like he'd just been crying, which obviously he had but I had no idea how long he'd been alone in the cold, dark with nothing to do but dwell on the fact that he was now an orphan hiding from people who likely wanted him dead, with his now potentially brain-damaged sister passed out next to him, beating himself up for being responsible for said potential brain-damage.

"It's okay, I'm fine it's not your fault, I'm fine." I felt myself welling up at the words, trying to reassure both him and myself that I was okay.

"Fine?" He sounded skeptical.

"My head hurts a bit, but I'm okay." I whispered, trying to ignore the sense of panic, wondering if I really was okay.

He held onto me for a little while longer, before I eventually asked him, "How long was I out?"

He let go of me and looked at his watch, I'm pretty sure he was squinting but it was hard to tell since our only light source was a tiny amount of light seeping under the car from the streetlamp on the pavement next to us, which would've been why he was squinting.

"About three hours. I think."

"That's not too bad then, is it?" I asked, despite the hammering I could feel on my skull. The movement of my jaw as I spoke jarred it slightly too.

Tripp was silent for a minute, before saying, "Theoretically." Sounding like he was trying not to sound too concerned. "Can you move all your limbs? Your toes and fingers?"

I moved my ears up and down a few times to check, then moved down through my body to my toes. Everything seemed to be working fine.

"Yeah, all good." I tried not to move too much. Everything was able to move, but it all ached too. Tripp put his fingers on my neck to check my pulse, then my forehead to check my temperature.

"Can you remember everything?" He asked, still concerned.

"I- I think so." I said, recalling the terror I'd felt right up until I went down under the car. Things had become hazy, but I remembered. I told him what had happened, and he listened, making sure I got it all right.

"What's your full name?" he continued, checking everything was still there, not just the immediate past.

"Iris Christina Reynolds." I said certainly.

"And mine?"

"Tristan Alexander Reynolds." I started calming down as he kept me talking.

"What's our nickname for each other?"

"Rainbow."

"What's your favorite band?" He sounded more confident in my health as we went on.

"Scouting for Girls."

"Which you find hilarious because?" I heard the shadow of a smile creep up on his face at this question, and I did the same as I answered.

"Ironically, neither of us are." I said, satisfied.

"Good. Tell me if anything starts to feel off. Anything at all." He said insistently.

"I will. Are they still here?" I squinted and looked around, my vision was a little blurry but I blamed that on the dark.

"They came back a couple of times, went to the house again, and I'm pretty sure they went into the pub and asked about us." All traces of smiles or happiness were gone.

"Because we live in the world of *Tangled*?"

"Exactly. I think they're properly gone now though. They know we're not hanging around. They'll be looking for us elsewhere, probably going to relatives' houses, then later they'll likely tell school that our parents-" He choked up and took a deep breath. "Tell them about the accident, except they'll say it was a car accident or a factory fire or something, and that we've been taken in by an aunt who lives far away and they need the school to give them all of our academic records to be transferred to our new school. They'll already have a lot of information on us and our situation, so the school will easily believe that our records are being given to the correct authorities and hand them over with few questions asked for privacy reasons, since we will no longer be students there. So SCREB will know even more about how our brains work and might be able to predict where we'll go more easily. We will almost definitely be caught and killed in the next six to eight weeks. We're screwed. The universe has screwed us over, royally." He finished. He'd clearly thought this through a lot.

"Not necessarily." I croaked, not very convincingly, trying to be just a tiny bit optimistic.

"I've had a lot of time to think this through." He sounded deeply pessimistic.

"Yeah, but with your sad brain." I continued the pointless endeavour of trying to be an optimist. Thoughts and plans can't be formed properly when the brain is fogged with this much grief.

"No, Rainbow, just my brain. Imbecile."

"You're an imbecile."

"You're the one that got a concussion."

"I thought that was your fault for pushing me?" I managed to almost smile as I won the exchange, before Tripp gave me a gentle thump in my stomach. I returned the gesture. Then we lay there, staring up at nothing in particular, thinking our thoughts, allowing ourselves to cry about what our lives had become in such a short amount of time. Just one phone call changed everything. If our phones had been on silent, we might still be up, competing in Mario Kart and knowing we were up too late but not worrying because our parents were going to be away all week and tomorrow was a non-pupil day. We could still be living in a world where on Friday night, we'd bake some flapjacks and greet our parents at the door, happy to see them for the first time since Monday morning. But that wasn't going to happen, because Tripp had answered his phone. Answered the person who changed the course of our lives in just a two minute phone call. Answered the person who made it so that we were orphans.

I'm not sure when exactly I drifted off, and it was so cold and hard on the road that I don't think I would've if my head was okay, but as it was I couldn't stop myself from entering a dreamless sleep that I was awoken from by Tripp shaking me.

"We fell asleep, how's your head?" He sounded frantic, whispering as loudly as he could while still actually whispering, and I knew why. Daylight was approaching and we had to be gone before the rest of the world woke up and people started stirring. I tried to put together coherent thoughts in the ten seconds I'd been awake. "Ugh- okay, I think."

"You really should be just resting for the next couple of days, but we have to go. Are you gonna be okay to walk?" He asked, as if we had another option. My head didn't feel very different from how it had before I fell asleep, though the throbbing had gone down slightly.

"Yeah, I'll be fine." I propped myself up on my elbows, sitting up as far as I could for Tripp to put my pillow-towel back in his bag.

Only now did I realise there was blood on it.

We rolled out from under the car and were able to stand up, looking around cautiously. The prospect of being seen by anyone - SCREB or otherwise - made me fully awake and alert very quickly. We were standing in the tiny car park behind the chiropractor's office at the end of our road, a car park that is so unextraordinary you could walk up and down the street twice and not remember it was there if you weren't specifically looking for it.

The wind had died down now, but it was still cold and the street was cast in a frosty, blue haze as the darkness began to subside. It was still dark enough to move under the cover of the night, but it wouldn't be for long.

"Time?" I asked. Tripp looked at his watch, able to see it better now.

"Quarter-past-six." He looked over at me. "You sure you're gonna be okay? Walking is one thing, but once we meet up with Zen and Delta-"

"We don't really have another choice. We have to be gone as soon as possible, and I've already slowed us down enough. I'm okay, I swear." I tried to mean it. My head

15

wasn't exactly killing me, I'd be okay to walk. If it was summer, the heat once the sun hit would probably be too much, but right now in mid-November, I'd be able to cope with walking. Walking meant I'd keep my feet on the ground. The next bridge, I would cross when we came to it.

Tripp didn't look happy but he nodded as he put his rucksack back on. He knew that we had to get moving, he knew very well, he was just worried. We started walking away from the car we'd been sheltering under, in the opposite direction from last night. He'd been smart about that, I hadn't twigged it in my dazed state, but if our roles had been reversed, if I was guiding him to safety, I would've taken us this way - towards where we were going now - and almost definitely gotten us caught. But Tripp knew we wouldn't be able to get far enough away in such a short amount of time so he took us to the tiny car park that no one ever paid any attention to, and tucked us away under a car in the corner.

We didn't talk for a while as we walked, which was perhaps not a good idea as it meant we had little to distract ourselves from what was going on. I felt both utterly empty and ready to burst at the same time, I didn't really want to walk anywhere. Not because of my head, because I just wanted to curl up in my bed and cry and sleep this all away. I looked over at Tripp, he was looking down, but I could see that his eyes were red - he, like me, was on the brink.

I listened to the seagulls beginning their morning squawking that I'd heard pretty much every morning of my life. The neighbors hated it, but I never minded. It was just seagulls being seagulls, like how you put on a private concert for all your invisible fans when no one else is home.

At the end of our road we turned the corner to make a quick stop at the ATM. I retrieved my wallet from my pocket and took out the bank card before removing every last penny from my bank account (well, everything that could be taken out in notes, there was about £3.50 left in there). I probably wouldn't need much, for now at least, but anyone who was after us could find exactly where we were by locating where we were getting our money from, so if we got it all out now, we'd be safe on that front if no other.

Tripp did the same and we both wadded up the cash and put most of it in the inside pockets of our rucksacks, just slipping a few notes into our wallets so that they would be more accessible.

We turned around and continued our 30-second trek to the train station at the end of our road. My vision sharpened as we walked, which made me relax a little about my possible brain-damage.

As we passed, we looked back at our house, at the house in which we'd lived for our entire lives and would maybe never see again.

Thank you, House I thought, because I thought that if I spoke out loud I'd probably cry. We stood and stared with a melancholy longing, before we had to go, time was not on our side.

Chapter 3

At the station we bought two single tickets to Totnes on the machine to avoid unnecessary human contact. The train was set to leave in half an hour, but it would arrive at the station in twenty minutes. We waited on a bench on the platform and shivered. There weren't many people around; a girl who looked a little older than us and smelled of weed, and a few adults in business suits with coats on top, holding briefcases. I was glad to be sitting on a bench, we hadn't been walking much but my head was beginning to get worse, a sort of dull ache pulsing throughout.

When the train arrived we got on and moved into the next carriage, no one followed us so we had the whole thing to ourselves. We sat opposite each other in the window seats on either side of the table and put our bags on the aisle seats.

Neither of us said anything until the train started moving, but Tripp looked distant, empty and absolutely miserable.

This obviously came as no surprise and I probably looked in a similar state.

I was still in shock over it - they were gone. I tried to process it properly but it was just so unbelievable. I saw them, I said goodbye to them just hours before they died. "What was the last thing you said to them?" Tripp broke the silence, his mind clearly in a similar place to mine. His voice sounded flat and slightly croaky. No talking, just thinking by ourselves had indeed been a mistake.

I looked out at the buildings appearing and disappearing just as quickly as the train rushed on, as I thought back to yesterday morning.

"Love you." I always try to make that the last thing I say when saying goodbye to someone I love, in case it really is the last thing I get to say to them - I just never imagined it actually would be, or at least not for a long, long time.

Tripp nodded, indicating that he'd done the same. That brought me the tiniest amount of peace. Well maybe not peace, but at least they hadn't left while we were in the middle of an argument.

"What are we doing?" Was Tripp's next question, in a very existential crisis-y way.

"What?"

"What's our plan? We're running away, then what? We just live as runaways forever? We meet Zen and Delta, and-"

"We'll figure out what we're gonna do next once we're with them."

"So we have no Idea." He leant on the table, resting his chin on his propped up arm, trying to think of what to do. "We're buggered. Our lives are done." He was right of course, I knew he was; unless he wanted to work for our parents company - which we didn't - or be killed because we knew too much - which we definitely didn't - we would forever be on the run, hiding from the consequences of the 'terrible accident'.

"We'll travel everywhere." I said. "We'll see everything and look after animals that need help. We'll work on getting rid of SCREB. There must be other people who disagree with them, who want them gone like us. We'll be okay." I tried to sound more upbeat than I was, to believe what I was saying.

"That's a nice little story." Tripp gave a weak smile, humouring me and wishing he could believe it, then we said no more.

As I stared out the window, now at fields and sheep, my eyelids grew heavier with the movement of the train and I found myself struggling not to let them shut completely. I looked across me to see that Tripp had dozed off right there with his head propped up on his arm. He hadn't gotten as much sleep as me under the car and he wouldn't be deeply asleep in such a short amount of time, so I left him like that and just focused on not doing the same so that we didn't miss our stop.

The announcement that we were about to arrive in Newton Abbot made him wake up and sit up with a slightly shocked intake of breath.

"Did I fall asleep?" He sounded sort of confused, despite the obvious answer to his question.

"Only a tiny bit. We should get to the door." I began to get up and hoist my rucksack onto my back, and he nodded and did the same. As we left the train a few more business people got on and the weed-girl got off from the next carriage up. We now had a twenty minute wait before our second train would come and get us to finish the journey. We walked up the steps and over the bridge to the platform that our next train would get us from and waited on a bench again in the cold. We huddled together for warmth and tried not to let our eyes shut because if they did for too long we likely wouldn't be able to open them again. This made blinking quite difficult.

We also looked around for anyone who might be looking for us. Not that they would know we were here, or we would know what they looked like but we were still anxious.

There were a few more people waiting at this station, as this was a slightly less ungodly time to be getting a train, which meant we couldn't say too much about our situation. Not that we had much else to say on the matter. But we should do something to distract us and keep us awake.

"Do you think Kerry and Brian will ever get together and actually stay together?" I asked out of the blue. It was completely irrelevant to everything, but it was something to talk about. Tripp thought about it for a moment, considering the people who we so loved to observe at school.

"I think they'll keep being on and off for ages, starting again over the Christmas holidays, at least one of them will cheat on the other, which means they'll split up for longer than ever and it will 'definitely be for good' but then eventually they'll come to the conclusion that they're soulmates and run off into the sunset."

"Hmm, it's unfortunate but you're probably right." We talked for a while longer, avoiding the subject of ourselves and our family.

Once the train arrived at the platform, we got on, shoved our rucksacks on the overhead luggage holder and sat down underneath, looking around for anyone who might be after us. I knew this was most likely paranoia, we had nothing to be tracked by and we were about to leave Newton Abbot, but I was still nervous about being spotted, and I could see that Tripp was too.

There were a few people dotted about the carriage this time, but no one that was obviously suspicious. No one that had the SCREB look. I wasn't sure what the SCREB look was exactly, but none of these people seemed to have it.

The train started moving and I stared out the window, passing more nondescript fields and trees. It was much brighter now, though the sunlight was sort of hollow, it didn't fully portray the idea of light and warmth.

I leaned back in my seat, trying to make myself comfortable but my head wouldn't let me. I ended up just turning to face the window and tucking my legs up to my chest while I rested my head on Tripp's shoulder.

"You're not very comfy." I informed him. "I expected better service."

"Apologies madam, but it's not often we have to cater to such a low standard of customer." He sounded sleepy and I contorted my head around to see that his eyes were almost closed.

The rest of the train ride was fairly short and uneventful, I tried to both avoid thinking because it would make me sad, and think about what we would do next because we hadn't planned at all in advance.

The disembodied voice of the driver announced that we'd arrived in Totnes and reminded us to make sure we had all of our personal belongings and mind the gap.

I sat upright and shook Tripp awake. He jolted up and opened his eyes wide like a frog having an existential crisis.

"I'm awake." He announced.

"Yep, I'm very proud of you. We gotta go." I passed him his rucksack and got down my own. We hurried to the door and dismounted the train, stepping out into the cold, crisp air. There were quite a lot more people in suits now, proper grown-ups getting on and off the train to get to work. This made me more anxious about being seen by someone we didn't want to be seen by. But no one yelled our names and shot tranquiliser darts at so we were off to a good start.

We left the station and started walking towards town to get some final supplies. Namely lentil chips. There wasn't much point in going to Dartington yet, we wouldn't be able to do anything while it was light, and while we weren't yet being searched for here - as far as we knew - we wanted to take advantage of the shops.

"How's your head?" Tripp asked as we walked.

"Meh. It's getting worse now that we're walking, but not terribly." I tried to word it so that he wouldn't worry, but I don't think I did a very good job. At his request, I took a water bottle out of my rucksack and took a few sips which did make me feel a little better.

"If you start to feel sick or dizzy, or your vision starts to go weird or anything, tell me and we'll stop for a while."

"I'll let you know, but honestly I feel okay." We carried on, my worst ailment apart from my head being an empty stomach.

Once we made it to the high street and started scaling the long, steep hill I did in fact start to feel dizzy and had to ask if we could sit on a bench for a while. Tripp looked grateful to be sitting down, he was still tired. I took the opportunity to redo my already half-fallen-out bright pink hair. in a loose braid. This way the hair wasn't too tight so it shouldn't worsen my headache.

As I braided, I was disturbed by feeling dried blood and a rough scab on the side of my head.

"Our tickets didn't get checked at all. We could've done that whole journey for free." I realised, trying to distract myself from the wound.

"Bloody typical." Tripp replied. "Next time, we should just get on a train and see how far we can go without paying for anything." We both let that hang in the air. What a nice little thought 'next time' was, for anything.

The quest for the lentil chips was a success, along with a few other bits and pieces including flapjacks and water bottles with built-in filters so that we could refill from the rivers and streams we would come across. No one paid us attention, and no one seemed to recognise us.

Afterwards we walked to Dartington, now in full daylight and therefore on high-alert. We tried to walk quickly, but Tripp was so tired and my head was in such a state that it took us about twice as long as it would've if we were in good condition. We talked, about nothing in particular, and kept focused on anything other than the last twenty four hour's events.

Finally, once we got there I realised just how empty my stomach felt. In one of the forest areas, with nobody around, we constructed a massive nest out of sticks and logs in which we ate lentil chips, apples and bananas and drank a lot of water. I asked Tripp what time it was, and it was only half-past ten. Still, he'd been awake all the time I was unconscious, and most of the time that I was asleep again under the car. He got maybe two to three hours' sleep then, and about ten minutes on the train.

He looked really tired too. His eyes were puffy and half shut and he was moving slowly. Any other time it might have been quite funny but right now it was just pitiful.

"Go to sleep." I commanded. He shook his head.

"No, Rainbow, it's not a good idea to leave you without someone to look after you've just had a concussion. You might pass out and fall on your front and choke to death on a mouthful of leaves." He was struggling to keep his eyes open and his thoughts rational.

"Rainbow, I think you know that that's not what's going to happen. If I start dying I'll wake you up and you can hold me and sing *Died In Your Arms Tonight*."

He didn't need much convincing. The going to sleep part, not the serenading me to death part. He was already starting to lie down on his side, up against the biggest fallen log of our structure.

"Okay, Wake me up if anything happens, or when you need to sleep, or when it gets dark enough."

"You got it, bud." I sat down by Tripp's feet, and he was dead to the world within a second.

Chapter 4

It became slightly eerie, sitting there, effectively alone while I knew that a very dangerous corporation was after me. I picked up a twig and started drawing shapes in the mud while I hummed to myself, trying to ward off the bad feelings, but I couldn't stop constantly looking around to check that we weren't about to be ambushed.

I started crying too. I didn't bother trying to stop myself, I figured it was better to get it done while I wasn't doing anything important. I didn't sob, I didn't weep or cry out or anything, I felt oddly numb to all that, I just allowed the tears to ebb and flow as I thought about everything I had lost.

I still had Tripp though, as well Zen and Delta. I looked over at my brother, breathing heavily, eyes glued shut and left foot twitching. I couldn't help but smile a little at that - I'd forgotten about his sleep-twitch. Only ever the left foot, no one quite knew why it happened, but I'd always found it so funny when we were little.

The bird songs were pretty, but sad at the same time. Or maybe that was just the way I was hearing them. Or maybe there were no birds singing at all and my bad head combined with my tiredness was playing tricks on me. I wasn't as tired as Tripp obviously, but my eyelids grew heavier as I stayed sat down, just drawing in the mud. I needed to move around so that I could stay awake. It was so cold though, I couldn't motivate myself to stand up so for about half an hour, I just sat, telling myself that I needed to get up and that I would in just a minute, mentally revving up to movement.

Eventually I managed to make myself stand, with the promise that if I did this, I would get to eat another apple afterwards.

I started walking around, picking up bits of fallen tree that I could maybe use to build a fire. I hadn't built one in ages but I was pretty sure I'd remember how.

I made sure to never stray too far, to always keep Tripp in my sight. I knew I was probably being over-paranoid but I didn't care. I was on edge and not willing to risk losing anyone else I loved.

I managed to find six good-sized sticks and put them down, back in the region of the nest before going out again in the opposite direction, where I found a thin fallen branch about seven-feet long and a couple of inches in diameter. I dragged it back, trying to be as quiet as possible which didn't really work since the ground was completely carpeted in dead, crisp leaves that crunched under my feet and very unkindly announced the fact that I was dragging something behind me. I hit Tripp with it by accident when I reached him as I turned around to sit with my back against the big log and swung my branch a little too far, he was too deeply asleep to even flinch though.

I took an apple out of my bag and saw there were only three left. I wasn't exactly starving, and I had no idea when we'd next be able to get food so reluctantly, I put it back. I started digging around for my penknife - I knew I'd packed it - and eventually found it nestled in with my socks. I sat back down again with my knees up and pulled my fallen branch up so that I could begin cutting through it. This was going to take a while - my blade was, while useful for string and labels etc, a bit small and pathetic and had no serrations. I started moving the knife back and forth about a foot away from the thicker end of the branch, but the knife was so small in comparison and unsuited for this job, my arms ached by the time I was only a quarter of the way through cutting this first piece. I carried on, making slow progress until eventually the foot-long log came off the main branch enough for me to just snap the last splintery bits holding on. I tossed it onto the pile of logs that I'd collected and sat back, putting down the knife and the branch to rest.

My arms felt like they were on fire with bandages tightening around them. My head was getting worse too. I'd been feeling pretty good just sitting, and eating had definitely improved matters, but now I was feeling lightheaded again. I took some deep breaths and tried to focus on just one thing at a time; that particularly orange leaf on one almost-bare tree, the pair of trainers tied together and hanging from another.

Oh, that's not good I realised. It was probably nothing, but we should still make sure we were gone by dark.

Before I started on the next piece of branch, I looked at Tripp's watch on his limp wrist.

Half-past one.

I had no idea what time I'd started the first one, but I guessed it was around an hour ago. I opened up one of the flapjacks in my bag and took a couple of bites before going back to my branch-cutting spot.

I tried swapping to hold the knife in my left hand to give the right a slightly easier job, but that got me nowhere and just made everything harder so I had to keep going like I had been before.

I know I absolutely could've just kept looking around and saved myself the trouble and effort of this, but I wanted something to do that would definitely take a while. It probably wouldn't take me that long to just find a few more logs and build a fire ready for later, I'd certainly be done long before Tripp woke up at least, but then I'd be left with nothing to do, so I carried on sawing.

I hummed to myself as I did, and I thought. I thought about what happened to my parents. We hadn't been told the nature of the accident, but it was easy to make an educated guess; I knew they were part of a team carrying out the transportation and experimentation of something, some creature, and things had clearly gone wrong. Things had gone very bad. The creature - though they hadn't been allowed to tell us what it was - was a dangerous one, they'd said, but they were taking the "appropriate" precautions to remain safe, whatever that meant. Hadn't worked, obviously.

I wondered what had become of the creature. Had it escaped? Or been captured and 'taken care of'? I really hoped it managed to get away unharmed. If it got captured again, that would mean my parents died for nothing, but if it had enabled an animal to be free, well that was something.

That sounds awful. I was trying to think of anything to make me feel better, to make me able to live with the fact that they were gone, to make that more palatable, and that's what I was able to think of, so please don't go thinking I'm glad my parents died because it meant an animal got to go free, it's just that I've forever wished that they worked for someone other than the Supernatural Creatures Research and Elimination Bureau.

I realised I was crying again as I thought about this, so I started sawing harder and letting the tears burn down my cheeks - for how long, I didn't know, I just kept thrusting my frustration and sorrow and anger and sadness into cutting the branch. It wasn't cutting as quickly as I'd like. I kept speeding up, making my arms hurt more as the tiny little fireballs fell down my face, until eventually I couldn't stop myself from letting out a great cry of anguish. I stopped cutting and looked over at Tripp. He stirred a little and muttered something that I couldn't make out, but he stayed asleep.

Four hours and five fire logs later, as I was cutting the fifth, I got jumped by the sound of Tripp's waking voice asking if I was okay.

I nodded but didn't look directly at him. I knew my entire face was all red and puffy, I just kept moving the knife through the branch, my horribly aching arms moving slower and less powerful than earlier.

I was glad he woke up by himself. I was tired and needed to sleep, but I didn't want to wake him before he'd recharged enough.

"Rainbow, you know there are plenty of pieces lying around on the floor, you don't need to do it like that."

"I know, but I felt like doing it this way." I snapped more harshly than I meant to, instantly regretting it. He stayed quiet but I felt like he understood why I was doing this.

"Sorry. I-I'm just-"

"I know." He said as he put a hand on each of mine and stopped me from cutting through the branch. I looked at him and he spoke insistently.

"Get some sleep. I'll finish the fire and wake you up when it's time." His blue-green eyes looked sad and worried, and he tried to plaster on a reassuring smile before he gave me a tight hug. Tripp's good at hugs and stopping me from being too sad so I just held onto him for a little while until I realised I was almost going to sleep leaning on his shoulder. I pulled away and folded up my knife to put back in my bag. It had gotten colder, I could now tell, since I wasn't burning through my arms anymore. I now also realised that my head was throbbing again and as I got up to go and lie down where Tripp had been, I felt dizzy and my balance completely disappeared so I just fell over. Tripp rushed to my side, but I was okay. I crawled to the spot where he'd been sleeping and curled up. As I laid down, the ground was still a little warm from Tripp which was nice, and I was too tired to really care about the temperature, now that my body knew it was time to shut down. My coat was warm enough to not let me get hypothermia at least, and for now that was good enough. I saw Tripp get up and start looking around for other fire supplies as my eyelids drooped and at last I was able to sleep.

Chapter 5

I woke up to see Tripp crouching over a blazing orange light with his back to me, having not dreamed at all. Or at least, not that I remembered. It had gone dark and much colder. I started shivering right away, despite the small fire burning only a few feet away like a tiny volcano on an island in the middle of a frozen sea. I sat up and rubbed the sleep out of my eyes feeling groggy, but I was hoping that was the effects of only just waking up rather than my head being bad.

Tripp turned around when we heard me stirring and came over, checking his watch as he approached.

"I think it's time. Do you feel okay?" Tripp said as he helped me up.

"Yeah, fine. Are you sure?" I asked.

He nodded. "Quarter to eleven, and we need to get gone as soon as possible."

We both went to our packs and dug out a pair of old lip
balm tins, and walked back to the fire, standing over it
like cult members about to make a sacrifice.

I carefully unscrewed the lid of my tin, letting out the
incense-y aroma that had become a familiar and welcome
scent to me and Tripp. I took a small pinch of the
contents; scales. Each one was about the size of a
two-pence-piece, in varying shades of shiny, electric blue.
"You first." Tripp said, stepping back slightly. I held my
arm out right over the fire - the heat would've burned me
slightly if I hadn't been wearing several layers, as it was I
just felt somewhat overheated, no scorching pain.

As if feeding the goldfish my friend had when I was ten, I
sprinkled the scales onto the fire and watched as they hit
the flames. I hastily stepped back to join Tripp as the fire
gave a great crackling pop and hundreds of tiny, glowing
blue sparks flew upwards into the night. The smoke began
to turn blue as it rose upwards, disappearing into the dark
sky as soon as it left the range of the firelight.

After about thirty seconds, the sparks died down and the
smoke turned back to it's normal colour as Tripp stepped
forward and unscrewed the lid for his tin.

The scales he picked up were bright white and silvery, like
little tears cried by the moon. I always loved watching
Tripp do this, because the sparks that his scales gave off
looked like rain that got confused and started going the
wrong way. The tiny explosion was like a cloud sneezing,
though the smoke didn't show that much of a difference
in colour. That's why I always went first - if anyone did
happen to notice the blue smoke and get suspicious of it,
it wouldn't be long before the smoke returned to a colour
that could be perceived as normal, so whoever saw my

smoke could hopefully believe they just imagined it, and keep looking at the smoke without seeing anything out of the ordinary. That was something that Tripp pointed out, another thing that he realised and I likely wouldn't've, and made me grateful that he was around.

Once the white scale sparks were gone and the smoke had probably changed back to normal (it was hard to tell with these scales), we both made sure everything was in our rucksacks and sat down on the log to wait. It was difficult to see anything in the dark, the fire only provided so much light.

"Are you sure you're gonna be okay? Flying is a bit of a terrible idea so soon after hitting your head, we can walk for a while, until you're feeling better." Tripp looked worried, a look he'd had a lot over the last day, and the firelight dancing across his cheek made his words seem ominous. I knew he was right, I knew I must be crazy for going ahead with this and would definitely end up regretting it, but my head was okay right now, and I didn't want him to be so worried, we needed to get moving as soon as we could. I tried to give him a reassuring smile.

"I'll be fine. I know you're anxious about it, but honestly, I'm feeling okay now and it's seemed a lot worse than it actually is." That was a lie. I hadn't told him just how bad it had been earlier, when we stopped because I was feeling so rough. "If I need us to stop I'll tell you." I meant that part, I really did. Tripp didn't look happy about it but he nodded and started staring back into the fire, he knew we didn't have much else in the way of options.

I was now getting a pit of dread inside me. What if his fears were right and something really bad occured? Things like that happen, where someone hurts themselves but then they don't look after themselves properly while they're recovering and then they end up worse than they had been before.

I stared into the fire, at the flames dancing about and thought about the time we saw an old phoenix burning up when we were eleven. Our parents had taken me and Tripp for a tour around one of the SCREB units to see some of the research facilities, they didn't want us to see the elimination part at that age, but we were old enough to at least start seeing parts of the company where we would take our parents places in the future. We hadn't realised the full extent of what went on over there back then.

There were other kids around our age with their parents who worked there, it was a sort of induction day for all the children above age ten whose parents worked there. Part of it included being taken to a phoenix-studying room, where there were five of the magnificent birds at different stages in life. The induction had been scheduled on that day because the oldest phoenix was due to burn and the organisers were hoping that we'd be able to watch. It was quite incredible to see, would've been terrifying if you didn't know about the life cycle of phoenixes. He looked so frail and weak and in pain - he looked ready to go, but his eyes still shone and glowed like tiny suns. He started to walk on matchstick legs and I wanted so much to reach out and stroke him, to tell him that he'd be okay again soon. His eyes began to dim and everyone was told to stand back behind the yellow line as the phoenix erupted into flames that appeared out of nowhere and consumed him entirely. I heard him let out a noise, not quite a squawk of pain, just a sort of final goodbye to this version of himself as I watched him crumble away to nothing. I remember starting to cry slightly and scolding myself for doing so; I knew he was fine, I knew this had to happen but I hated to see such a beautiful creature being destroyed. I was happy in a way as well though, knowing that soon he'd be able to start again in perfect health and strength, without being in pain anymore. I would've felt better if I'd gotten to see him reborn, but once the flames died down, we swiftly moved on to the next part of the tour, being told that the ashes would take about ten minutes before forming back into a baby bird. I'd only seen a phoenix once since then, this summer we got taken to another SCREB unit where we got to see a glimpse into the elimination part that we were allowed to see since we were now sixteen. That time I didn't scold myself for not holding back tears. That time, the phoenix wasn't saying goodbye just to this version of himself.

I heard a twig snap from somewhere in the distance and sat bolt upright, turning to look behind us from where the snap had come. I couldn't see anyone, but I couldn't see very far anyway with just the firelight. I looked over to Tripp and we made a nervous eye contact. I tried to breath as quietly as I could while we both stood up slowly and carefully.
I could now hear definite footsteps. They were quiet and it was impossible to tell how many people were there, but they were there alright. And they were coming this way. *Just some late-night walkers.* I told myself, trying not to think the worst. Whoever it was, they had to be gone soon, otherwise Delta and Zen would be seen and who knew what would happen then? They never took long to arrive

when we called them and I knew they would be here any second, in full view of anyone who happened to be right here right now.

The footsteps got closer, but still quiet, like whoever was making them was trying to move silently, but the dead leaves everywhere wouldn't allow that.

My heartbeat got faster and my breaths got quicker and shorter as the fear of who that might be grew and grew. No, it surely couldn't be them, they had no idea where we were going, the last they saw us we were leaping off the roof of our shed and into the dark alley behind our house. And yet somewhere inside me I knew it was them. It was always going to be them.

Three bodies came into view, though I could not yet make out the faces, but I knew who the one in the middle was. A tall, thin figure, the woman who'd come out into the backyard calling our names last night, and the two huge guys who'd accompanied her. These were clearly the agents who'd been assigned to bringing us in and making sure that one way or another, we kept the existence of SCREB a secret.

There was no point in hiding, they'd have seen our fire from far away and they could now easily see it was just the two of us alone and unarmed, our only chance was to run. So we did.

I was terrified that I'd go into a state of pure panic like last night and be frozen to the spot, and I think Tripp was afraid of that too. He grabbed me by the wrist tightly and practically dragged me along for the first few feet. He seemed to realise I was moving on my own and loosened his grip and we kept running.

No idea where as we couldn't see anything except the vague shapes of trees, we just knew that we were running away. The footsteps behind us quickened and got louder, no longer trying to be quiet and sneak up on us, suddenly we were rabbits and the were foxes closing in on us quickly. I thought I heard yells but I wasn't sure what of, and I realised in horror that my hearing was going again. It wasn't that I couldn't make out all the different sounds because of the rushing through my ears, my hearing was actually disappearing and my head was starting to feel like jelly, I was going into a similar state to last night, I was screwed.

Thank God Tripp didn't completely let go of me, my senses were messing around and I wouldn't have carried on if he hadn't been guiding me. I started to feel weightless which was even more concerning, and I could feel something wrapping around me.

I was going into shock wasn't I? It was warping my perception of reality, I knew that what I'd felt around me was the arms of my captor, though it didn't feel like human arms. I closed my eyes and just prayed for this all to be over as my stomach flipped and my head started spinning and I suddenly felt the rushing of frosty wind all around me, including the soles of my feet, where the ground usually was. I realised I could hear my name being yelled, but in a voice more triumphant than threatening. "Iris! IRIS!" It was Tripp's voice. I made myself open my eyes and was greeted by a sight equally terrifying and euphoric. I was soaring over the trees and tremendous speed, held securely in the claws of my dragon, Delta. I screamed and wrapped my arms tightly around one of the great scaly arms that held onto me, knowing deep down

that I was safe in his grasp but the suddenness of
everything threw me into panic.

I couldn't not smile however, when I looked over at Tripp
grinning, cheering and looking on in awe as Zen gripped
him tightly. I tried to relax (shockingly, that was easier
said than done in this situation) and focus on the
adrenaline rush of flying that I had longed for but hadn't
felt for three months, but it was impossible to feel safe
with my legs just flailing around rather than seated
properly on top of Delta.

I then made the mistake of looking down at the world
hurtling at high speed below me, like a conveyor belt
waiting for me to be dropped onto it.

The wind stung my eyes and constricted my breathing and
hearing, I had only just heard Tripp yelling my name but
now that we'd picked up speed all I could hear was the
wind screaming at me painfully.

That's when the vertigo got worse than ever, stabbing at
my head and spinning it round at the same time on the
inside, but on the outside I was being compressed by an
invisible helmet getting tighter and tighter until it got too
much and I had to shut my eyes as I felt myself going
limp. All the food I'd eaten that day came back up, though
I couldn't tell where it went after it was out of my mouth, I
just felt that burning sensation in my throat. Delta's grip
around me got firmer but I didn't feel much more stable,
though it was nice that the last thing I felt before I
blacked out again was an act of protection.

Chapter 6

The noise that I woke up to was one that I hadn't realised how much I'd missed; dragon snoring. It's sort of a cross between a horse sneezing and a cat purring, and it's weirdly relaxing. I was much warmer now, lying in my sleeping bag, against the gently vibrating hide of Delta, lending his body-heat to me. Yes, body heat even though he's a reptile. It turns out dragons can do this thing where they keep an internal fire burning inside themselves while they sleep if they want to, to keep warmth going. It's thought that this was something they evolved to do during an Ice Age, when going to sleep was potentially a death-sentence. They could involuntarily slip into a coma, or just take an extra long nap, until they would freeze to death. So the fire-in-tummy method came to be and they never lost that characteristic, and now Delta was lying down around me and warming me up. On the ground might I add, which I was very grateful for. We were in a forest again but not the one that we'd narrowly escaped capture from last night.

Last night? Maybe. I didn't have any indication as to how many hours, days or nights had passed, but I could tell that it was morning.

The birds round here - wherever here was - sang more happily than those back home.

I sat up and immediately regretted it as the world started zooming in and out, doing barrel-rolls and swaying underneath me as my brain liquidised. Instead of lying back down, I bent over and held onto Delta's scaly side, shutting my eyes and holding on tightly for what felt like hours but what probably only about two minutes. It was comforting to hold onto the dragon that I hadn't seen since the end of summer, that I'd longed to ride on and fly far away into the clouds on.

As I scrunched up into a ball against Delta, I could smell what had been brought up just before I passed out on myself, a scent that usually accompanied having a stomach bug.

I flinched as I felt a hand on my shoulder and turned around to see Tripp kneeling down in front of me, having just stepped into the circular nest created by the giant reptile lying with his head on his coiled up tail.

His eyes were still puffy and bloodshot, and I could feel mine were in a similar state. He pulled me into a tight hug, ignoring the sick that was spilled down my front, and spoke straight into my ear.

"I'm so, so sorry. I was an idiot to let you fly."

I held onto him and didn't say anything - I wasn't really sure what to say, I just held onto him. He pulled away and held onto my shoulders as he looked me up and down. I could now tell that I was actually fairly clean compared to last night, he'd clearly wiped as much off me as he could while I was sleeping.

"You're really pale," he said worriedly. "how are you feeling?"

"Like there's a magnet in my head, and a load of slightly smaller ones surrounding us as equal distances, and the one in my head is trying to get to all of the others."

"That's colourful. Why can't the surrounding magnets just go to the one in your head?"

"Because they're anchored to the ground, obviously."

"Obviously." Tripp nodded in understanding, though he kept eyeing me with concern and handed me a tissue. "Your nose is bleeding."

"Thank you." I took the tissue and pressed it below my nose. I hadn't felt anything, but that was probably down to being numbed by the cold. The tissue came away with a red bloom seeped into it though. "I think I'll be okay in a couple of hours." I said. I had no idea whether or not that was true, but I needed it to be.

We both sat with our backs leaning on Delta's warm, still-sleeping side and I rested my head on Tripp's shoulder, still holding the tissue up to my face. "What time is it?" I asked, realising I had no idea how long I'd been unconscious. Tripp looked at his watch.

"Quarter to nine."

"What day is it?" I lifted my legs so that I was able to remove the sleeping bag and start rolling it up.

"Wednesday. Don't worry, you were only out a few hours." I breathed a sigh of relief at this.

"But I have no idea where we are. I couldn't tell which way they were taking us, but we were flying for about forty

43

minutes. I think." He put his arm around me so that we were nestled up together. It seemed strange and a bit wrong given our current predicament, but I felt so cosy at that moment.

A great melancholy still hung in the air around us, and perhaps it always would, but I didn't feel like crying anymore. I didn't feel happy by any stretch, but I was empty of tears for now and felt comforted by the presence of my brother and dragon.

"Rainbow, what are we gonna do?" I asked, surprised by how low and croaky my voice came out. I coughed to clear my throat as Tripp twiddled his shoelace in thought.

"I don't know." He paused, still fiddling with the shoelace. "If we go home, we're screwed."

"Royally."

"Exactly. So I think," I heard a smile creep into his voice. "we're officially runaways."

Suddenly there was a growel as Tripp's stomach announced that it was breakfast time and we both laughed a little, which still felt wrong, but it also made the weight feel a little lighter.

"So what I don't get-" I said between mouthfuls of flapjack, sitting atop Delta as he delicately sharpened his claws on a clump of stones.

"Is how the hell they found us?" Tripp finished as he took another bite of his own flapjack from opposite me. Underneath him, Zen looked behind her and flicked her shimmery tail, it's fin flattening the fern that had been tickling her so rudely.

I nodded, but kept my attention on the sugary-oat-concoction that made literally everything better. I'd been thinking about it all morning, and I was sure he had too, but we only vocalised it now. The being found, not the flapjack.

"Do we have anything on us that they could've been tracking?" I asked.

"No, I'm sure we don't." Tripp shook his head. "Maybe they saw us on the train station cameras and found out which train we got. I guess it wouldn't have been too hard to narrow down where we would go once they knew we were going to Totnes. I think they know us better than we're giving them credit for." It was a perfectly reasonable explanation. It made sense and seemed likely, but it didn't sit quite right with me. "We'll just have to make sure to be more careful next time." He added.

Whatever 'next time' meant.

"We should put our hats on if we go through more public places." I said. "In case we get caught on camera again." To be honest it would be more helpful to strip the bright pink dye out of my hair, but that would require us to go and locate a Superdrug which could take a full day or two judging by how the forest and it's forest-ness seemed to never end.

Then there was the fact that that would cost money, and we may have a few thousand pounds between us but that would run out eventually, we should save it as much as possible for food. Plus we didn't wasn't to risk being seen if we could avoid it. A public alert could've been put out for us, or there could be agents anywhere out looking for us.

"Cover up the fact that you're a wannabe Lava Girl?" Tripp asked, giving me a small, mocking grin. I'd've gently elbowed him if we were next to each other, but

45

instead I just said, "Shut up, I *am* Lava Girl. We could always dye yours pink instead, to confuse them, keep 'em on their toes." I looked at his brown, slightly overgrown hair and smiled, imagining it matching the fuschias in our Auntie's garden that I'd partially taken inspiration from. Aside from Lava Girl.

"Only if I get to have turquoise highlights with it." He declared, not entirely sarcastically.

"Seriously though, there are SCREB branches all over the country. We'll be found if we stay in the same place for too long. The flight bought us some time but we should go get moving again as soon as possible." I knew he was right but I wanted to stay here. The forest we were in was so beautiful and stretched out as far as the eye could see. The trees seemed to hum inaudible little melodies of happiness that the birds harmonised with and the sun, while providing minimal amounts of warmth, made everything look like a painting of a scene from a fairytale as it dove through the treetops.

"We're not flying though, are we?" I asked, trying not to sound as nervous as I was. I adored flying, I really did, but I'd passed out twice within the last forty-eight hours and my head was still gently pounding away - the magnet inside still trying to reach all of the surrounding ones. Last night had been full of the worst headaches I'd ever experienced and I really thought I was on the brink of death while Delta carried me at about three billion miles per hour. The fact that I didn't seem to be suffering any real brain damage was a miracle.

Tripp shook his head decidedly. "Absolutely not today. We'll walk for now, and we can ride these two on the ground if they're up for it, so that we can keep moving quickly during the night."

Delta grunted as if in agreement and I stroked his scaly neck.

"I'm sorry." I said, knowing that we would go so much quicker and further if we were flying, though I couldn't help breathing a sigh of relief at Tripp's words.

"It's not your fault, Rainbow," Tripp shook his head again. "and we've got a good head start. At the moment, no one knows where we are, so we can take our time moving, just as long as we *do* keep moving." He sounded like he didn't mind, but I still felt like a liability. If my head was okay, we could stay in one place during the day and then fly our dragons to anywhere else during the night.

"I'm gonna get changed before we do anything. I've been wearing the same clothes for two days and I feel icky. Not to mention-" I gestured at what was spilled down my clothes, before screwing up my flapjack wrapper and gracefully sliding off Delta, snapping a few twigs as my socked-feet hit the ground. I'd taken my shoes off to let my feet breathe, having been wearing my boots for a full day and a half. I pulled some clean clothes out of my rucksack and began walking around to the other side of my large-car-sized reptile out of Tripp's view.

"Yep, good idea. Maybe we can find a stream or something to wash these clothes at some point." He said as I heard him slide off Zen's back and onto the ground. It did not sound like a graceful landing. I heard what was definitely the sound of someone missing their footing and falling over.

"Tripped!" I proclaimed, grinning.

"Shut up!" Came what was definitely the voice of someone standing up and trying to sound like they hadn't just fallen over.

Chapter 7

"You know, we could've been dropped here at any moment in the history of all time," I mused as we trudged on through the sad, dormant foliage. "and we would have no way of knowing when or where we are." The strange wintery mist that had been present earlier was settling down, now as if we were walking on a giant sheet of dry ice and someone was gently, gradually pouring warm water over it.

"So what you're saying is, if what essentially has just happened, happened, then what is pretty much happening, would in fact be happening." Tripp graciously and sarcastically summed up my point for me.

"Killjoy." I said. I didn't look at him, but I could feel him smiling triumphantly. "Time?"

"Eleven-thirty." We'd been walking for nearly two hours. My feet were getting sore, my head kept pinging at random moments with sharp bursts of pain, a deep, dull ache hanging like the forest mist in between.

Delta and Zen were off hunting, since they couldn't really do anything with us during the day. All we were doing for now was trying to find a body of water to wash our clothes and ourselves. Having not showered since Sunday night, I felt a little riddled. With what, I don't know, just riddled. "Do you think Mum and Dad planned for us to be taken in, in the event that they-" Tripp asked, out of the blue and unable to finish the sentence, lowering the mood dramatically. Unable to say the word 'died'. Neither of us liked saying that word. When it happened to our Grandfather a few years ago, we couldn't say that word for about three months after it happened, as if not saying it made it less true. We always say slightly less direct things; *passed on, gone to sleep, gone to be with the angels.* I didn't know how long we'd be unable to say it in the case of our parents.

"What, you think they wanted us to be kidnapped?"

"No, no not that. I just mean, we know too much to be trusted alone, and they knew that, so do you think that when they found out that- that they might not come back," I could practically feel the tears stinging behind his eyes. "they asked for us to be taken in and looked after to make sure the secrets are protected." His voice sounded dangerously close to catching and breaking, and I couldn't answer for a few moments, out of fear that words might draw tears forward.

"No. They wouldn't do that. They wouldn't have people sent to capture us, they would've known and trusted that we'd keep the secrets. SCREB sent those people to us all alone, our parents had nothing to do with it. They probably specifically asked for this not to happen." I rushed to get the words out before it got too much and I

had to make the choice between shutting up and crying. I realised I'd sounded quite certain as I spoke. Too certain, like I was lying and trying to convince someone that what I was saying was the truth, and it seemed that that someone was me. I refused to believe that our parents would do a thing like that. "They would've asked Auntie Em to look after us, or Grandma and Grandad, or-"
"They knew that we know too much." Tripp repeated. He seemed set on the idea that our parents wanted us to be taken into the corporation that we so despised.
"No." I shook my head, acutely aware that tears were gently rolling their way down my cheeks. So much for being empty and not feeling like crying anymore. "This is all SCREB." I was adamant.
We carried on walking in silence, not sure what more to say. I wondered what would happen after we completed our current mission. We had absolutely no plan. We left home, knowing only that we had to leave but with no idea where to go.
We still had no way of knowing where we currently were, and we had seen no signs of other people apart from from a single odd glove a little way back that had clearly been lost there a while ago.
But for now it certainly seemed that we were homeless, and had nothing away from home that we could go to. Our whole lives had been there, our whole family, we had nothing else. Maybe Zen and Delta would take us somewhere safe, wherever they go when they weren't hanging out with us.
That was something we'd never known about them. Ever since they were hatchlings, we knew everything there was to know about them, but once they were old enough to

leave the nest they disappeared to an unknown location and returned to us when we summoned them. Maybe they didn't have any permanent place to go, maybe they just wandered the world and went wherever they pleased. Tripp and I hadn't really discussed what was going to happen with us now, but I knew that he would've been thinking about it too. There didn't really seem like a good outcome though so we just avoided the subject.

As we walked, I felt heavy. Not physically, even though my rucksack was pulling down on my shoulders, but heavy in my soul.

At least my head was beginning to feel normal, that was something. Before we'd set off Tripp had dug around in his rucksack and found some Paracetamol to help with the pain, like the tiny Irises in my head were managing to stick the brain back together. Maybe it was a bit of a placebo-effect, but it seemed to be working.

I thought back to the last time I hit my head badly, after falling off my bike when we were seven. It was a hot summer day and we'd just managed to ride without stabilisers for the first time and were so excited about it. Mum was helping Tripp into his helmet and pads as Dad checked the air in his tyres. My tyres had already been approved and I was waiting my turn to put on my armour. I sat on my bike seat, pretending I was rushing down the hill that seemed so steep back then. I kept my toes on the ground and gently rocked myself back and forth until I accidentally propelled forwards just a little too much and my toes came off the ground. Suddenly I was sent into a terrifying descent, gripping my handle bars and fighting to gain control over my wobbling front wheel but it was too sudden. I had ridden without stabilisers twice before, and both times had been slow and on a flat surface. This was to be our first hill, going slowly and with our parents walking next to us to grab if we started to fall. But I was going all on my own, completely unprepared and inexperienced and I tried to keep going straight, but the wheel turned sideways and I didn't. My bike toppled over taking me with it and I hit my head on the tarmac of the deserted road, scraping my arm as I went down. I lay there and started crying out in pain as I felt like my head might crack open any moment. I heard my parents calling out to me and saw them running towards me, Tripp trying to keep up behind them on his little legs. When they reached me, they each grabbed an arm and pulled me into a sitting position, moving the bike off me and pushing it aside. I kept crying as my parents asked if I was okay. I nodded, trying to make myself be okay by saying it was true.

"Why did you do that?" Mum asked me. I was taken aback by how calm yet accusatory she sounded. "If you'd held still like I told you to, this wouldn't have happened." Her face was hard to read, sort of a cross between concerned and, well, cross. Dad inspected the arm that had been scraped across the ground and tutted.

"I'm sorry, Mummy." I said, still sobbing and now feeling a crippling amount of guilt about ignoring my instructions.

"Does sorry make it feel better?" She asked, now more clearly cross than concerned, but still completely calm. I shook my head as I was brought up to my feet, the physical pain in my head going down slightly.

"Think, Iris." Dad said, in a scarily calm voice. He picked up the bike and began walking back to the top of the hill without another word.

"Come on, I've got plasters in my bag up there, and let's put your helmet and pads on so that you don't get hurt again if you're being silly." Mum said coldly as she turned to follow.

I began trailing behind when I felt Tripp grab my hand and give it a squeeze. I was still crying but that made me feel the tiniest bit better. I looked at him and he gave me a sad little smile. We turned and kept holding hands as we followed our mother up the hill. I felt so bad and so sorry that I'd annoyed my parents. I never meant to, but I knew it was my fault, I'd been being stupid and they were right to be cross with me. Now, nine and a half years later, I'd hurt my head again, and again it was my fault, this time for freezing up and Tripp having to push me over the garage door. That felt like forever ago now, two days seeming like two years. You'd think it would feel like less since I'd spent a large amount of that time passed out which was annoying. I had to be careful until I was okay again not to pass out, it wasn't fair on Tripp.

Snap.

My heart sped up at the sound of a twig, several feet behind us. Tripp and I stopped walking and grabbed each other's hands, frozen with fear.

"Someone's coming." I whispered. I reached into my coat pocket and pulled out my white knitted hat. The footsteps got closer and I let go of Tripp as I put the hat on and tucked my fuschia waves up inside it as Tripp put his own hat on. The footsteps drew closer behind us, each one like the ticking of a bomb.

"We turn around on three, pretend to look at my watch, and keep walking so that we're not getting followed." Tripp whispered. "It's probably not SCREB, in which case we keep walking and just pretend we're hiking."

"And if it is?"

"We panic and run."

"You really think we can keep outrunning them? We don't have a carpark or dragons to save us this time." I resisted the urge to start running now.

"Don't worry, I don't have to outrun them. I just have to outrun you."

"You know you can't outrun me, and if you leave me to be killed I'll make sure you're the first person in the world to be genuinely, undeniably haunted."

"One. Two. Three." We both turned around.

We did not need to worry or threaten each other after all. Approaching us was a man in beige cargo shorts, a bright orange fleece jumper and a dark woollen hat. He had a backpack on - about half the size of each of ours - and a very nice camera hanging around his neck. Clutched in his hand was a walking stick, he was clearly an actual hiker. I let out a deep breath that I hadn't realised I was holding in as we walked towards the man with a sense of relief. As we got close the man smiled at us and came to a stop.

"Decided to brave the cold too, eh?" He said, smiling like a friendly maniac. His accent was clearly Scottish, but that didn't necessarily mean we were in Scotland. I smiled back and tried to think of something someone who was out for a hike would say.

"Means most people are scared off so we get to enjoy it by ourselves." I said.

"Plus the frost adds a certain atmosphere to the forest that you can't get in the warmer months" Tripp added, also smiling.

"You're certainly both right there, can't beat the winter air. Been out long?" He continued. Tripp and I looked at each other.

How long is a reasonable time to be here? I stared.

I have absolutely no idea. He replied.

We made ourselves look as though we were trying to recall how long we'd been out, then I remembered we'd geuinely been walking for quite some time.

"A couple of hours." I said.

"Glad to see young'uns gettin' out and appreciating the world around you!" He looked so happy at this. The presence that this man gave off was great, the look in his eyes seemed both wise and slightly insane. I liked that. Suddenly his eyes narrowed slightly as he said, "You two not in school today?" I panicked and began to open my mouth to say something but Tripp interjected.

"Non-pupil day." He said. I breathed a silent sigh of relief as I realised that was actually true. "Our parents-" He faltered slightly saying that. Not enough for an outsider to notice, but I noticed. "Think this is an important part of life to spend time with nature, so whenever we can, we get out here." He smiled and I nodded along earnestly.

"And right they are too!" The man said, positively excited by this. I couldn't help smiling at his sheer joy and I immediately wanted him to be my best friend.

He suddenly but gently took my hands in his and looked into my eyes. His were a deep brown that looked like they were young, yet had seen thousands of years, all in the sixty or so years that looked like the rest of him had seen.

"You listen closely and learn to tune in to the right place, and you'll hear the trees tell you things." He said in a quieter, knowing voice. I stared at him in a trance and wasn't sure what to say. Was he some kind of angel sent to give us cryptic advice on what to do next? He let go of my hands and picked up Tripp's, looking into his eyes now. "They'll tell you the things you perhaps don't want to hear, but the things that you need to hear." Then he let go and straightened back up as we both kept staring at him. "Well my dears, I'd best be on my way. Perhaps I'll see you again coming through this way, have a lovely rest of the day." He said back at normal volume and the spell was broken. He gave us a small solute and began walking in the direction he'd been going.

"You too!" I called out hastily, not wanting him to think we'd been rude and just ignored his leaving. After he'd gotten further away I turned to Tripp and said "I love him."

Tripp nodded in agreement.

"Do you think he was a wizard?" He asked in awe. Then before I could reply he started laughing.

"What?" I said. He pointed at my hat, hiding all my hair. "You look like a shocked mushroom."

I laughed too and took the hat off, letting the pink hair tumble out and fall annoyingly around my face and in the way. I preferred not wearing the hat, because it made my head and ears feel a little claustrophobic sometimes, so I began to tie the hair up as Tripp continued, "Why take the hat off? Is it too tight because there's not mush-room?" He looked mock-sad.

"Just not much of a fun-guy." I shrugged. We both laughed hysterically and continued on our way.

Chapter 8

I never did think dragons were the kind of animal to purr before I adopted one, but they do, they really do. I never had a pet cat - or any other kind of pet - but I always wanted one, and now it was like I had a massive, able-to-burn-me-to-a-crisp-in-under-ten-seconds, weirdly scaly cat!

I stroked Delta's face as he continued the contented low-hum and sharpened his claws. He likes sharpening his claws.

"Plan for the morrow?" I asked as I threw another stick onto the fire. This one had been considerably easier to light as it just consisted of Delta breathing out slightly more violently than usual.

Tripp sat against Zen and eyed me, thinking. In the dark, with just the flames lighting his serious expression, he looked terribly ominous again. Or teen-angst-album-cover-y, either worked.

He shrugged, then looked down to our bags.

"How much food do we have left?" He sounded concerned. I thought back to what we'd eaten throughout the day. We both finished our flapjacks for breakfast, and had eaten a load of apples, bananas and veggie crisps over the course of the day. We'd eaten too much, and we both knew it. Not too much as in we stuffed ourselves; too much as in we should be preserving our food more than we were, we only had a limited supply. The day had been uneventful, we walked, we met the wise-old-man whom we suddenly wanted to be best friends with, we kept walking and eventually found a stream. We hadn't had much to do, much to keep us busy from eating, we did it to pass the time and now regretted it.

"Too little." I said. He nodded as I confirmed his thoughts.

"We should see if we can find our way into the nearest town. We'll find a Tesco or something, and stock up on fruit, and stuff that won't go off." He was clearly not looking forward to the venture.

"We might be able to find somewhere to shower too." I suggested.

We'd managed to wash our clothes in the stream, and they were now lying down, half-dried, ready to be packed up again in the morning. Cleaning ourselves however, would've been near-impossible without a high chance of getting hypothermia. My hands had seized up and went numb from the cold while washing my clothes, so God knows how bad I would've been if my whole body was made to do that.

Tripp nodded in agreement about the showers, and seemed to remember something as he got up to get something from his backpack. He came over and handed

me my bamboo toothbrush and a tube of toothpaste. I
hadn't realised he brought these, and completely forgot to
ask. I'd kept passing out rather than getting ready for bed
so it was easy for this to slip my mind. That reminded me,
I hadn't passed out tonight, I'd broken my two day streak.
Yay!

"Thank you." I said, squeezing the toothpaste out onto my
brush and handing it back to Tripp. I got up and Delta
lifted his relaxed head, looking at me with hurt in his eyes
and whimpering slightly.

"I'll be right back, I'm not leaving you." I said, in the same
tone I would've used to call my brother an idiot, but I
couldn't say that to my dragon.

We both moved over to the stream and suddenly, as if my
thoughts about not passing out were a trigger, hundreds
of invisible needles started poking into my head, like some
mad acupuncturist was trying to reach my brain. I took a
deep breath in and knelt down over the stream, but the
needles kept coming.

"You okay?" Tripp asked, concerned. I nodded, sure that
once I was down again I would be.

We brushed our teeth, in the strangest makeshift sink I'd
ever used but didn't rinse our mouths out with the stream
water, having no idea how clean it was so even if we
weren't swallowing it, it wasn't something we wanted
getting into our systems. Instead we each took a few swigs
from our bottles of water and rinsed it around our mouths
before spitting into the stream. I felt a bit bad about that,
but it shouldn't really cause any harm.

I jumped when I felt something nudge me on the
shoulder. Delta was staring at me with his huge green,
hypnotic eyes full of worry. He'd stepped over Zen to get

to me and was standing on all fours, wings drooping sadly at his sides. Zen continued to lie down, awake but seeming not to have noticed that anyone had even moved. I stroked Delta on the chin.

"It's ok, I'm coming back now, it's bedtime." He poked my forehead with his snout, letting out a small, pitiful sound. A sudden stab came with his poke, and I took in another sharp breath and shut my eyes and the needles concentrated there for a few seconds. I continued to stroke him and tried to guide him back to where we'd been lying down but he wouldn't let me, stamping his front right foot and nudging me again, insisting that I stayed where I was.

"What's wrong?" I asked, getting quite worried now, he was clearly deeply bothered by something. He made the same pitiful sound again, like a sad velociraptor.

"What's the matter?" I asked again, and Tripp came over to stroke him too, trying to calm him down.

Delta gave me lick on the forehead which I could've done without, but it was out of love so I went with it. He shuffled himself backwards slightly and looked down at his front paws. I knelt down to see what was wrong and to my horror, Delta lifted his right hand, extended his freshly sharpened claws and moved the deadly sharp talons towards his left hand.

"Delta, no!" I cried out, but before I could stop him, he sliced a quick line through the palm of his scaly paw and looked at the indigo blood rising up and spilling out. I reached for his skin to try and hold the fresh wound together, stop the bleeding, but he put his hand up and held it to the side of my head, letting his blood mingle with mine. I realised what he was doing.

Hands shaking, I reached up and held onto his wrist, as Tripp knelt down next to me and rested one hand on top of Delta's, the other stroking the dragon's head. I shut my eyes as I felt the blood stinging slightly, but that was all. Just the stinging from the dragon blood. No needles, no magnets, no spinning, just the magical, healing dragon blood. My Delta had sensed how bad my head was and cut himself to heal me. Even when the stinging had stopped and I felt perfectly well, I continued to hold his hand pressed against my head.

"Thank you." I whispered as I released his hand and let it fall to the ground. I knew his wound wouldn't take long to heal, being filled with dragon blood but the pain it must've taken to cut through his thick skin must've been awful.

He started purring again and nuzzled me, definitely seeming to be smiling.

I wrapped my arms around his neck and nuzzled him back before we both walked back to our spot and got down onto the ground, where he seemed happiest and wrapped himself around me protectively.

Even before the stabbing-needle pain, I hadn't realised how fogged my brain had felt. It was like someone opened a window to let out a load of smoke that I hadn't realised was blinding me until it was gone.

Tripp went back to sit with Zen opposite me, and she continued to lick herself clean, not noticing that anything had happened.

"Does it feel completely healed?" He asked in amazement.

I nodded, smiling at how much lighter my head suddenly felt, how little effort it took to nod.

I looked down at Delta's hand, wrapped up in my own. The bleeding was already stopping, it hadn't been a deep cut, thank God. The blood at the wound was clotting and would likely be an almost healed scab by morning, if it wasn't completely gone already.

"I might be able to fly again." I thought out loud, as Delta adjusted himself around me and rested his heavy head on my crossed legs for me to scratch between his ears.

"We can test tomorrow." Came in the voice of reason, my brother. "We don't know if any permanent damage was done and, as magical and amazing as it is, the blood might not have been able to fully fix it. It could be more of a temporary relief."

Delta and I huffed in unison.

"Are you dissing Delta's healing powers?" I asked, it came out sounding more annoyed than I intended, I knew he was probably right.

"No, no, sorry, I just-" He seemed to relax a little. "I just don't want you getting hurt again. I was really worried about you. It was terrifying, not having any idea when you'd wake up or what state you'd be in."

I realised my shoulders were really tense and I, too, relaxed. I hadn't thought about it much from Tripp's perspective. If he'd passed out twice and had headaches throughout his time being conscious, I'd be worried too. I'd be more than worried, with no real doctor, no medicine besides painkillers, and no idea how much damage had been caused, and we only had each other now. Apart from our dragons.

"Sorry, I'm just excited. Thanks for taking care of me and not leaving me for dead." I said, bowing my head slightly. He smiled at me.

"Thanks for waking up and still being able to function." All was quiet for a minute until, perfectly in sync, we both stared into the fire and started to sing Spongebob's *Campfire Song Song*. We gradually picked up speed and went on for several rounds before finishing. We probably sung out too loudly, laughed too elatedly, but we'd seen no sign of people since the man who spoke about trees, and we were tired. Not just in need of sleep, tired in our souls. We missed our lives, so much having changed in just two days. We hadn't felt happy for what felt like years, but in that moment it was as if we knew no other emotion. We were orphans, but in that moment we sang as if we were part of the biggest, happiest family in the world, as if the trees surrounding us were our big happy family. In that moment, we were home.

Chapter 9

Doctor Strange. For some reason that was my first thought
when I woke up. Today, Thursday the seventeenth of
November, we were supposed to go to the cinema after
school with our group of friends to watch the new movie
Doctor Strange, then tomorrow again for the opening night
of *Fantastic Beasts and Where To Find Them*.
I wondered what my friends had been told about our
disappearance. I missed them. I wondered if anyone
would've guessed that something was wrong, whatever
they'd all been told. They didn't know what our parents
did for work. No one knew for real - everyone believed
they were scientists at a big pharmaceuticals lab, and that
was that. That was their cover, that they stuck to
religiously when they were around 'normal' people. That
was what Tripp and I had been trained to tell people who
asked about what our parents did ever since we were old
enough to understand what their job was.

Well, back then, we didn't know the full extent, not at all, we just knew that they worked with magical animals but it was a secret. That was all we knew for a while. It was a shock when we found out what SCREB stood for; when we found out about the whole 'elimination' thing. From then, it changed from telling people our parents did something else because that was what we'd been taught to do, to telling people they did something else because we were ashamed of what they really did and didn't want to be associated with it.

I'd half wanted to be able to tell my close friends the truth for a long time so that I wasn't lying to them, but I knew I never could without getting into a huge amount of danger. Our parents had warned us that if anyone were to ever find out about the secret agency, something would have to be done about that. They'd looked deep into my eyes in a way that sort of scared me, and made it clear that there would be consequences if anyone were to find out. And now because of that, no one knew the truth of what was happening.

I didn't have a lot of close friends, I didn't need a lot, but I wanted to be able to explain to someone what had happened. I wondered if Tripp had been right, and everyone we knew would be told that we'd been sent away to live with some distant aunt that conveniently we'd never met or mentioned to anyone.

I sat up in my sleeping bag and rubbed my eyes, feeling groggy but with a much clearer head than the last few times I'd woken up. I blinked several times and surveyed the surrounding area.

Tripp was still asleep in his own sleeping bag opposite me, Zen snoring behind him and Delta behind me.

The burnt out remains of our campfire lay between us, like a sad little phoenix who never did manage to come back.

But there was also snow.

Floating down and coming to rest in a thin blanket as if a bunch of fairies had gotten over-enthusiastic with the confetti at a wedding.

It was more snow than I'd ever seen back home, and much earlier in the season than it had been before. I stood and stared in wonder for a few minutes, shedding my sleeping bag as I rose and holding my hands to catch some of the magical snowflakes, completely awake now, as if I'd suddenly taken a double-shot of coffee. There was a circle completely clear of it around me and Delta, and another around Tripp and Zen, where the dragons' body heat that had kept us alive while we slept wouldn't allow it to land, but still it fell, before melting into water when it got too close.

I pulled one of my grey gloves off so that I could see the snowflakes in my bare hands, and didn't care that I was shivering and my teeth were chattering.

I realised that I was doing this alone and rushed over to prod Tripp with my foot. His face screwed up a little and he groaned (not in pain, he just does that when he's waking up, I promise I didn't kick him hard) as he began to enter consciousness once again.

I pulled the hair tie out of my now more-out-than-in ponytail and started to re-tie it more securely as I knelt and used my knee to keep nudging him awake. He started rubbing his eyes and winced as he felt the same frosty welcome into the day that I had.

"Snow!" I announced triumphantly. He made another nondescript sound.

"Snow I tell you, get up!" I couldn't contain my excitement anymore as I grabbed his hands and yanked him upwards.

"Whyyy?" He whined as I pulled him up onto his feet; he was clearly still in sleep-mode.

"Because when was the last time you saw snow that wasn't really ice that we pretended was snow?!" I retorted. He opened his eyes properly and looked around, unable to keep a smile from creeping up on his face.

"You gonna keep chucking massive balls of ice directly at my face?" He asked, the smile turning a little evil.

"That was ONE time!" I sneered, gathering up a snowball and lobbing it at him. He turned around and it hit him on the shoulder, making it look like a tiny star had exploded on his navy blue duffle-coat. He turned back to me and instead of retaliating with his own snowball as I'd expected, he charged at me. I turned to run but he'd been too close to start with and I was tackled to the ground, kicking and squirming and laughing, still filled with the happy energy that last night had brought us. I rolled over, wrestling Tripp to the ground but he kept the momentum going and I was suddenly plunged into the frosty stream. A thin layer of ice had formed on the top that shattered as I made what would've been a splash in the summer, but was now more of a crash. I screeched from the shock of the cold.

Luckily it wasn't deep so only my rump and the backs of my legs got wet, but the sudden impact of hitting the water shocked my nerves.

"Why would you do that?!" I shrieked, my voice much higher-pitched than usual.

"Crap, I'm so sorry!" Tripp exclaimed. He did not look sympathetic or filled with regret as he said this. He laughed at me as he stood and helped me up. I couldn't not laugh as well, I tried, I really did but it just felt so good to laugh. I stood, shaking and dripping but smiling. This morning didn't feel real, it was like we'd woken up in a reality where nothing bad had happened, where everything was fogged by a sweet, perhaps a tiny bit too sweet, mist that calmed the air and made everything pure. Delta woke up at the sound of our laughter, and sneezed as he inhaled too hard and a load of snow went up his snout. Zen continued to sleep like a log, gradually camouflaging into the surroundings as the amount of snow grew.

I ran over to Delta, remembering the events of last night, and knelt down beside him. He looked at me with his big, bright green eyes that seemed almost permanently worried.

I gave him a smile to try and soothe him, then took his paw in my hand to look at where he'd cut himself for my head. There was no evidence of any kind of wound whatsoever. If you looked at it without knowing what had happened, you could've almost thought it belonged to a newly-hatched. I felt Tripp looking over my shoulder and he reached out to stroke Delta.

"You doing okay, buddy?" He asked. Delta put his head down and licked where his wound would've been.

So many times I wished he was able to talk to us. It was clear he could understand us perfectly well, which was hardly surprising since I'd raised him, and I was usually able to tell what he was trying to say to me, even if he didn't actually speak the words but I longed for us to somehow speak the same language to each other.

He looked back at me, and this time his eyes didn't seem quite so concerned. He seemed more sort of at peace, less worried than I'd ever seen him.

"How long do you think it'll take us to get into town?" Tripp asked, as Delta stood up and started walking around, stretching his legs.

"Well considering I have no idea where town is, what the town is, or how far from town we are, I really couldn't say." I responded, hunting in my backpack for the packet of tiny ricecake-triangles that I knew I hadn't eaten yet.

"Alright!" Tripp said, in the mock-annoyed way that we say it to each other. "They might be able to figure it out. Or they might just know." He said as he threw a snowball at the still heavily-sleeping Zen. She didn't move in the slightest and Tripp threw his hands up in a sort of *what the hell?!* kind of way. "You could launch a cannon at that creature and she would stay sleeping."

We both kept throwing snowballs at Zen while she continued not to notice.

"Do you think they're normal? As dragons go?" He sounded genuinely curious. It was something I'd thought about a lot, but having never met another dragon, even during SCREB events, I couldn't really answer. They weren't what I'd expected, they had so much more personality than I'd ever pictured when I was younger. I always thought of great, ruthless beasts who ripped through the air with ease and cast shadows from the sky as if it were the apocalypse. Who breathed fire with no rhyme or reason, without aim or intention, just for the sake of breathing fire. I thought of destructive creatures whose only goal in life was to be the survivor. What I had not expected was an oversized house cat with wings who had anxiety and didn't know how to not be worried about something. On the other end of the spectrum was Zen, who could've slept through both world wars if she wasn't hungry when she went to sleep, and often couldn't really be bothered to do much that didn't involve bedtime or food, unless Tripp was in danger. We didn't know what 'normal' meant for dragons. We'd never been given the opportunity to find out.

"It depends what normal is. They both have features of every literary and cinematic dragon that I know, but none of those are exactly the same so who can know?" I said. Tripp nudged Zen and she snorted as she abruptly came back into the world and stood up, shaking the melted snow off her like a wet dog.

"We need to go into town, Zen. Do you think you and Delta would be able to tell which way to go?" Tripp asked as he scratched behind her ears and horns.

"The snow should be enough to cover us and we only need to fly low. If you can just get us close enough, we'll go and do what we need to do and you two can go off and do what you want to for a while." I stroked her nose.

"But we'll move later today, we can't risk staying in one place for too long." Tripp added. Zen started into my eyes with her glimmering bright blue ones, like a fishing hole in a frozen lake against the pure silvery white of her scales. She turned her head to Tripp and gave him a big lick over his face. He tried to smile for her, but it really was a grimace. She seemed pleased with herself.

Thump.

Something landed by my feet. I looked down and jumped back with a small shriek. Delta had come back with four dead squirrels. I looked away and gulped, trying not to listen to the sound of the two dragons devouring the creatures and simultaneously keep my own food down. I tried to think of something else to distract myself with. How about that time my parents- *NOPE!* Not thinking about that. About them. That was off limits until things were more...stable.

My own stomach began rumbling at the sounds of eating and I started thinking about what we could get to eat in town, while spending as little money as we possibly could. Once the noises had stopped I turned around, at the same time as Tripp, who had a grim expression on his face, no longer trying to conceal it with a smile for Zen. I looked down at the small pool of blood that had gathered on the ground where the squirrels had been, the only clue that they had been there, and mentally apologised to them. Delta nuzzled me and I made myself stroke him, trying to put out of mind what had just happened. It wasn't his fault he was a carnivore. He was just doing what was necessary for him and his sister to live.

We took one more look around to make sure there was nobody to see us before we hoisted our backpacks and climbed atop our dragons. I was feeling nervous about this now, the excitement of last night had worn off. Last time I'd flown I threw up then passed out and I wasn't looking forward to any kind of a repeat.

"You okay?" Tripp asked. I looked over to him, where he reminded me of my favourite fictional character, Hiccup, a weedy brunette boy sat on top of a dragon ready to take flight.

"I think so." I nodded. He looked concerned.

"It's only gonna be a short, low flight, but if you feel bad at all, get Delta to take you down and we'll follow." He instructed.

I nodded again and tried to give him a smile. I hated this feeling. I used to look forward to flying so much, it was the greatest thing I'd ever experienced and suddenly I was terrified of it.

I swallowed hard and shut my eyes for a second, envisioning the last time that we'd flown when it had gone well. Late August, when our parents believed we were on the beach for the evening with friends to mark the end of summer, and indeed we had been earlier on in the evening, we just hadn't gone straight home when everyone else had.

I wanted to go back to that time, when the only thing to worry about was starting A levels in a couple of weeks. And now, just three months later, we were runaway orphans who hadn't washed in several days, were being hunted quite possibly for death by the government, and had just stood next to a small squirrel massacre. I opened my eyes, worried that if I thought about things too much I would cry, and I'd really had enough of crying. I met Tripp's gaze and forced a determined frown onto my face, trying not to let on how fast my heart was beating, or how much I was sweating under all my layers, or how every instinct was telling me to get onto the ground, curl up into a ball and stay there for all eternity.

"Ready?" Tripp asked. I nodded and leaned forward so that I could wrap my arms around Delta's neck to grip on as he flapped his enormous wings and we soared into the sky.

Chapter 10

I'm not sure I had ever been more certain that death was upon me than I was when we ascended. Not that anything went wrong, in fact it was one of the smoothest lift-offs I'd ever taken with Delta - he was probably being extra gentle on purpose for me - but the panic that was set off in my brain topped that of anything we'd encountered over the last few days.

I clamped my eyes shut and held on as tight as I possibly could; if dragons were any less robust I would've been strangling Delta.

The snowflakes turned into miniscule firebolts shooting at me from everywhere and nowhere as the world disappeared beneath us and I felt myself screaming out and tried to stop but it was the same feeling as being attacked in a dream and being unable to run no matter how much you try, it was like someone else was screaming out of my mouth and I was powerless to stop it.

But my head felt fine. It took me by surprise, but the only thing that happened to my head was the rush of the cold, crisp air going past that I always felt when flying. No pain, no queasiness, just purely psychological panic. After I realised this, I tried to open my eyes, but they just wouldn't. I had no idea how high up we were but I guessed it wouldn't have been that high so I tried to force them open, but they just wouldn't. This sent my body into panic again, even though my mind was calming down. I started shaking all over, my grip loosening involuntarily as I heard the scream that wasn't completely mine stop, and be replaced by my frantic, tiny breaths that each carried their own screeches with them.

Time sped up and I realised we were descending.

I felt myself slipping as my grip became practically non-existent, in my mind I yelled and screamed at myself to hang on but my limbs would hardly respond.

The frost bit at me, daring me to let go and see how close we were to the ground, to test the limits of human resilience. I started slipping down off the side of Delta, just hanging on as my eyes stayed glued shut.

NO! I yelled in my head.

HANG ON!

I slipped further.

PLEASE! I cried to myself, to the universe, to anyone and anything that might be listening.

THUMP-ump.

Delta hit the ground, then I hit the ground.

We made it.

I lost my grip entirely just as he managed to make a messy landing. The snow on the ground cushioned me and was quite a comfy way to become reacquainted with the earth.

I still couldn't open my eyes for some reason, and I had stopped screeching but I was still hyperventilating. I laid down on my side, half curled-up as my muscles and joints locked so I couldn't move, I just lay there as my body tried to process everything.

I felt Delta sniffing and nuzzling at me, making distressed noises and trying to see if I was okay. I heard the soft landing of Zen a few metres away and the thud of Tripp jumping off her, before hurried footsteps towards me. He knelt down beside me and put a tentative hand on my shoulder as I continued to shake.

I flinched at his touch. I didn't mean to, but at the moment I didn't really seem to be in control of my own movements.

"Delta, Zen," He said, in a direction other than at me. "you two should get out of here before you get seen."

I heard Delta make his velociraptor-esque noise that meant he didn't want to go anywhere.

"She'll be okay, I promise I'll look after her and we'll meet you tonight. Thank you so much, guys." He spoke in a calming voice that made me relax a little, even if he wasn't saying anything to me.

Delta made another disgruntled noise but he backed away and I heard the great flap of four incredibly powerful wings as the dragons went to find more food and safety away from humans for the day.

"You okay?" He asked me. He asked so casually, as if we were just passing each other and in perfect health, rather than one of us having a minor fit on the ground. I managed to nod and I could feel the shaking calm down as I found my eyes opening.

The daylight was bright and slightly blinding now, but I could see my brother quite clearly, looking concerned but absolutely certain that things would be okay.

"Do you know what happened?" He pulled my fingers out of the fists I didn't realise I had clenched.

"Minor p-panic attack. B-body went into shock." I managed to say. "I think it remembered last time we flew and just responded b-badly this time." My voice quivered.

Tripp nodded, like I'd just confirmed what he'd been thinking.

"But your head?"

"F-feels fine." I made myself sit up and lean against a tree behind me, taking in our surroundings for the first time. We were still in the forest, but clearly at the edge of it, we'd be able to make our way into town without getting lost in the trees.

Tripp took off one of his gloves and put a frosty cold hand on my forehead.

"Deep breaths." He said. I tried to slow my breathing, holding in each breath as long as I could.

He dug around in the front pocket of his rucksack and pulled out a little brown spray bottle with a bright orange label - calming herbal spray. I opened my mouth and he pumped the lid down twice, giving me two sprays of the sweet, comforting taste that burned my tongue slightly.

"Thank you, Doctor Reynolds." I said as he put the bottle back in his bag. He helped me to my feet and gave me a hug.

"Do- do you think this will be a permanent thing when I fly now?" I asked, not really sure I wanted the answer.

Tripp was quiet for just too long before he answered.

"I don't know. It shouldn't, because you've always been fine with flying. But..." He trailed off, not looking me in the eye.

"But we don't know what was done to my brain when I hit my head. It could be my new thing." I finished for him. He nodded, a sad smile on his face.

"Exactly. Just take it easy for now, tiny flights, low to the ground when you can, and gradually build it up from there. It could just be a case of relearning." He tried to sound reassuring.

Maybe he was right. Maybe I'd be fine. But the way I lost control over my body scared me and I prayed that it wasn't the new normal for flying.

"You ready to go into town?" Tripp asked, changing the subject to the task at hand. I nodded, now feeling pretty much back to normal as I took my mushroom hat out of bag and tucked my bright pink, very unsubtle hair up into it.

Tripp too put on his dark grey woollen hat; his brown hair was much less distinctive than mine, but the less recognisable we looked the better. Plus it was damn cold. We started walking, my shaking had stopped but the echo of it remained with every step I took towards civilisation.

Chapter 11

We walked for about half an hour before we were able to find a Tesco, figuring out from signs that we were in the village Meaden in Gloucestershire, and had been hiding out in the Forest of Dean.

The edge of the forest took us to a road with just some houses along it, no people around - everyone being at work or school on a Thursday late morning.

This road lead us to a bigger one where we had to choose right or left. We went right but after a while it looked like there was nothing in that direction. A man with long curly hair was coming towards us, so, keeping our heads down as much as possible and not looking him in the eye, we asked him which way any shops were.

He smelled very much of alcohol.

He pointed behind us, in the direction from which we'd come and seemed to find our ignorance quite funny.

"Not from round here then?" He asked, as if it wasn't obvious. He didn't seem to quite be able to focus on us,

and before we could give him an answer, he pushed between us with his unsettlingly warm hands and stumbled along on his merry way, talking to himself about 'stupid tossers' while turning off to the right and not checking for cars before he crossed the road. He was lucky there had been hardly any cars around here so far.
Tripp looked at his watch and gave an impressed whistle. "It's only half-past ten." We both gave the man a silent mock-applause and saluted him.

Once we reached Tesco, we kept nervously checking all around us and probably looked very suspicious.
I had no reason to suspect anyone from SCREB would be here, but I was still extremely anxious. We were out in the world and we had no dragons around to pick us up if things got bad.
There were a few people gathered around the bus stop outside, including an older woman with short black hair talking to the whole group about how she was worried about her cat getting rickets and making everybody look very uncomfortable as she announced it loudly so that everyone present, whether they knew her or not, knew about the fifteen year old cat who didn't like going outside so wasn't getting any sunlight.
We kept our heads down as we continued walking through the carpark and towards the entrance of the shop, bypassing the cat-ricket lady.
I could hear tense violin music playing in my head as we walked, as if an attack was imminent. Usually coming into Tesco we would've started skidding and skating around as the floor was almost always like an ice rink, but today we

just trudged on through, carrying too much weight to do that.

I went to check through the ingredients on a loaf of bread even though I knew it was almost pointless, while Tripp looked at the newspaper stand by the door. I put the loaf down after seeing the word 'egg' and heard Tripp with pure terror in his voice.

"Oh god."

I looked to where he stood and walked over to join him. "Oh-" Any more words got caught in my throat as I stared down at the frontpage. Our college ID photos stared back up at us, along with a report of "Missing Teenagers Still Unfound" by Kevin Smythe. I read through the report and my legs grew weaker as it went on.

Twins Tristan and Iris Reynolds, 16, are still reportedly missing with no known sightings since their disappearance. The pair were last seen going into their Paignton home at approximately 5pm on Monday 14th November, 2016 after coming home from college on the bus, by a neighbour. Although unknown to them at the time, tragedy struck the two earlier that day when their parents Adam, 54 and Jennifer, 51 were victims of a fatal car accident while travelling. The microbiologist couple were heading to Bristol to work on an unspecified project for the rest of the week. Authorities got in touch with the twins later that night to break the news to them by phone, letting them know that a social worker and Devon & Cornwall Police officer were on their way to take them in and deal with the new situation, but when they got there the twins were nowhere to be seen. Nina Parr, a social worker of seven years, arrived at their home at around 11:30 Monday night to find nobody answering the door. "I rang the doorbell several times, I tried phoning both of

them but there was absolutely no sign of either of them." Nina said. "I called the police of course and told them to hurry up, I was so worried about the two. Who knew what state they might be in after finding out what had happened?"
But when the police arrived and got into the house, Tristan and Iris seemed to be nowhere. Almost all of their notable belongings seemed to be present and untouched, save for the teens' mobile phones having been taken apart and left in their bedrooms.
Neighbours reported hearing screams and shouting not long before Nina arrived and alerted the police, but were informed that they were already on their way. Friends of the missing duo have been questioned for anything they might know say that they are 'seriously worried' about their friends, 'praying that they come back soon and safe.' An investigation is well underway and has all but confirmed this to be a kidnapping, police say that the likelihood of finding the twins alive is decreasing by the day. Juliet Williams, a friend of the two, described them as being "average height and slim build, facially very similar and they look a bit like pixies. They both have brown hair but Iris dyes hers bright pink."
The investigation started in Devon alone but given the time that has passed since the last sighting, the search area has been expanded to the whole South of England. Police are urging anyone with information to come forward.

I looked down at the pictures. As well as the two of us, there was a blonde woman who I vaguely recognised. The caption read *Nina Parr, worried Social Worker on the case.*
Nina Parr did not look worried. Nina Parr looked cold.
Nina Parr.

I knew that name, but I couldn't think why. I looked at the picture again. She was the woman who'd come to our backyard, who'd chased us in the forest, who was hunting us. But I was sure I knew her name, and possibly her face, from something else. I put the thought out of my mind when I took a good look at my own picture. I'd seen the picture almost daily for the last two and a half months on my ID and bus pass, but somehow it had changed. The girl looking back up at me seemed distant now. She was smiling brightly, with an excited twinkle in her blue-lined eyes because her brother had just told her a stupid joke to get her to laugh too much and ruin the picture, but she managed to compose herself enough to not completely lose it until after the picture was done. The freckles across her nose and cheeks stood out after being in the sun so much and her hair that had been dyed pink for the first time just a few days ago after being gradually lightened for weeks was more vibrant than ever. I didn't realise how different I felt now until I saw this picture. I looked at Tripp's next to mine, he too was holding in laughter, freckles almost as vibrant as mine, both of us having been caught in moments of happiness.

Now, we looked at each other with dread.

"So they didn't tell everyone we went to live with some distant aunt." Tripp said, resigned. His eyes glistened with the threat of more tears and went even redder than they were already. Maybe that was a good thing though, his face looked so red and puffy that to anyone who didn't know us, he probably couldn't be recognised as the smiling boy from the picture.

There were dark circles under his eyes from how hard it had been getting to sleep. Mostly we'd just been lying down and trying not to think too much about anything, eventually gone to sleep for as little time as our bodies could get away with before waking up and not being able to get back to sleep.

I guessed I looked pretty much the same, and I could feel the prickle in the back of my eyes that always comes before crying while wishing not to. I sniffed everything back as Tripp looked back down at our article.

"You look a lot rougher at the moment, people won't know it's you with your hair hidden." He said, his train of thought following the same track as mine.

"You don't look much better yourself." I said and we both gave the tiniest little laughs. The sad kind of laugh that isn't really a laugh, but that people do when they want to pretend they're not as sad as they are. Or to imply that they're laughing at themselves for being ridiculous. You know the one.

He put the newspaper down and gave his eyes a quick wipe before he spoke in a hushed tone.

"We should see if we can find some glasses to wear while we're in public." He looked around to make sure no one was listening, but there weren't many people around. I nodded in agreement and we stepped away from the newspaper stand. We kept our heads down as we walked through the shop, picking up as much unspoilable food as we'd be able to carry. The weight of my rucksack had been making my shoulders and back ache, but it had practically been glued to me for the last few days so I wasn't noticing much now. I would when I took it off later though.

We got some fresh fruit and some tinned, along with a packet of oats. When we got to the potatoes we got one bag of big ones and a roll of tin foil so that we could bake them. Or rather, get our oversized reptiles to bake them for us. This was more than we could fit into rucksacks so we called it quits and went to pay but got slightly distracted on the way by a wide range of sweet stuff, including flapjacks.

"Check the ingredients!" Tripp exclaimed, taking the potatoes from me so that I had a hand free to pick up a pack of six big flapjacks. I searched through the writing on the back until I found the ingredients list. I started scanning but was quickly stopped in my tracks.

"Butter." I declared, disappointed.

"Check the other ones!" Tripp demanded.

"I *am* checking the other ones!" I frantically put the ones I was holding back down on the shelf and picked up the next, same-sized packet, from a different brand. I started looking. I didn't see butter. I didn't see anything that wasn't plants.

"They're vegan!" I shrieked, higher-pitched and louder than I intended. Tripp grinned and looked at the shelf to see how many there were. Five other packets remained. We looked at each other. We made eye contact. We forgot everything else in the world and how sad we'd been not ten minutes ago and knew exactly what to do.

We grabbed all the flapjacks.

Chapter 12

We made it out without being recognised, the fact that we looked so rough and worn out definitely helped, but I put it mostly down to the fact that the girl on the checkout was looking at her falling-off acrylic nail more than at us. Walking towards what we assumed was the High Street, there were a few more people who didn't pay us any attention.

We were planning to find somewhere quiet and unfilled with people in order to eat something but we got slightly distracted.

We passed a chip shop. The smell floating out was one I hadn't realised how much I missed. It took me back to going to the beach at sunset in summer, when sunset was about nine o'clock at night. We would all go together and stop for chips on the way until we were about twelve, then Tripp and I would walk down together with our body-boards and Mum and Dad would meet us there with the chips as we got older. We would jump around in the waves and dig holes in the sand, and I got that feeling that you get when you're with your favorite people, and everything feels right and wrong at the same time but still it's a wonderful feeling and you want to spend the rest of your life making more memories with these people but you also want this moment to never end. I think you probably know the feeling I mean; when looking back you will definitely think of 'the good old days' I missed that. It was a feeling I got a lot this summer, when Tripp and I went out a lot together and things were good and everyone was alive and hadn't run away.

Yeah, the smell of chips made me nostalgic for that.

I looked at Tripp and could tell he was thinking the same thing. They smelled so good, and we didn't know when we would next get this opportunity.

"We could." I said, checking the outdoor price list. "It'd only be four pounds." I tried to make pitiful, starved eyes. Tripp looked at the canvas bag of vegetation we'd just bought and then back at the chip shop. He couldn't hide his smile and dug two pounds out of his pocket.

"Only one of us should order them, we'll be less easy to recognise if we're apart." He said.

I nodded in agreement. "I'll go, I look less like me without my hair. You just look like *you* wearing a hat."

"You made that sound like an insult somehow, but either I'm not intelligent enough to see it or you weren't intelligent enough to form it properly." He half-smiled, but also looked slightly confused. I took the coins out of his hand and fished around in my own pocket for two more.

"Let's just go with we're both equally intelligent, however much or little that may be." I said, though we both knew

damn well that Tripp was more intelligent than me.
"That works. I'll see if there are any shops up that way
that sell reading glasses. I'll get the weakest ones and we
can wear them while we're in town. You gonna be okay on
your own?" He asked. He looked so much like he had a
hangover, it was a little weird seeing him look concerned.
"Yeah, I'll start walking up that way if you're not back by
the time I'm done." we nodded in agreement and he
turned to walk up the gentle hill as I headed into the
source of the late-night-sunset-memory smell.

There was someone reading our newspaper inside.
He was looking at a page on the inside, rather than our
front-cover spread but it sent a bolt of electric fear
through every nerve in my body.
The man was leaning against the opposite wall, waiting
for his order and didn't look up as I walked in. I took a
deep breath and looked around. Not that there was much
to look around at. The shop was small, just a takeaway
place, and there were no other customers in sight. The
woman behind the counter was pottering about getting
together what I assumed was the man with the
newspaper's order. I realised I wasn't just stood looking
around, I was frozen, I couldn't move, I was freaking out
so much. The tiny Irises in my head were screaming and
trying to offer a load of different pieces of advice.

Get out now.

*Go order anyway, you look so terrible right now they won't
know it's you.*

It's not worth the risk, just leave quietly before they notice you're here.

They aren't paying any attention to you or the front page.

So hungry, just act normal, they won't know it's you.

What if he's looking to see if there's any more information about you and Tripp?

What would happen if he did see me and recognise me from my picture? Think this through logically, what would actually happen?

There would be a second where we stared at each other in confusion, as his brain computed that I really was the girl from the newspaper. Assuming I had regained the use of my legs by then, I would turn to run out, but I'd be in such a clumsy, panicky rush that I would inevitably trip over myself and this guy might well lunge forward to either help me up or hold me still so that he could call the police. Let's say I managed to get out, but the man had still recognised me and ran out after me. I would have to keep running until I managed to get out of his sight, even if that meant going back to the forest and hiding in the undergrowth. That meant I was separated from Tripp and he had no way to find me. Plus he was left in the town where I would be known to be, where word of my appearance would surely be spread, so the people would be on the lookout for him and he would have no idea. Then the police would be called. They would know exactly the area we were in, it was broad daylight so we couldn't get Delta and Zen, and I couldn't go too far because Tripp wouldn't be with me. The police would come to this chip shop, where I had definitely been seen, and maybe bring sniffer dogs to follow my trail which meant that I would undoubtedly, inescapably be found.

Then SCREB would get involved. I didn't know what they planned to do once they'd caught Tripp and me, but I didn't want to find out. Maybe they'd make us work for them with threats. Maybe they'd capture Delta and Zen and 'eliminate' them. Maybe they'd just kill us and say that we were insane and unstable since our parents died, and commited a double-suicide.

Maybe that would be easier.

Jesus, that's a dark thought.

I mentally kicked myself for going there. That was a horrible thing to think. Something I wouldn't have thought of, or at least not so quickly, a week ago.

Anyway, in the space of about five seconds I'd run through the entire story of now up until my hypothetical death in the scenario where I stayed. The risk far, far outweighed the reward, no matter how hungry and nostalgic I was feeling. The woman behind the counter looked up at me, slightly surprised.

"You alright, love?" She asked. My heart nearly stopped as she looked right at my face, at the face that was being shown to the nation for anyone to find.

Did she know the picture was me? Had she even seen the picture? Was that flicker of her eyes recognition, or just surprise at the fact that I probably looked like I was high? I could feel myself blush horrendously, my face burning up as I tried to think of what to say. There was no way I was ordering something, I just needed to get out.

It was so hot in here, and I was bundled up in layers to combat the outside world.

I started to back out, trying to think of something, anything to say so as to not be rude.

The man reading the newspaper looked up and I completely panicked. I turned around and tried to pull the door open, but as predicted, I was in such a rush I managed to trip over nothing in particular and crashed into the minifridge next to the door, knocking off a stand of flyers in the process. The man started coming over to help me, so I grabbed all the flyers and the cardboard stand and hastily shoved them back onto the fridge, not bothering to get the flyers back into their stand.

"S-sorry!" I managed to half say, half splutter as I pulled open the door and threw myself out onto the street, the cold air hitting me like a violent hug.

I hadn't realised how hard I'd been finding it to breath until I got out and took several deep breaths, as if someone had been holding me underwater and suddenly let me up. The man stepped out and put a hand on my shoulder.

"Are you alright?" He asked. I nearly screamed as I pulled his hand off me, a lot harder than I meant to, and began a quick sprint in the direction Tripp had gone. The man ran after me, calling out, "Hey! Are you okay?" I ignored him and kept running, but he didn't seem to follow me for long. I felt like a really shitty person after that. That was so incredibly rude, and a major overreaction.

But he didn't know it was me in the newspaper. I was sure of that. Even if he went back and looked at the picture, he'd see a smiling, healthy-looking girl with pink hair and a bit of makeup and mental stability. He would not see the slightly crazy, drug-addict image that I just presented to him in that little display.

I didn't realise how little time had passed until I clocked the fact that I ran past Tripp in my efforts to get away from the chip shop. I knew I ran past someone, but for a second, that's all he was - someone.

I squeaked as I felt hands on my shoulders, my fragile legs crumpled and I fell to the ground again.

When I looked up and twigged who my attacker was I calmed down. Tripp had fallen with me but was now helping me into a sitting position, a look of worry and fear on his face.

"Rainbow! Are you okay? What happened?" He asked quickly, looking around for whatever had threatened me. I looked over his shoulder and nearly jumped out of my skin, heart pounding uncontrollably. The man who'd been reading our newspaper was jogging towards us. I guess he kept watching me and saw the two of us go down. I scrambled to my feet as I shook my head in answer to Tripp.

"Nope, very much not okay." I managed to say, before the man reached us and looked at us both with concern.

"Are you alright?" He asked me. I avoided his eyes, I looked down so that he couldn't really see my face. I took a shaky breath, racked my brain trying to think of what to say, knowing that my voice would come out high pitched and pathetic.

"Sorry, we're just running late for something." I heard Tripp say. His voice sounded calm, but I detected an edge of panic that I think only I could've heard. He grabbed my hand and gently but swiftly led me back on the path up the hill, as I tried to mutter an apology under my breath. The man didn't follow.

"What happened?" Tripp asked again, now out of earshot, though he still said it in a hushed tone.
"I'm sorry, that guy was in the chip shop and he was reading the newspaper."
"Oh god. The one that we're in?" Tripp's voice went cold and fearful.
"Yup. he wasn't reading that page, but I just freaked out when I saw it. Sorry." I kept looking down at my muddy boots, not wanting to look him in the eye after the scene I'd just caused. He stopped walking and looked at me.
"Why sorry?"
I made myself look up and meet his gaze. He didn't look annoyed as I'd expected, he looked worried. I felt hot tears behind my eyes again, this frustrated me as there was no real reason right now. I tried to think of how to answer his question. *Why sorry?* It was obvious, wasn't it?
"Because I went into panic mode and-" I broke off, not sure what to say.
"And what?" Tripp said, after a pause.
"And-" I tried. "I knocked stuff over going out, and he could've recognised me." I tried to take deep breaths, but I still felt unable to relax.
"But he *didn't* recognise you, and you *did* get out." Tripp declared. "You panicked, which is a completely natural reaction in that situation, and you got out as quickly as you could. Did you think you did something wrong?" He stared at me, his face distressed but somehow comforting.

"I don't know. I just-" I bit back the words, not sure where they were going as I couldn't help the tears rolling down my cheeks. Again. "I want to go home." I whispered.

I dropped my gaze to make it less obvious how much I was crying now, but I don't think it really worked. Tripp pulled me into a tight, warm hug that made me feel like I was being protected from the whole world. Did I mention he gives very good hugs?

"I miss Mum and Dad." I started properly sobbing into his shoulder as he rubbed my back and held onto me. I could tell he was crying too, but trying to be subtle about it.

"I know." He said gently. I didn't mean to break down like this, but once I started, I couldn't stop. We just stood there in the empty street, two snivelling wrecks.

Chapter 13

I had not looked at my reflection since Monday. It was
now Thursday and I looked *rough*.

Although, Tripp was right - in this hat I did look like a
shocked mushroom.

I hadn't paid any attention to what little I saw of myself in
shop and car windows, and now seeing myself in the
mirror of the toilets at the leisure centre came as a shock.
My eyes were about three times their normal size and
bright red, almost matching the shade of the rest of my
face. I had a bunch of new spots on my chin and forehead
that were taking advantage of me being unable to see
them and do something about them. There was also dry
skin appearing on my forehead and around my nose. Not
to mention my lips. I'd felt them getting upset from the
cold but not realised how bad the damage was. They were
completely dry, with splits and cracks all over and a
decent amount of dried blood. The cold had always gotten
to me but I always had lotions and potions to put on and

fix things. Now however, it looked like I'd had sandpaper rubbed all over my face.

The thing that struck me the most, though, was how very much I looked like Tripp at the moment. Without my hair showing, with no makeup on and my face in my current disheveled state, it was uncanny. We'd always looked pretty alike, with fairly neutral faces both of which could've belonged to either a boy or a girl, which always made me think that if we'd both been boys or both been girls we would be identical twins. I know that's not exactly how the biology works but still, you get my point.

I looked into the blue-green eyes that also belonged to my brother and wondered what he was thinking. Probably wishing I'd stop bursting into tears and having panics, and just get through the day properly.

I wondered what he was feeling on the inside. If he felt the same as I did, but kept it to himself so that at least one of us was keeping calm and sensible. I wondered how he'd been all the time that I was unconscious. He'd cried with me in the street earlier, but gently and quietly, trying not to make it obvious, to comfort me. What would he have been like if our positions had been switched?

I quickly looked down at my hands in the sink as someone came in. She went straight to a cubicle and didn't pay any attention to me but I couldn't stop my heart rate speeding up. My hands were bad too. Knuckles chapped and irritated, even though I'd been wearing gloves throughout our excursion. The warm water from the tap hurt, but the cold had been even worse, though it helped when I splashed it over my face, bringing a sweet relief I didn't realise how much I needed.

I stood and just breathed for a moment, looking into the eyes of my reflection again before I wiped my face dry on my sleeve and put on the reading glasses we'd found in one of the shops. We'd gotten the weakest prescription like Tripp said, but my vision was still a bit weird with everything slightly magnified and obscured. I also learned that glasses absolutely didn't suit me when all my hair was hidden under a hat, and I looked less like a mushroom and more like some cartoon character, but I couldn't place who.

As I left the toilets, I hung back a little and looked round the corner at the reception desk. No one was looking at me, but I didn't know what the protocol was for going to the changing room without paying. Back home, no one would stop you because there was the café and the viewing area through the same door you go through to get to the changing rooms but I wasn't sure if that would work here.

"You okay?" I nearly jumped out of my skin at the sound of Tripp's voice behind me. I turned to look at him and nodded, surprised and annoyed at how well the glasses suited him.

"You?" I asked. He nodded too and we both turned our looks back to the receptionists. I heard him laughing slightly behind me and looked back in confusion.

"You look like the turtle wizard thing from Mario."

"Shut up. You look like a knock-off Harry Potter." I retorted.

"Harry Potter's hot."

"I said 'knock off.'"

"Yeah, but it's still Harry Potter." He sounded smug so I elbowed him.

98

Walk like you're supposed to be here, and people will believe it's true I told myself over and over again as I walked. I knew I was ridiculous for being so afraid, worst case scenario I paid a fiver and pretended I was going for a swim, but every step I took towards the changing room felt like I was on a tightrope of risk.

One receptionist was on the phone, the other was writing something on the desk in front of her. I tried to keep my breathing calm. I looked straight ahead and resisted the urge to look behind me at Tripp. I passed the desk, no one stopped me.

No one stopped me.

God, I'm pathetic aren't I? Of course no one stopped me, I walked through a public space that I was very much allowed to walk through. I breathed a sigh of relief as I passed and looked back to Tripp who gave me a kind of *See?* look, at just how fine we were and how no one had tried to arrest us for walking through a place that it was fine to walk through.

As we continued towards the changing rooms I prayed to the fairies that there would be cubicles to shower in. The pool nearest our home didn't have any, but the better one that was only about ten minutes further to drive to did. If there were no cubicles, I would just have to strip down to my underwear and pretend I was wearing a bikini, even if there was no one else in there.

Thank any form of higher power that there might be that there was no one in the changing room while I was getting undressed. There had been two old ladies getting ready to go into the pool and chatting about pineapples and rocks when I got there, but they left almost as soon as I arrived.

To say that I did not smell great would be an understatement. I would feel an unbearable urge to apologise to anyone present if there had been anyone. I knew it hadn't been great yesterday when I got changed, but we'd done a lot of walking since then, and I was under a lot of layers that, although kept me warm from the cold outside, I got really hot inside while moving about a lot and consequently, not washing for four days was taking a toll. I grabbed the bar of soap Tripp had picked up from home, shoved the clothes I'd been wearing into the rucksack and wrapped the towel around myself before leaving the changing cubicle, picking up my boots and trying to make sure the towel didn't come untucked and expose me to anyone who might walk in.

I was just able to squish my rucksack, shoes and clothes into a locker and shut the door. It would've probably fitted no problem had I folded everything and shut it properly, but I was only having a shower and then would be getting it back out to dig through pretty soon so there didn't seem much point.

I then cursed myself for not remembering that lockers eat money and getting out a pound before I got this far. I pulled out the rucksack and put it on the floor, digging through to get to my cash and trying to keep my towel on, while my hair flopped over my face now that it wasn't hidden away under my hat.

I said a couple of rude words under my breath as I flipped my head to get the hair out of the way and had to hold it at an awkward angle to keep my visibility while my hands were occupied until I finally found my wallet. I pulled out a single pound coin and folded the tattered wallet up before shoving it back into the rucksack and shoving the rucksack into the locker, cursing both of them more than was reasonable as I put the coin into the slot and slammed the door shut. This was the point at which my towel had had enough of my leaning around and moving and fell to the floor. I shrieked and prayed that no one would enter while at the same time knowing for absolute, undeniable certainty that a large group of cleaners, or inspectors on a tour, or a children's birthday party, or every female member of the royal family was definitely going to come in and witness me unnecessarily getting myself into a state. I hastily picked the towel back up, grabbed the key from the locker and ran to the showers.

There were cubicle ones, I checked when I came in.

I don't think soap and warm water had ever felt better than it did right then and there. You know the feeling of having a warm shower after a long day in the dead of winter? Well multiply that feeling by about fifty and that's about how it felt now. It felt like one of those "oddly satisfying" videos you see online where something is getting cleaned.

I realise that I was finding it more exciting than it actually was after only four days, but those four days hadn't exactly been fun and this was a nice break and relief from everything.

I would've washed my hair properly given the chance, but I didn't have any shampoo or conditioner, we hadn't thought about that. I did as best I could and gave it a thorough rinse but it was hard and took a long time because my hair is not only quite long and thick, it's also wavy and a bit curly in places, plus hadn't been brushed for several days so was full of tangles and I found myself feeling like Rapunzel.

I didn't want to leave, it was so nice and warm but I must've spent about twenty minutes in the shower and I was getting hungrier. I heard one of the non-cubicle showers start just as mine ran out and I pulled the towel down from where I'd chucked it over the divider and tried to keep it from getting water all over it. I squeezed out my hair and made sure the towel was done up tight and secure before opening the curtain to a sight I was not prepared for.

Why is it that old women at swimming pools are so very okay with being naked in the showers? I mean I applaud the self-confidence and it's great that they feel so comfortable in themselves but I think we can all agree that the whole situation just makes everyone else involved deeply uncomfortable and unsettled.

I tried not to look at her, but not look like I was specifically not looking at her in case she thought me rude. I was suddenly very aware of the large distance between me and the door back into the changing room, and the fact that she was roughly halfway between. Then it happened.

Eye contact.

I don't know how it happened, but somehow our eyes met and she smiled at me in a friendly way. I returned the smile, though it probably came out as more of a grimace by accident, felt my face turn red and scuttled away, pretending I had any amount of dignity I could hold onto. There were a few more people in the changing room now, including a woman and two girls, one around my age and one who looked about seven, who I presumed were her daughters, and I darted past them to get to my locker. As I hurriedly unlocked it I remembered that my hair was now exposed and still very visibly pink, which would be the most recognisable thing about me from the description. Back in my cubicle to get dressed I dug through the dirty clothes in the top of my bag to get to the clean ones underneath. I could've worn the same jeans I'd had on today and just changed my shirt and underwear, but since I'd just gotten clean I felt I owed it to myself and the clothes to put on fresh ones, like when you change your bedding and you just *have* to wash your hair and put on fresh pyjamas. Otherwise it's disrespectful to the bed. After I got dressed and applied deodorant, I wrapped the towel around my hair while I put on socks and laced up my boots.

Putting on my coat, I suddenly stopped and all of my muscles seized up when I tuned into what was being said by the family outside.

"But won't their mummy and daddy be wondering where they are?" Came the voice of a little girl.

"Their mum and dad are dead, Chloe. That's what the guy on the news was saying." Another voice, the girl who looked about my age, I assumed.

"Quiet, Abi." Said the mother. "Once the police find them, they'll sort out who'll look after them and where they'll live."

"*If* they find them." Abi said.

"Abi!" The mum was clearly trying to get Abi to shut up.

"What? I'm just saying it's already been four days and there's been no sign of them-"

"That's enough now, just put your stuff in the locker." The

conversation ended. I tried to believe that they weren't talking about me, tried to tell myself that it could be anyone who'd gone missing four days ago and had dead parents. Somehow, I couldn't shake the feeling that they might just be referring to me and Tripp as my heart thumped and my pulse quickened. It felt so weird to be just ten feet away from the people who were talking about (most likely) me, believing that I was missing somewhere in the middle of nowhere, possibly never to be found. People who'd just seen me being talked about on the news as people were out searching for any trace of me and my twin.

Hang on, *that's what the guy on the news was saying*, were we now being announced on national television as well as newspapers? Right now? I snapped out of my listening-freeze and quickly put my glasses back on and tucked my cold, damp hair into the hat. I rushed out of the cubicle and hoisted my rucksack onto my back, being careful not to let anyone see my face properly.

Tripp was sitting on a bench outside the changing rooms twiddling his thumbs, wearing his hat and glasses and his same old navy blue Paddington Bear coat, but in different jeans now. He looked up when he heard me rushing towards him and his face turned worried when he saw me. I could see the café was ahead of us, directly in our path so I grabbed Tripp's hand and pulled him along with me as ran, a hunch telling me to go in there.

"What? What's wrong?" He asked as we went. Before I could answer, we'd reached the café and looked up above the counter, where there was a small TV mounted to the wall, with the news playing. The news did not contain something I wanted it to. My blood froze and I stood still,

Tripp and I both gripping each other's hands in disbelief. There, on that screen, was the old Scottish man from the forest.

Chapter 14

"And they said they were out for a hike, but I've not a shadow of a doubt in my mind that it was those wee nippers you're after." He looked as sure as could be as he looked just off centre of the camera. Across the screen below him, his name, *Neil Westcott*, was written.
"No. That's not fair!" Tripp said.
"Why, Neil?" I chimed in. "Why would he do this to us? I really thought he was our friend!" We both sighed in resignation at the screen. Of course this was a horrible new development that was terrifying and made us more likely to be found now that everyone knew we were in this area, but we both felt an overwhelming feeling of disappointment in the wise old man that we'd thought was possibly a spirit sent to give us some kind of Bob Ross-style advice.
"What their truth is, I don't know, but I surely hope they've got their minds intact." He finished. The screen cut back to news reporters on they're comfy looking

settee, again showing our photos and asking for any information anyone could offer, before they started on something to do with Brexit. I hoped they would all sort that out soon. It had been going for four months now and nothing seemed any clearer yet.

I gulped and felt slightly nauseous, the glasses just making it worse. I was suddenly extremely aware of how many people were now here, able to see this screen just as well as we could. We were so, so vulnerable.

"You guys alright there? Can I get you anything?" The woman behind the counter asked.

I started to panic. She could see us very clearly right now, and had just been able to see us very clearly on the TV. I looked to Tripp, panicking over what to do.

"No, it's alright, thanks." he said, in a voice several tones lower than his natural one. He kept his head down and turned to leave the café, while I followed and kept hold of his hand. We seemed quite rude but we had to get out. We held our gazes firmly to the ground, only looking slightly forwards to make sure we didn't walk into anyone, as we hastily made our way back towards the main door.

"Security cameras." Tripp whispered, afraid. He wasn't issuing instructions, but thinking out loud as all sorts of thoughts of being caught and taken away swam through our heads. Past reception we went, feeling like we were being suffocated by the presence of people who could so easily call someone who would come and 'take care of us'. Bursting out into the cold, crisp outside world was a literal breath of fresh air. We ran to the edge of the car park and sat down on the edge of the pavement, panting and looking down. I could feel myself shaking slightly, and the two of us leaned on each other for support.

"We need to get out of here." Tripp said. I nodded as he continued, "As soon as Zen and Delta get back tonight, we're moving." I thought for a minute about that. I didn't want to say it, I didn't want to be a liability any more than I already had been so far.

But, I knew that if I stayed silent it could just make things worse.

But, maybe I'd be okay after all and I should keep quiet so as to not cause a fuss.

But what if I wasn't okay? What if I got worse than ever?

"I don't-" I began, not wanting to say what I knew to be true. "I don't know if I'll be able to fly. Sorry." I stared down at my feet, no longer to not be recognised, but to avoid eye contact. We'd move a lot slower without flying. A lot more inconveniently, because of me. I felt a burning of guilt in my stomach as I waited for Tripp to say something, but he just put an arm around me and held me tight.

"It's okay." He said in a comforting voice. "We'll be alright." I could hear a smile in his voice but I couldn't quite tell what sort of smile. Maybe a sad one, maybe a fake one designed only to stop me feeling bad, maybe a genuine one just because we were okay.

"How do you feel after showering?" He asked.

"Lighter." I said. Tripp laughed and I couldn't help smiling as I went on. "But some of the dye washed out so my hair is gonna look really bland once it's dried." Tripp put both his hands on my shoulders and turned me to face him, looking deep into my eyes.

"Are you gonna be okay?" He sounded so concerned.

"I don't think I am, Rainbow, I really don't. My hair is about sixty percent of my personality." I said and we both laughed, before he reached into the food bag that he'd held onto and handed me an apple. I took it, only just realising again how hungry I was.

"Thank you." I said as he took an apple out for himself and held it to mine, we clinked them together as if we were toasting with wine glasses.

It wasn't the best place to sit and eat apples, it wasn't a *good* place to sit and eat apples after our faces and story had just been freshly broadcast to the nation. But we had our Mario Turtle-Wizard hats and our knock-off Harry Potter glasses on so sit and eat apples we did. There were very few people out here anyway, and they weren't paying us attention. Anyone inside who had seen our news report wouldn't be expecting to see us here, so they probably wouldn't see us here.

* * *

We were almost back in the forest when we saw her. Heads down and walking through town, we would just have to make another left turn to be on the road that led straight forest-wards.

We'd spent an hour and a half retracing our steps, getting lost and trying to find our way back to the forest while being seen by as few people as possible and finally, we were so close and recognised everything around us from this morning.

I didn't even notice her, I was focusing so much on not stepping on the cracks in the pavement (or on other people's feet, it had become busier later in the day), which was particularly difficult with the glasses on. I had to stop abruptly when Tripp slammed his hand into my chest to make me stand still. I looked to him and opened my mouth to speak, but before I could get any words out, he clamped his other hand over my mouth to shut me up.

I frowned at him but he looked panicked and I was just able to make out him staring, frowning and keeping his eyes locked ahead of us.

I looked. I squinted through the glasses that were supposed to be only for reading, trying to make out who or what he was looking at.

Nina Parr.

How the hell had she found us? I know the news had just told the country that we were seen round here, but that hadn't been that long ago. And she wasn't just in the area, she was *right* there, about ten feet from us.

My heartbeat sped up, my legs began to feel wobbly, I didn't know what to do. She wasn't looking at us, she was facing side-on, staring at some kind of tablet or iPad thing. She was wearing black trousers and boots, with a white puffy coat, her blonde hair scraped back into a neat bun.

I looked back at Tripp, my eyes wide this time, trying to ask him what we should do. He took both his hands off me and looked around.

Nina was blocking our way back to the forest. There would've been other ways, but we had no idea how to get to them. She kept staring at the tablet, tapping on the screen as a young, tall guy dressed all in black stood next to her and looked at it over her shoulder. They were pointing at the screen and talking, but it was impossible to tell what they were saying. I was completely frozen with fear, and the tiniest bit of recognition still niggling away at me. I grabbed Tripp's hand and held on tight.

"What do we do?" I whispered.

Nina and the guy started to turn in our direction, still looking down at their tablet.

I tipped my head down a little, tucking my chin in towards my chest so that I could look out over my glasses at them. My whole body went numb as I realised they were in fact looking at us. They couldn't tell it was us though, not yet at least. They were frowning, thinking, trying to decide whether or not they knew who these kids in glasses and woolen hats were.

We didn't want to wait around for them to figure it out.

"Run." Tripp commanded, and we both took off like rockets.

We bolted down side streets and lanes, no idea where we were going, just one goal in mind; away.

We passed through areas of housing, a small park and what I'm pretty sure was a drug-deal at one point, swooping through every location and leaving as quickly as we'd entered without taking time to look around or comprehend our surroundings.

I don't know how long we ran, it probably wasn't that long, we were in a fairly small village but it felt like forever.

I wanted to stop and breathe so much, just rest for a moment but my legs wouldn't let me stop, I knew I had to keep going, get as far from where we had been as possible.

I looked back behind us as we ran, no one seemed to be following so we slowed down to a jog.

I tried to breathe more normally, wishing I had better stamina as we eventually came to a stop on a little lane next to a big old house on a street full of cafés and little shops. Tripp and I both leaned down with our hands on our knees and took big breaths.

"Christ, we're unfit." Tripp wheezed as we stood up straight and looked around, laughing and gasping for air. They might be following us, they might not, neither of us knew and we didn't care to find out.

We walked out into the street, taking care to look around us and simultaneously keep our heads down, both to avoid recognition to to look over the glasses at our surroundings. The big building we stopped next to was not a house, but a pub. We looked up at the sign that told us to come inside the Red Lion and watch sports.

"Would it be worth hanging around in there for a couple hours?" I asked. "Wait until it gets dark, let them look around town for us and hopefully move on to somewhere else?" To be honest I'm not sure how much of that was genuinely being helpful and trying to hide and how much of it was me just wanting to sit down, but Tripp nodded at my words and looked around again, then looked at his watch.

"It's half-three now, what time does it start getting dark?" "Around five?" I suggested. He nodded again before he spoke, his eyebrows knit together slightly in thought. "If we start making our way back forest-wards around then, I think we'll be okay." He sounded very much like he was trying to reassure the two of us. "There should be a lot of people going home from work and like you said, they'll have had time to search for us and move on." We looked at each other and said the word at the same time.

"Hopefully."

Chapter 15

What I was hoping for when we walked in was something akin to the *I've Got A Dream* scene in *Tangled*, but that wasn't quite the vibe that this place gave off. It was dimly lit, and the light coming through the windows was grey and sad so it just felt like those days when the sun is hiding and the air is cold and you don't feel like doing anything, and not the cosy kind.

The tables were stocked with older people drinking their sorrows away and wondering if the next sip of stale beer would taste any better.

I pushed my glasses up my face so I had to look through them rather than over them now. It would be annoying to not see properly, but I really didn't like the idea of the people in here seeing my face.

There was a big TV screen up behind the bar that might well have had the news on earlier, when our faces had been shown to everyone. Now however, a small group of men were gathered around and watching some form of sports, but with the glasses on, I couldn't tell what sport it was. Probably football.

The rafters hung low, like an old barn and I still could feel the cold wind even inside. Looking around, I was able to see a free table near the corner at the back. I couldn't tell separate, empty chairs from one another, but I could see that it lacked the amorphous blobs that were people.

We walked through the tables towards the empty one at the back, and I felt an uncomfortable jumpiness at not being able to tell where anyone was looking. I could feel eyes on me, but I couldn't tell if that was just because I expected to.

There was very little conversation going on, so I felt weirdly exposed as we walked. The men around the TV cheered and everyone's attention seemed to turn towards them.

Tripp and I sped up so that we got to the empty table before people started looking away from the screen. We sat down on the once-plush sofa bench behind the table, that was now worn out and had some questionable-looking stains that we avoided sitting on.

"This is the kind of place Lola would hang out." Tripp whispered. Despite my discomfort, I couldn't help snickering at the mention of our friend's older sister who'd made some...interesting life decisions. I shouldn't have laughed, but I couldn't help it. Actually I *really* shouldn't have laughed as it made me take a deeper breath than I had been and the strong scent of alcohol nearly made me gag.

I took my rucksack off my back and put it down on the seat next to me, rolling my shoulders around now that the weight was gone. Taking it off always caused a shock of

sudden weightlessness through my spine, not realising
how heavy it was until it was gone. It damn-near pulled
my hat off with it, the top zip getting caught in the wool
and I had to quickly pull it back on to cover up my hair.
"Do you think it would be okay to take the glasses off?" I
asked quietly. "We could sort through the crap in our
bags." Tripp looked around, peering out over his glasses
like a judgemental grandfather who disapproves of your
painting that you just showed him, even though it was
exactly like the one that Bob Ross did and he
complimenting it only ten minutes ago. Not that I'm
bitter. He nodded, like the grandfather did in fact approve,
but wasn't very affectionate.
"Just make sure your hat stays on and try and do it quietly,
don't draw attention."
"I know, I won't." I said, more coldly than I'd intended. As
I took off the glasses, I avoided looking at my brother's
face out of fear that I'd been too harsh in my tone and
stung him.
"Hey, you know what I just realised?" He said, clearly not
fazed by my words.
"What?" I asked, looking up at him, seeing his real and
uncovered face looking slightly amused.
"If we see Simon again, we can tell him 'I told you so.'" He
sounded slightly triumphant. I thought back on our
frenemy from school whom we got on with, but also
insulted and were permanently in competition with. There
were many things we could say to Simon, but that didn't
necessarily mean we would. What specifically had we told
him though? I looked at Tripp and tilted my head.
"Because...?" I asked, unable to place what he was talking
about. Tripp stuck his head forward slightly, in a sort of

'Really? You don't remember?' gesture. I stuck mine forward in more of a *'No, I'm sorry but I really don't, what are you on about?'* gesture.

"We've won the bet!" He exclaimed.

"Ooohh!" I felt a rush of realisation that we had in fact won a bet. "We *have* won!"

We had been sitting down with our friends at lunch one afternoon several months ago, entering a conversation led by Simon asking who would survive longest living out in the wilderness.

"We'd last pretty long." Tripp had interjected as we took our seats. "I have the medical knowledge to keep us alive if we get hurt, Iris can run really fast if we get chased, and we both like camping so we'd be naturals. Plus we live entirely on plants so finding food wouldn't be an issue."

"Okay, fair points. But," Simon challenged. "What about if you're on your own?" He raised an eyebrow.

"No, we count as one person." I declared. Tripp nodded in agreement.

"Besides," He added. "We would only run away *together* so being on our own would never happen."

"Yeah, but you guys would never have the guts to run away anway." Simon retorted. Neither of us had said anything more on it, the conversation soon changed but I remember we both look at each other, sort of offended. *Why wouldn't we have the guts? We could so run away if we wanted to, and we'd be really good at it.* I'm not sure why it got to us so much. But there was something that was getting to me now, too. 'Iris can run really fast.' I could, back then. Back in the spring. Back then I had been part of the running team at school, I was one of the fastest there, running fast made me feel more alive and even

116

though I didn't care that much about winning or losing, running competitively had been one of my favourite things. But I'd let myself slip. I hadn't done any real running since June and I hadn't realised how much it had affected me. How out of breath I got running to this pub had scared me a little, how hard I'd found it today, when six months ago I felt like a cheetah. I knew for a fact it was because I hadn't done any of it, I hadn't kept up with any form of training, but I felt like it had gotten even worse this week.

There was something else I hadn't thought of before now. "I haven't dreamed since I hit my head." I stopped, frozen still, halfway through unzipping my rucksack as I realised this. Tripp stopped too and looked at me.

"Not at all?" He asked, concerned. He understood why this was freaking me out now that I thought about it. We *always* dream. We'd had crazy, wonderful or terrifying dreams every night without fail for as long as I could remember. I shook my head, distressed.

"To be honest," Tripp said, thinking as he talked. "That's probably not a sign of anything bad. We've been through a lot since then and things in your head will have been affected because of that as well as the fall." I couldn't tell how much he meant this and how much he was saying it to make me feel better.

"So I've got brain damage?" I asked, panicking slightly. He shook his head, frowning in thought.

"Very very minor. Maybe not at all actually. It could just be that subconsciously you don't want to go into a deep-enough sleep to dream, because you're afraid of not being able to wake up if you're that deeply asleep. Your brain and body are scared of being unconscious again." He said matter-of-factly. I hadn't thought of that. Not that I'd been thinking about the whole not-dreaming thing, but if I had been thinking about it, I wouldn't have come up with that explanation, I would've just assumed that part of my brain had been chipped off, I was perhaps riddled with tumours and my end was definitely near. I liked Tripps's conclusion a lot better.

I looked down at nothing in particular, deeply, unreasonably upset by this realisation. My dreams were amazing.

"Oi!" We both jolted at the voice. The bartender man was leaning over the bar and scowling across the room at us with his big, werewolf-ish eyebrows.

We both looked up at him and too late, I realised that neither of us were wearing our glasses.

The man looked angry as he continued, but didn't seem to recognise us. "You two ordering anything or just using my table as your own workspace?" He barked. All my muscles tensed up as I looked down at the table, at the stuff we'd gotten out and put on it while trying to sort through them and organise them a bit to make them any smaller and lighter if possible. We weren't doing a very good job with the organising. I looked back up at the bartender who was glaring at us.

"Uhh..." I began, looking to Tripp who was making a face that visually depicted what I'd just said.

"Um, two- two orange juices, please." He said. From the look on his face now I could tell that his thought process was along the lines of: *Please, please, please let them sell orange juice here.* We both relaxed and breathed sighs of relief as the man nodded in irritation and went to get a couple of glasses. Tripp and I both started digging around for money in our pockets while we waited for the now rather annoyed old man to bring them over to us.

Tripp also elbowed me gently to get my attention. I looked at him and saw he was putting his glasses back on. I hastily did the same, annoyed with myself that I hadn't remembered this.

Two glasses of orange juice were plonked (a little violently, I thought) down on the table in front of us, a few drops flying out of each as the hit the wood of the tabletop.

"Three-sixty then." The man said as he stood, a certain huffiness to his voice. I could feel him judgmentally stare down upon us, disapproving and wishing us gone as we each held up a five pound note. The man sighed as Tripp and I looked at each other, fighting for politeness-dominance with our eyes. Neither of us backed down, and eventually the bartender took Tripp's money and went back to the counter to get his change.

I sighed a little to myself in annoyance. Tripp had already been so responsible for me since we set off together. I didn't want him to keep having to look after me.

"Thank you." I said as I put my fiver back in my pocket. The bartender came back and chucked the few coins onto the table, before stomping off. Maybe I was wrong, but I felt like he was overreacting a tad. Perhaps he just didn't like teenagers - we were the youngest people in this building by at least thirty years. We both said our thanks as he walked away, but I don't think he heard or cared. We looked down at our items on the table, surveying what we had and what we could get rid of to make carrying easier. There were a lot of food wrappers that we hadn't put in the bin yet, but apart from that it was just a few pieces of clothing, toiletries and the food we bought earlier today. Still, we folded up the clothes and put stuff away back in the bags as best we could to save space. We were able to fit all the food into our rucksacks and dispense of the separate food bag which helped.

"Where are we gonna go next?" I asked, as I put the last flapjack in and zipped up the bag.

"I don't know. We need to find some form of permanence somewhere." Tripp said. He sounded sort of resigned from life. He really had no idea what we were going to do. Neither of us did.

"Maybe Zen and Delta have a safe place they go when they're not with us and they could take us there?" I wondered aloud.

"If there was somewhere safe, I think they would've taken us there by now. They probably just move around all the time." He pointed out. I knew he was right. I'd known that before I spoke, but I couldn't help hoping.

An hour went by, and then another while we talked about nothing in particular, trying not to dwell on what was actually going on in our lives. The light coming in through the windows, gradually getting dimmer and dimmer, the feeling of a non-productive, grey day only getting stronger as time went on. We both kept nervously glancing at the door, knowing that at any moment someone could come in - someone who could destroy us.

We were both avoiding the fact that we needed to go. We *had* to get back to the forest as soon as possible so that we could move to a new location. Everyone in the country could know that we were in Meaden and it was only a matter of time before our luck with being unrecognised ran out.

As long as we stayed in this pub, avoided stepping into the outside world, we were safe and nothing else needed to exist. But Zen and Delta would either be looking for us or waiting for us, soon if they weren't already.

We overcompensated how much we laughed over stupid jokes that weren't funny even to us, and made sure to jump in with another light-hearted statement if the conversation came to an end, so as to not have an awkward silence in which our thoughts would be able to roam.

We had to accept that we needed to leave though when it was almost completely dark outside. It was six o'clock, more people were coming in and sitting down, making the whole place feel slightly claustrophobic and we both knew that we'd waited here long enough. We needed to move. We were procrastinating - which we're very good at - as much as we could; digging through our bags to make sure had everything, checking all over the floor to see if we'd dropped anything, looking at the TV to see if we could figure out what was going on, but the acceptance that we needed to leave kept thumping it's way nearer.

We would've gone anyway, I swear we would've, but something happened that made us simply have to leave.

Chapter 16

We kept our eyes on the door the whole time we were revving up to leave, and thank god we did. Amongst the almost-drunks who were filtering in and out, a familiar and extremely unwelcome face appeared, waltzing on in through the door. Actually two; Nina and the bloke who'd been looking over her shoulder at the tablet earlier. I vaguely recognised him too, but that was hardly surprising. Tripp and I had been to the SCREB building several times in the past couple of years and met several of the people. That was definitely why I recognised Nina, but there was something more about her. A definite, particular memory of her that was somewhere lodged within me, I just couldn't reach it and figure out exactly what it was.

The second I saw them enter I nudged Tripp, who was digging through his rucksack again.

"Shit!" He said, then clamped a hand over his mouth.

We both ducked down under the table and crouched, watching them. I held my breath as I saw them looking around, surveying the scene, somehow knowing we were here.

"How the hell do they know?" I whispered. This was really frustrating me now. Of course I was petrified because they kept finding us, but I was getting annoyed that I didn't know *how* they kept finding us. Yes, I know it was on the news earlier that we were here, but Nina and her friend weren't just in Meaden, they were right here, in this pub, exactly where we were hiding and had no actual reason to be. They'd found us, somehow.

We slowly, gently, pulled our rucksacks down from the seats and held on to them, squashing them up against us and poised to run as soon as we got an opportunity.

I studied Nina carefully. Her slightly hooked nose and strong jawline reminded me of how I always pictured the witch in *Hansel And Gretel* and now that was a terrifying parallel of our current situation. Her eyes squinted a little and her lips pursed as she looked around, she knew we were here, but she couldn't tell exactly where. My heart started racing even more as she began walking forwards. *Its' fine.* I told myself as she got closer to us.

She's just walking forwards. This was slightly easier to believe when I realised she was still looking around the whole pace, not directly at us, it just so happened that our table was almost exactly opposite the door.

I started hyperventilating a little, but tried to keep it under control, just as I could feel Tripp doing the same right next to me. I looked at him and mentally asked what the hell we should do now. He didn't know, so we both looked back at Nina and the guy. Standing still now, just ten feet from us and looking around for us. They turned and started walking towards the bar.

Once they got through the small crowd of people ordering drinks, they started talking with the barman.

"Rainbow, what are they saying?" Tripp whispered, hastily.

"I don't know, I can't hear them." I replied.

"No, but you can lip-read!" Tripp sounded somewhat desperate.

"I haven't done it in ages!"

"Just try!" He said, his voice at least an octave higher than usual.

I leaned across him so that I could get a better view of what was going on at the bar.

"Uhh- '*I- I know. Terrible.*'" I voiced what seemed to be being said by the bartender, trying not to get flustered and praying that I was getting it right. "'*Makes you wonder what-*' um- '*what led them...this way.*'" I kept squinting as Nina spoke but I couldn't tell what she was saying, I was at the wrong angle.

"Who was that?" Tripp asked, holding me up as I stretched across him so that I didn't topple.

"Barman." I said, still watching and trying to move my head in a way that would grant more vision.

"What's Nina saying?" He adjusted himself to try and let me see better.

"Can't tell. Probably asking if he's seen the two kids who were on the news this afternoon." I guessed. Tripp shifted around some more, trying to get at an angle where I could tell all that was being said, but it was no use, we were in completely the wrong place.

I stretched forwards again on instinct as the barman started talking again.

"'No...but...you said about...disguises...hats...' Oh my god, oh my god he's pointing over here we're gonna die!" We both retreated back as far as we could, looking around for any form of escape route. We shuffled as quickly as we could around to the other side of the table as Nina turned to look at where we had been sitting. I looked next to me, desperate to find anything that could help.

The buzzing of voices all around began closing in, taunting us over how happy and normal everyone else's evenings were, making everything seem not quite real. We moved, still on the floor, sideways and out of the booth in a pathetic attempt to escape while we watched our trackers approaching. They had to move slowly and carefully as the pub was getting even busier now, and people kept walking in front of them, through their path and making them have to wait. It bought a precious few seconds and I gained just the tiniest bit of hope when I realised they hadn't seen us yet.

We were still low enough and behind a group of people at an angle that blocked us from their view. They were just walking towards us because that was the direction in which they were pointed, they were still looking around and scanning the room for any sign of us.

We kept moving, up against the wall, my hand out and holding onto Tripp's. I felt like we were on the roof at home all over again, trying to escape the evil clutches of this woman who wanted us caught, maybe dead. The difference was that this time we had no plan. We had no idea how we were going to make it out of this one.

No idea, that is, until a miracle happened.

The toilets.

Inching across the floor, back pressed up against the wall, I suddenly felt myself falling backwards as the wall disappeared. Without meaning to, I pulled Tripp down along with me and realised we were falling onto a tiled floor, and that the wall had not actually disappeared; I'd come across a door without noticing and fallen right through it while keeping my attention in front of me.

Once we fully both clocked what was going on, we moved out of the way and shut the door quickly, without speaking before getting up, gathering our rucksacks and frantically putting them back on our backs. We stared at each other for a second, in awe of the fact that we'd actually made it out of the situation alive. We still needed to figure out how we could get out without getting caught, and we were far from safe, but we might actually have a chance now.

A woman with bleached-blonde hair, patchy fake tan and huge, drawn on eyebrows that covered roughly 30% of her face was washing her hands at one of the sinks. She looked over at us and frowned. Specifically at Tripp.

"I think you're in the wrong one, love." She declared, sarcastically and much louder than was necessary. She glared at him some more, daring him to stay and argue while at the same time threatening that he should leave. Tripp stared back at her, neither of us sure what to say. Facially, we both still looked like we could've been either gender, but I think the clothes made it more obvious.

"Hello?" The woman moved closer, the scent of alcohol coming from her slightly sickening. Before Tripp could respond, I jumped in. It wasn't my proudest moment and I don't think it was necessarily the right thing to say, but it was the first thing that came to mind and my mouth was saying it before my brain had time to register it as a thought.

"She has a hormone disorder and she's very sensitive about it!" I blurted out defensively, then realised what I'd just said.

What?! Tripp said to me in a facial expression, and I said to myself in my mind.

I'm sorry, I don't know where that came from! I looked back at him, as the woman began drying her hands.

"Eh?" She asked, her face contorting with confusion. Tripp and I looked back at her, and after a second of awkward silence, Tripp nodded earnestly.

She scowled and tutted at us while she finished drying her hands and barged past us as she made her way out. I don't think she was sober enough to care once we were no longer in the centre of her vision.

"Well done?" Tripp said quietly, surprised that it had actually worked, or at least gotten rid of her even if she didn't believe us.

"Cheers." I replied, before whipping round to look at the line of toilet stalls when I heard one of them flush. There was no one else out here to see us, but any second there would be.

The nearest stall was empty, so I grabbed Tripp's wrist and pulled him inside with me, shutting and locking the door behind us.

I turned around to him so that we were face-to-face and we stared at each other for a few seconds, suddenly realising the weirdness of what was going on, and hoping more than anything that no one noticed the fact that two

people had just gone into one stall. I dreaded to think
what this could look like from an outsider's point of view.
"What now?" Tripp mouthed at me.
"I have no idea!" I shrugged.
We both jumped slightly when we heard the door into the
toilets open again and a pair of boots started slowly
entering. Slow enough that we knew it wasn't someone
coming in to use the facilities, it was a predator who knew
very well that her prey was nearby.
I quickly nudged Tripp's feet with my own and gestured
for him to get on top of the toilet so that one of the sets of
feet would disappear from the view of anyone outside of
the stall. He quickly got up on top of it and hunkered
down in place, like a little goblin hiding from a giant. His
eyes were wide and he looked more scared than I'd seen
him look in a very long time, like he finally didn't feel as
though he had to be the brave one of the two of us.
He looked vulnerable.
I tried to give him a reassuring smile before I turned
around so that my feet were facing the right way, and took
a long, deep breath. I listened to where the boots were
treading. With every step she took, my heart sped up and
my blood pressure rose as I expected her to kick open our
door and take us away, or maybe shoot us right here.
The woman who had flushed the toilet nearby was now
washing her hands and I was able to hear something being
said over the running water.
"Excuse me, sorry to bother you," That was definitely
Nina talking. The sound of her voice made the hairs on
the back of my neck stand up as she continued. "but I've
lost my niece and nephew and I was just wondering if you

might've seen either of them at all?" I felt insulted and patronised by her calling us her niece and nephew.

"They're only thirteen," She continued, lying through her teeth and making my skin crawl at the falseness of her words. "Yay tall, and I'm quite concerned because they're a bit, well you know." She broke off and I guessed she was making some kind hand gesture. The other woman, the one washing her hands, made a sympathetic 'Aww' sound before Nina went on explaining about her missing niece and nephew.

"I really hate for them to be left on their own, they just can't look after themselves, they have the minds of six year-olds. I'm really getting worried." She almost sounded like she was holding back tears. I turned to look at Tripp and we both mimed putting our fingers down our own throats as the other woman tried to console Nina.

They left, leaving us as the only people in the toilets, but we remained in the stall in case they came back, or anyone else came in.

"I can't believe she's just done that." Tripp said in astonishment at how comfortable Nina had seemed telling such lies.

"What do we do now?" I asked desperately. I tried to peer through the crack in the door to see if anyone else was coming in, but no one seemed to be.

"You go see if they're out there." Tripp said.

"Why me? Why do you get to wait here?" I asked. He raised his eyebrows expectantly, then spoke.

"Because I'm a boy, Iris. We need as few people as possible to see me in here and someone will inevitably come in and see me if I do the looking."

"Right, yes, of course. Sorry, didn't think of that."

We nodded at each other and he patted me on the shoulder as if he were general sending his finest soldier off to the battlefield.

"Go forth bravely." He said and we nodded together once more, before I turned around and exited the stall.

I didn't really need to tiptoe across the mucky-looking tiles, but I couldn't help it, my heart pounding with every micro-step I took. I probably would've looked horrifically suspicious to anyone looking, with my hunched over posture and hands held up in front of my chest like a T-Rex. I berated myself for walking like this, I was the one who was actually allowed to be in here.

The door opened and I immediately changed my course from the door to the sink, assuming the gait of someone who was just going to wash their hands, not check to see if a glorified child-catcher was still here.

The woman who entered walked past me and we gave each other that awkward half-smile that we give each other in this situation because we're British.

She disappeared into a stall and I quickly ran for the door, trying to be as light footed as possible, and caught it just before it shut. I held it open a tiny bit, enough to see into the pub without having to stick my head out too obviously.

What I saw made me freeze in place.

Sat at the table that Tripp and I had been at just minutes ago, was Nina.

She was holding and inspecting something - our glasses. We'd left them on the table, ready to put them on when we finally departed but forgot to pick them up when we went down under the table. I silently cursed us both for being so forgetful. I knew it hadn't been said that we were wearing glasses in the news report, but I was still terrified by the fact that they'd been found. We'd left a direct trail to ourselves, all we could do was hope and pray that our pursuers wouldn't realise or assume that these were ours. They had no reason to do so, there was no record of us wearing them, but we'd really screwed up by leaving any trace of our presence.

I looked around, realising that the guy she'd been with wasn't with her anymore, and my heart sunk even further into the void when I saw him sitting at the table nearest the door, at a perfect angle to watch and identify anyone and everyone who came in or left. There goes the possibility of sneaking out unnoticed.

It was still bugging me that I couldn't remember his name; as I stared at him, I was now certain I'd met him before and it was gnawing away at me.

Nina and her friend showed no sign of leaving soon, it looked like they were sitting comfortably waiting for us. They knew we were here.

I made myself move away from the door, away from watching them and went back to the stall where Tripp was still hiding. I shoved my foot under the door to let him know that it was me and heard the little slide and *click* of the lock being unbolted. The door opened and I slipped inside so see him still on top of the toilet lid, hugging his knees.

It hit me all over again how unhealthy he looked. So pale, with dark circles under his bloodshot eyes, but at least he was clean now, which was more than could be said about this morning.

Huddled up into himself, he made me think of a homeless child in the Victorian times, afraid and unsure of what would happen next.

He looked at me with his wide, questioning eyes, asking what the situation was. I locked the door behind me before I spoke.

"We're screwed."

Chapter 17

The window simply wouldn't budge. There were no other doors. There was no vent in the ceiling or wall to climb through. We were trapped.

"I think we're gonna have to smash it." Tripp whispered, looking back at the window. He was no longer the scared little child hiding from the monsters, he was a problem-solver again, ignoring his fear in order to think straight and get the job done.

"No other option?" I asked. If we could get out without doing too much damage that someone else would have to deal with, I really wanted to.

"Well can you think of one?"

"No, I just don't want to have to break something. Plus that would draw a lot of attention so we wouldn't have much time to get away." I pointed out.

A woman came in and we turned our backs to her, peering out the window and pretending we were just looking at the view.

It was very dark now, and the snow was beginning to fall again, very gently at the moment, dusting the world in a blanket of hopeless hope. I might have called it beautiful at another time.

"Sorry, you're right." Tripp whispered, his tone gentler. "I just- I don't see another way out. Unless we just bolt-"

"But that way we'll almost definitely get caught immediately." I finished the thought for him.

"Precisely." He nodded.

"Then what?" I whispered as a couple more people came in. This was getting more and more inconvenient as time went on, more women kept coming in and out and we had to keep looking out the window to keep them from seeing that one of us definitely shouldn't - and didn't want to - be in here.

"Just run back to the forest?" I said, even quieter now.

"I guess so. It'll take us a while to find it again in the dark though. Do you think you can remember which way we came?" Tripp stared out the window longingly, wishing to know the way back.

"Theoretically, but probably not." I said, leaning on the windowsill.

Tripp nodded, agreeing despondently.

I glanced over my shoulder to see what was going on behind us. Three women were washing their hands, and I think two of the six stalls were occupied. I looked back at Tripp, who was clearly uncomfortable being in here.

"What do we smash it with?" I whispered. I knew we had a few tins of pineapple in our rucksacks, but I guessed those wouldn't quite cover it.

"I don't know. I'm not sure we have anything heavy enough." Tripp shook his head. We were talking so quietly now, I hoped no one reported us to the staff for suspicious behaviour. They'd have been perfectly justified to do so, but I really hoped that they wouldn't notice us, or care enough to tell someone.

I looked around, trying to be subtle about it, but searching for anything in our surroundings that we could use to smash the window. Upon doing this, I, once again, cursed the two of us for being so slow and stupid and not getting out sooner.

"Fire extinguisher." I said quietly, as I spotted and stared down at it, sitting in it's black holster against the wall. Tripp turned to look at it and nodded.

"Yes." He looked back at me, impressed. He took a quick glance behind to make sure no one was paying us attention, but as the evening went on, everyone who came in here was at steadily increasing levels of intoxication. I'm pretty sure that's the only reason we hadn't been reported and asked to leave the premises.

While Tripp surreptitiously removed the fire extinguisher from it's stand, I went to check if Nina was still out there waiting for us, just in case we didn't have to smash anything to get out.

"She's definitely still there." I said as Tripp and I rejoined at the window. I had an intense feeling of dread in my stomach, about what could happen to us if anything went wrong, and about the heinous crime we were about to commit. I racked my brain for any other, less destructive solution, but either there wasn't one, or I wasn't intelligent enough to see one. Both seemed equally possible.

We waited until there was no one washing their hands, the only people present were us and those in the stalls so that we could do it without being stopped. The waiting between people coming in and going out felt like a computer puzzle game we used to play where you had to select one of a spider's eyes and it would shut a few and open a few others, until you got the right combination so that all of them were shut.

While we waited, we moved our scarves from round our necks so that they were tied around the lower halves of our faces, protecting our mouths from the imminent flying shards.

Finally, once we were alone enough, I climbed on top of Tripp's back, keeping my rucksack on and clutching his in my trembling hands. He hoisted the fire extinguisher and positioned himself to strike.

"As soon as it's done," He said, his voice coming out slightly muffled. "Just drop, 'cause we will have *no* time to spare."

I nodded, then remembered he couldn't see me. "Understood."

He drew the extinguisher back, I squinted in anticipation of the small explosion, and I swear that with every second that passed I could hear both our heartbeats getting louder and faster, like they were waiting for a monumental sneeze to arrive.

The smash of the breaking glass was deafening. One minute time seemed to slow down and the world felt still, then suddenly there were tiny shards of glass everywhere, like a fairy hunting-party had just been released, each holding a dagger. I shut my eyes tight upon the impact, and felt several sharp little pieces hit me in the face around my eyes, stinging and giving me a load of tiny, bleeding cuts like freckles.

I heard the sounds of footsteps running, voices wondering what the hell was going on and before I knew it, I had pushed myself from Tripp, who flung me off to give me a boost, and clinging onto his rucksack as I tumbled out the window, onto the moss-infested concrete outside. It hurt, but the moss made it a bearable landing.

I got up immediately, the fight or flight instinct kicking in, and held out my hand to Tripp, who was already halfway through the window. I pulled his arm, giving him more momentum and helping him outside quicker.

I saw a flash of some angry, some bewildered faces coming to see what the crash noise had been. Nearly all the faces I saw, I glossed over. I didn't really register what they looked like, they seemed to disappear as soon as they were visible, so quickly did I glance.

But one face stood out. She didn't look angry, or bewildered, she didn't join in with the shouting over what just occurred, she just stared at me. Directly into my eyes in that way that seemed to last hours and sent shivers down my spine. A stare that would not give up, that was so blank and yet so chilling and disturbing. I thought I understood the term 'death-stare' before, but I was wrong, I didn't truly understand it until that moment. She wanted us dead.

The cold was a shock to me, even though I'd gotten used to it this week, we'd warmed up in the pub and the night had suddenly taken on a more vicious kind of frost. We ran like we had never run before, keeping a tight hold of hands, lest we lose each other in the night. We didn't fully know where we were going, but we had a vague idea of the direction, and, like a lot of the running away we'd been doing lately, we had one main goal; away. Running was harder now that the ground was slippery with frost and snow, and the darkness had crept in. I had to be so careful with how I placed my feet so that I didn't go sliding and falling over.

The cold bit at the already painful cuts on my face, making them sting even more. I knew Tripp would be in a worse state, having been so much closer to the window and I wanted to look, to see how bad it was and to ask if he was okay, but we had to keep running as quickly and as much as we could. I didn't think there was anyone following us at the moment, I'm pretty sure only Nina got a proper look at who did it, but the further away we got, the better. We tried to backtrack the way we had come, but I'm certain we took some wrong turns. We were going so determinedly though, so unwilling to stop and think about which way to go, we just kept going whether it felt right or not. We were slowing down though, as we got tired, as the way seemed less and less clear.

I felt a buzz in my legs, a familiar buzz that came from sprinting, one that I hadn't felt since my last race and gave me a sudden burst of adrenaline. I gripped tight onto my brother's hand and surged ahead, hardly able to see but letting my muscles take over and take us wherever they seemed to be going. The ground didn't seem so slippery either, now that we'd been going for some time, I got a weird sort of used to it and felt like I knew which way to go.

We had to stop after what felt like ages, both breathing heavily. While Tripp had a minor coughing fit. I looked back, but no one seemed to be following us yet.

Seemed.

Yet.

The words tugged at me, such uncertainty, such possibility for disaster.

"Alright?" I asked Tripp as he finished coughing, trying to see what state his face was in, but we were in a little alley with no street lamps, and the moon was covered by clouds. I was able to make out him nodding and looking at me, asking the same thing but not wanting to use any more breaths than he had to. I nodded and looked around.

"Hey, it's there!" I exclaimed, joyfully shocked when I looked up in front of us. Great trees towered up ahead, not too far away. We'd be back in the forest almost as soon as we left this alley and only at that moment when I relaxed a little, did I realise how tensed up all my muscles were; how high my shoulders were resting and how unhealthily fast my heart was racing. I took some deep breaths, trying to calm my body down as I told myself that we'd be okay. That we didn't just smash a window like a pair of delinquants. No doubt the newspapers would have a field day with us tomorrow.

"Well done." Tripp gave my hand a squeeze and somehow, I felt for the first time in a while, that maybe we really would be okay.

Chapter 18

We took too long resting.

We should've gone as soon as we could, we were so close and we could rest all night once we found the dragons, but no. We looked around and saw that no one was following us, so we sat down on the icy ground to catch our breaths. I turned my attention to Tripp, I couldn't make him out much, though I could hear him well, taking sharp, laboured breaths and trying to control them, the cold making both our breathing about ten times worse.

"You okay?" I asked, between breaths.

"Yeah, you?" He replied.

I nodded, my breathing normalising a bit now that I was sitting down.

"Are you sure you are? You looked really freaked out in there." I tried to sound more concerned than prying and accusing.

Tripp didn't answer me for a minute, his gaze down to the ground (as far as I could tell anyway).

"I think the realness of it all just hit me, you know. This whole time, it hasn't really felt like it's been real. Like it's a dream that I'm gonna wake up from. And then I just...don't." He sounded sort of empty as he said this. "Plus I wasn't exactly comfortable in the girl's bathroom." He said and we both laughed gently, trying not to let the weight of what he'd said before hang in the air too long. And then he was quiet again, but I sensed he wasn't finished. The silence wrapped around us for a moment, comforting while Tripp coordinated his thoughts and figured out what he was going to say next.

"I can't believe they're really gone. I just can't. Then, it hit me, the fact that we're being hunted. I mean, obviously I knew, and realised how dangerous it is," he spoke oddly quickly for what he was saying, like he was trying to get his thoughts out before they slipped away and he lost the words, while his hands fiddled with his shoelaces. "but that was the first time it felt real, when I really twigged that- that we could actually...die. If they catch us."

I realised he was crying.

"They won't." I said, moving closer to him and sniffing back my own tears that had appeared while he was talking, ready to emerge. "We've gotten this far." I whispered, as I put my arms around him and squeezed him gently. "We'll find somewhere to go, somewhere safe, where they can't find us."

We would've stayed there for who knows how long, in the cold and dark. Somehow though, the dark didn't feel too menacing now, as it had done the other nights.

Not until we heard the footsteps.

They started far away, but they were rapidly approaching. Both our heads snapped towards their direction the

141

microsecond that we heard them, like cats who've suddenly heard a fly.

They were most definitely Nina, coming after us. We both just knew as soon as we heard them, there was no point trying to believe anything else. We weren't safe and we'd let a moment of weakness put us in danger again by not moving to a less exposed location.

We both got up and, as quietly as we could, put our rucksacks back on.

The footsteps were getting closer.

My heartbeat echoed every step and we began to move. We held hands for both comfort and stability; the ground was so slippery it would've been foolish not to.

Only one set of footsteps, I realised. Two people were after us, but on one was currently pursuing. Nina was the one behind us, I was certain of that.

We sped up as the distance between us decreased and I looked on ahead, trying to see through the darkness to gauge how much longer we would have to go on. Not that far.

The footsteps got louder, closer. We were nearly at the end of this dark alley, then we would be back in the outskirts of the forest.

My legs were burning and my chest was tight, but the fear made me carry on whether I wanted to or not. Nina was so close behind us, I could almost feel her arm reaching out to grab the hood of my coat.

Too late, we realised where the missing, second set of footsteps had disappeared to.

As we finally burst out from between the walls of the alley that it felt like we'd been running through for hours, we were met by the guy who'd been with Nina and whose name, James, suddenly popped into my head as he closed in. Not that it mattered, it had just been really irritating me that I couldn't get it before. I didn't exactly have time to celebrate this though, he seized my brother and kicked me hard in the knee, making my whole leg buckle and possibly bend the wrong way, as I dropped to the ground. My whole right leg felt like it was exploding with pain and I tried to keep myself from screaming as I felt a pair of hands grab onto me and hoist me up so that I was being forced to stand, trying to keep all my weight on the. Sharp nails dug into the skin on my neck, a sharper voice dug even deeper into my ear.

"I've got you now."

I felt shivers go from my head all through my body as she said it so simply but with such a menacing edge in her voice. I whimpered involuntarily as my knee flared up again and I tried to break myself out of Nina's clutches but she held onto me tight, not letting me get away now that she did indeed have me.

I looked over to Tripp. I could see him a lot better now that we were more out in the open, street lamps bathing us in a light that wouldn't have been so spooky in a different context. He too was being held tightly, struggling to break free but being restrained by a man at least twice his size. One of his arms was being twisted and held at an awful angle, and I could see on his face that he was in a lot of pain.

As we made eye contact, we both stopped struggling, stopped moving and let ourselves be held. This seemed to satisfy Nina, as her grip on me loosened just the tiniest bit.

Tripp and I made a silent agreement and I tensed up my muscles, bracing myself.

Nina started to say something else, but I didn't listen to her. Her icy voice was strong and commanding, but as much as I was shaking from fear, I didn't let her words creep in and compromise me. I tried to plant my feet firmly, stand my ground, but it was hard when one felt like it was disintegrating from the knee and one felt like it was made of jelly.

Come on. I told myself.

You can do this. You have to do this. As I tried to get my nerves together to do it.

What if it doesn't work? What if it just makes her angrier and she kills you here and now? Myself told I.

Nope. That attitude wasn't going to work. I had no choice but to try and escape, whether it worked or not.

I screwed my eyes shut and brought my arm up, before thrusting it backwards and elbowing Nina hard in the ribs. She cried out in pain and the hand that was digging into my neck scratched through the skin as she pulled away, her hands going to where my elbow had hit her. I started freaking out, unsure what to do next, as I hadn't actually expected that to work.

Nearby, I was aware of Tripp doing something similar, but from the way James was keeled over, I guessed Tripp had hit something a little more sensitive to men.

I turned around, and although I had hurt Nina, she quickly recovered and began grabbing for me again.

"Stupid girl!" She affectionately called me as she tried to capture me once more.

I stopped thinking, stopped wondering what to do next and just let my instincts take over. I grabbed her hands

before they could grab me and held them tight as I
delivered a very messy kick with my good leg, wobbling
around standing on the bad one and almost falling over
again. Once more, Nina yelped in pain and pulled her
attention away from me in order to cradle her knee.
It would've been more satisfying If I'd gotten James in the
knee, but what can you do?
Getting almost excited that I seemed to be winning, I
flung my knee up at her chest in the split-second she was
leaning over. This was when I should've taken my chance
and run; Nina was hurting enough to give me time to get
away, but I was so thrilled that this was actually going my
way, I did something that felt equally badass and
unnecessarily rude.
I grabbed the tight, blonde bun and pulled her head up
with it, looked her in the brown eyes that had been so
scary but were now more surprised than anything else,
and I spat. I hoicked back a load of saliva and promptly
launched it at her face. This made her look even more
outraged and shocked. She shrieked, but I gave her one
last hit with my knee for good measure, the adrenalin of
the battlefield numbing the pain in my leg, slamming my
rucksack into her as I turned and ran.

I knew Tripp was running too. I wasn't sure exactly how
close to me he was, but I knew that I'd seen him escape
his assailant around the same time I had.
Maybe he was ahead of me, maybe behind, but I could at
least be sure that he had gotten away too. I would meet
him in the forest and we would find our dragons and fly
away and start a tribe with the squirrels and hedgehogs of
the world and all would be well.

But for now, I just had to run. I was getting tired of running, in both senses of the word, I felt like I'd spent the equivalent of half my life running these last few days, but my four years doing it competitively helped, even if I hadn't been keeping up with it lately.

I didn't know how long Nina and James would take before they started after us again, though I knew it wouldn't be long. They'd gotten to us quickly, and now we had enraged them and fuelled they're motivation to get us. I kept on going, knowing how close I was to my goal, but I was limping, as the pain in my right leg was creeping back in like a spider, every step sending a lightning bolt through the entire leg, each one bigger and more painful than the last.

Finally, I felt the familiar twiggy ground beneath my feet and I was back in the forest. I kept going for several yards, trying to get as much tree coverage as possible, before at last I stopped and took a deep, long breath. I had to sit down, my leg and the knots forming in my chest were too much. I shut my eyes and just focused on my breathing, feeling like I might pass out again and fighting for that not to happen.

When I opened my eyes again, the adrenaline rush was wearing off and I realised what was going on.

No Tripp.

No Delta.

No Zen.

No idea where anything or anyone was.

I looked around, and on my own, the forest was still beautiful, but now crippling creepy as well. It was eerily quiet, with moonlight seeping through the gaps in the trees and casting haunting shapes on the ground. The wind whistled around me, singing spooky little lullabies as it passed.

I began to shiver and felt like something was following me. I looked around but didn't see anything apart from the trees making the shapes of monsters. They were definitely trees though.

I let out a high-pitched shriek as I thought I felt something on me and jumped up, my knee buckling as I got up and making me fall over again. I began humming, almost involuntarily, just so that there was some form of familiar sound rather than the completely murderous emptiness that the forest was giving off.

I felt horribly exposed, unable to see what was around me. My neck twinged where Nina had scratched me, and I put a hand up to rub it. My fingers came away covered in blood.

My eyelids wanted to shut, to pretend that this wasn't really happening and everything would be okay if I just went to sleep, but I couldn't let that happen. I hadn't put enough distance between myself and my hunters. Slowly, so slowly, I got up onto my hands and knees, trying to believe myself when I said that there was nothing evil coming to get me.

There was though.

I tried to tell myself that this wasn't really that bad, that it wasn't that cold and scary.

It was though.

I let out a noise that was somewhere between a scream and a sob as I began to crawl forwards, trying to motivate myself with some form of warcry. I stretched out my right leg and put the foot on the ground rather than the knee, and slowly, pathetically got to the biggest tree in the area, about eight feet from where I'd fallen down.

I took off my rucksack and put it down next to me, turning around and resting with my back up against the tree. At least my back wasn't exposed now; that was one thing I absolutely couldn't stand. I always felt safer when my back was up against something.

I looked around again, but still couldn't see anyone coming to look for me, and all I could hear was the gentle, ghoulish wind.

"Tripp?" I called out. My voice came out small and hoarse, and I realised there were tears on my face again. Not the running kind, not the actual *crying* kind, the kind that are just there when you're frustrated and broken. Ghost tears.

No one answered my call, as I expected, and I suddenly felt very small and cold. I huddled into myself, trying not to look around too much, trying not to think about the true crime videos Tripp and I had been watching and obsessing over recently.

A cool mist was settling through the forest, like an echo of the snow that had looked so pretty earlier on, but now it all felt very macabre.

I looked to my rucksack, with the cosy dark green sleeping bag strapped onto it.

No.

This was *not* where I would stop for the night. I was just resting here, then, I would be brave, I would not be that weak girl that I so dreaded being. I'd get up, and I would go and find my brother.

Come on. I tried to force myself to get up, but I was glued to the tree. I felt myself shivering and tried again to pluck up the courage to go, but I couldn't do it.

You're pathetic. Said a voice in my head. I knew it was right.

To combat the cold, I opened up the rucksack and got out my other pair of jeans - the baggier pair. It took a long time because I was so slow, but I put them on, on top of the skinnier pair that I already had on, struggling to get them over my boots. If I wasn't getting in my sleeping bag - which I wasn't - I needed to do something to protect me from the deathly cold. I winced and had to be extra careful around my fragile right knee, as every touch felt like I was injecting it with a syringe of purest pain. I could tell that I'd have a large, colourful bruise right there in the morning. I would've put on another jacket if I had the option, but I was already wearing both of the ones I had with me underneath my coat. The last spare item of clothing I had was the other t-shirt I'd brought, and that hardly seemed worth the ordeal of taking off all of the top layers to get it on.

Chapter 19

I stayed up against the tree for I don't know how long, maybe twenty minutes, maybe two hours, all the while telling myself that I would get up in a minute. But the minutes kept passing, and I remained attached to the tree, where I felt the closest to "safe" that I was ever going to feel while out here on my own in the dark. The pit of dread in my stomach grew steadily as time went on, and the world around me just felt more and more haunted.
I sat up a bit and tried to pretend that I was brave, that I wasn't terrified of everything around me. I began singing to myself quietly, so that I wasn't just listening to eerie sounds of the half-asleep forest, as I managed to slowly and shakily make myself get up. My voice came out small and high, filled the fear that I was so desperately trying to ignore. I heaved up my rucksack and put it on my back, putting off taking any steps for as long as possible.

With the second verse of Vance Joy's *Riptide* I finally moved my quivering legs and started towards the heart of the forest.

As I put my foot down I frantically looked around, now feeling like every creature in the world was coming to get me, before I moved the other foot.

My voice got a little louder as I went, to give myself the illusion of being more confident.

The trees were so tall and menacing, staring me down and daring me to go on and see what horrors awaited, not just crumble.

I kept swatting at the air around me, feeling like something was on me, and letting out involuntary little squeaks of fear between lyrics. I knew I was being silly to keep singing as I walked through such a sinister place, but somehow it helped me. I was able to focus on the words of the song, and pretend I was in a music video rather than traipsing around looking for a brother I was unlikely to bump into.

Snap.

I froze in terror and silence as I heard a twig break behind me. I felt like screaming, crying, dying, just *anything* to not be here anymore. My heartbeat was going at a million miles per hour and seemed loud enough to reach the drunks back in the Red Lion. I opened my mouth to try and say something, but no sound came out and I felt like I was just choking on air.

Snap.

More twigs went as what or whoever was behind me drew nearer. I breathed in quickly and hard, hyperventilating and shivering. I screwed my eyes shut out of instinct and began to turn around.

Slowly, I made a one-eighty with my eyes still shut. I wanted to run as fast as I could, but my legs wouldn't allow it, so I just stood there preparing to open my eyes but never doing it.

Grunt.

I held my breath. That sounded familiar. That sounded friendly. I could feel the thing coming closer still and I slowly opened my eyes.

"Delta!" I cried out as he slowly stalked his way towards me. He sped up once he realised I was no longer afraid of him, the blue glow that he gave off getting brighter, and I began running towards him. I wrapped my arms around him tightly and held on for dear life, suddenly not feeling too afraid. I wasn't alone anymore, and I got an intense feeling of relief throughout me. I realised I was crying into his warm, scaly side. Not ghost tears anymore; real tears. Tears of happiness, at long last. Things were far from good, but this was most definitely an improvement.

Delta whinnied and purred, nuzzling me as I stroked and hugged him.

"Are you okay?" I whispered, holding onto him. He nuzzled me again, and put his forehead against mine, so that we would've been eye-to-eye, had his eye not been on the sides of his face.

He leaned forward slightly and stared at me, then moved his long neck round so that he was indicating for me to climb on top of his back.

"Thank you, little dragon." I said as I held onto his back and swung my leg up and round so that I was straddled on him like a horse.

He began walking onwards, slowly and carefully so that he could be quiet, and I leaned forward and held onto him tightly so that I could never let him go.

We'd only been trudging along for about five minutes when I started hearing more twigs snap, the tell-tale sound of something approaching. Delta and I both froze in place, and although I couldn't feel his heartbeat, his skin suddenly went cold, his ears rising along with the looser, feather-like scales surrounding his neck. I realised I was nearly strangling him with my tight grip, and loosened it as he slowly, silently began moving towards another big tree.

If this had happened ten minutes ago, before Delta got here, I would've hidden or tried to get away and felt nothing but fear, but now, having had Delta fine me, I dared to hope that it could be Tripp or Zen; or both.

I stayed planted firmly on Delta's back as he moved, but I kept my eyes ahead, where the sound was coming from. The feeling of dread returned to my stomach, stronger than ever and I realised with utter horror that it was Nina and James approaching. I heard them before I saw them. They were definitely talking, but I couldn't make out what they were saying, it was just a blend of their voices. My view of the forest ahead disappeared as Delta got us completely behind the tree trunk. The footsteps were getting closer. They were moving fairly quickly, like they knew exactly where to go and were wasting no time getting there.

Delta gently tilted sideways, indicating for me to get off. I slid down and tried to make as graceful a landing as possible, holding on to him for as long as I could to keep the resistance going as my feet hit the ground.

I knew what Delta was planning to do, so I quietly got down onto the ground and curled up into a ball, as tight as I could, which was extremely awkward with all my layers on.

Delta, constantly looking around with both his eyes and his ears, laid down on top of me, stretching out his magnificent wings so that I was completely covered. Then it happened, something I hadn't seen him do in a long time. His skin, naturally such a vibrant, glowing electric blue, began to change; dulling down and camouflaging with the terrain around us.

It was always a fascinating process to watch, although I couldn't see it very well in the dark, all curled up underneath him, but it was still impressive. The grainy brown started at his heart and bled outwards, like a drop of ink in a bowl of water.

Delta tucked his head down, so that his forehead was against mine again, and I tried to calm my nerves, knowing that I was being protected, but unable to stop the fear and dread inside me.

They came closer, so close that I could feel the vibrations in the ground as they put their feet down. With every step I drew in a sharp breath, hyperventilating but trying with all my might to not be heard. I was in conflict between feeling safe and secure with Delta guarding and hiding me, and wanting with every part of me to scream and run, or curl into a ball and die. Well, I was already halfway to that one.

I stopped breathing completely and just held my breath when they were right above us, and I could hear what they were saying.

"Well you can see that she's around here, can't you?" Nina was saying, a sharp, warning edge to her voice.

"Yeah," James argued. "But she's clearly *not*. Maybe the forest is messing with the signal."

What signal? What have they been using to track us?

"The signal is fine." Nina shut him up. They were both quiet for a moment, allowing my thoughts to spiral out of control. I could feel my pulse all throughout my body, every part of me overheating and shaking. I started to feel claustrophobic, and it took all my will power to remain still and silent.

"She should be here." Nina said, softly. Deadly soft, scarily calm. I sensed her take a step forward, and that step happened to be onto the edge of Delta's wing. He didn't squeal as he did the few times I had accidentally stepped on his wing or tail, but I felt him go completely tense, his eyes shut and he let out the tiniest amount of breath, just a slight trace of smoke snaking up from his nostrils. With the hand of mine that I wasn't lying on top of, I took his paw and rubbed him gently, which seemed to make him feel better.

"Well, she's not. So we should go look somewhere else. Or go back to base and see if there are any updates." James sounded both bored and cocky. I heard the sound of a *thump* and a grunt of pain and submission.

"Shut up." Nina said, briskly. "If you hadn't let them get away, we wouldn't be here in the first place."

"Me? I got kicked in a sensitive area! You-" He cut off. Maybe by the threat of another hit, maybe just by a stare,

but I could hear the regret in his voice as he stopped.
The leaves and twigs around us moved around slightly, as a weight was put on them.
She was kneeling down, directly in front of me. I heard her sniff the air, and imagined her looking around with her evil, cat-like eyes, just inches away.
"Where are you, Iris Reynolds?" She asked quietly, more to herself, but her saying my name sent shivers through me and made me want to vomit.
I shut my eyes tight and screamed in my head for her to go away. Not just now, forever, just leave us alone.
I noticed that my left hand - the one that I was lying on - was clenched tight in a fist, so tight, I'm pretty sure the palm was bleeding as the nails dug in. I loosened it, but I could feel the blood gently spilling out, making a little pool.
The ground made more sounds, as, I assumed, Nina got up.
"Carry on that way." She commanded. "Maybe she dropped something here on her way." They began walking away.
I let out a deep, long breath as their footsteps got further and further away.
"Thank you, Delta, thank you so much. I love you." I whispered into his ear. He purred at me quietly, his version of *you're welcome, I love you too.*
Once the footsteps had travelled far, far out of ear shot, Delta slowly rose and changed back to his natural blue while his glow gradually brightened, allowing me to see better. I got up, trying not to look too relieved, but I hadn't realised how hot I'd gotten until I was now suddenly cooled down to a more bearable temperature.

I looked down at my left hand. It wasn't that bad, The cuts would scab over soon and the blood wasn't coming out too quickly. I wiped the blood off on my jeans and looked at Delta.

"You're such a good boy Delta." I said as I gave him a hug once more. "Are you okay to go and find Tripp and Zen, do you think?" I asked. He looked worried again, his big eyes seeming smaller than usual, and not as bright. He was tired. He had been when he found me, and after having to hold a camouflage, he was exhausted. I was too, but adrenaline and fear had kept me from thinking about it.

"Zen will be looking after Tripp, won't she?" I mused out loud. Zen may have been lazy, but she loved Tripp more than anything in the world and would make sure that he was protected. She would've found him just as Delta had found me.

Delta didn't nod, but I could tell he was agreeing with me. He skulked around the tree and I followed him, on the other side was a crater in the ground, a dip where there perhaps had been a big rock at some point. He clambered down into the ditch and I followed. Delta curled around in a spiral, and I lay down in the middle, putting my rucksack by his tail. I couldn't be bothered to get into my sleeping bag, plus my body temperature was still confused about it's surroundings. Besides, I was leaning on Delta, and his warmth kept me at a good temperature.

Chapter 20

I was torn between going to sleep and getting rest while I could, and staying awake and alert. Delta would be sleeping very lightly, if any danger started approaching, he would hear and wake up, but I didn't like the idea of both of us being asleep and vulnerable.

I lay there for what I thought was a couple of hours, though my sense of time was pretty warped at the moment. Even if I did want to sleep, I was finding it hard not to be awake. I kept worrying about Tripp and Zen, and thinking about what James had said.

The signal.

So they must've been tracking us somehow. Maybe on some visit to the SCREB building we'd been secretly chipped somehow? I honestly wouldn't be surprised if that were the case. Maybe they could track Zen and Delta? We had gotten them from SCREB, maybe there had been trackers put in their eggs and they had kept them somehow when they hatched?

But they'd kept saying "she", and Nina had addressed me by name, so it couldn't have been Delta. They were hunting me.

I was now caught in that strange world halfway between awake and asleep, where everything felt like a dream but you can tell it's real. Where you suddenly realise that you have blocks of about twenty seconds that you have absolutely no memory of because you completely zoned out.

It felt like an awfully dangerous state of mind to be in at the moment. If I went to sleep while Delta was sleeping too (and who knows how long he might stay asleep) I was scared that I might not wake up, Tripp had been right. What if I went to sleep and Delta cooled down so the cold got too much for me, or James and Nina found me again, or the stress got too much and my heart exploded? If I went to sleep, it really could be forever.

I opened my eyes properly again, and wiped away the dribble that had slowly been accumulating down my chin and cheek. I felt an odd sort of need to be awake now, more than I had before, thinking about how much I needed to go and find Tripp and Zen.

For now, while I wasn't fully in a state of consciousness, things didn't feel as creepy, it was just like being in a dream where nothing bad could actually happen, however bad things seemed.

I blinked a few times and looked ahead of me. There was a curious bluish light, very far into the distance, but gradually getting closer.

I snapped into fully-awake mode as the light drew nearer, but somehow I didn't feel afraid. If Delta hadn't been right here with me I would've guessed it was him, it was pretty much the same shade of blue light that he gave off.

But it wasn't Delta, so I knew that I should've been afraid, I should've been up and running in the opposite direction the second I saw it, or waking Delta up and clambering atop him so that we could escape together, but instead I just sat and watched, waiting for it to come closer. As it crept through the trees and came into my view, I was able to see it's source.

Skipping and dancing towards me, was a small humanoid being, maybe two feet tall, made entirely of white-blue vapour. It drew nearer still, flitting across the ground as light as a feather and barely making contact.

Ghost? It looked like the spirit of some kind, but too friendly to be a ghost. Although, I've never met a ghost in person so maybe it was.

I sat up, my eyes widening as I stared at it in awe and extended out an arm in a greeting. It got about six feet away from me when I realised it wasn't made of vapour, but flames.

A wisp!

A Will-o'-the-wisp. It continued to frolic towards me and I felt warmer, not just because it was made of fire, not because of Delta, it just gave off such a pleasant, comfy energy.

I smiled at it as it reached me and stared up at me. Was it smiling back, or was that my imagination? I decided that it was most definitely smiling back, and it rubbed it's cheek on my outstretched hand. It tickled and gave me just a tiny bit of an electric shock, but more of a tingly sensation than a painful one. I couldn't help giggling at this.

I stared down at it, it looked so magical and impish, I wanted to adopt it. Maybe Delta could accept having it as a little sibling.

Delta.

I tried to remember something. I'd come out here all sad that I didn't know where Delta was, but now I was happy because he was right here, but I'd been sad about something else too. I couldn't quite remember what. Someone else I wanted to find, maybe? I wasn't sure, but it didn't matter, I had this little wisp with me so everything was fine.

The wisp began moving away and I felt my smile fade slightly. Where was it going? I reached out forward again and the wisp turned around, he seemed to beckon to me. I decided it probably was a he, but I think that's because all of my previous experience with wisps came from the TV show *Willo the Wisp*.

I got up and slowly, shakily started walking towards him. I had to be quiet so as to not wake up Delta, I didn't want to disturb him while I was just seeing what the wisp wanted, maybe it knew what I was looking for and could lead me there. I'd be back soon.

My knee wasn't so bad now, on the pain level at least. It still twinged, but it was now just at a level of a dull discomfort. The pain in my neck and hands where nails had dug in hardly registered anymore, just stinging a tiny bit as I moved.

I hopped across the fallen twigs, following in the wisp's path as it snaked through the trees, wondering what I'd been so afraid of before. There wasn't anything to be scared of really, was there?

I wondered where the wisp was leading me, perhaps somewhere lovely where I didn't need to be cold or afraid of anything anymore. Perhaps to whatever I was missing. I had vague notions of a boy whose face looked like mine, who I needed to find for some reason, but I brushed over the thought as the wisp continued to amble onwards, like a fairy, fluttering delicately over the forest floor.

Irisssss I heard it's whispers in my head, the "s" of my name elongated like a snake. It's voice sounded sharp and icy, but it called to me so clearly I couldn't not follow it. Plus the wisp was so pretty and light, and I'd never seen one in real life before. It must be taking me to safety.

I'm not sure how long I followed it, it felt like a small lifetime, but we went twisting and turning in so many different directions, following an invisible path that the wisp seemed to know well. It kept calling to me, his voice still sounded like icicles stabbing my ears, but that didn't seem to matter. It needed me to follow it.

We got to a small clearing, and with the light that the wisp gave off, I could see that we were at the bottom of a hill. The wisp started floating up it. I got an impending sense of doom, but as quickly as it appeared, it was locked away and forgotten about as I scrambled up the steep hill to follow the wisp.

He crept upwards, looking over his shoulder to make sure I was following, and holding out an airy arm. I needed to reach it, to hold onto it.

The hill was so steep, I had to go on my hands and knees and crawl, but I went quickly, desperate to get to the wisp. I was going so frantically, I got clumsy and slipped back down as I misplaced my foot but managed to catch myself by putting down my right knee to steady myself. A great pain flared up throughout my whole leg and I let out a small screech, but I quickly started going up again, even quicker now that the wisp was almost disappearing over the top. I *had* to get to it.

Irisssss it called to me again.

"I'm coming!" I called as I dashed up the hill, sending a load of fallen branches rolling down as I went.

As I got to the top, I reached out my left hand to the wisp, trying to catch it, but it slipped right through my fingers, leaving them cold and shivering. My hand began to sting more, where my nails had dug into it, and it felt like the blood was heating up and burning. I stared down at it, and the blood seemed to be bubbling and fizzing slightly.

Irisssss I looked up at the call and gasped. Stretched out ahead of me, back down the side of the hill was a magnificent lake. It must've stretched about twenty metres across, with deep blue water that was almost purple, shimmering and sparkling, and a big silver patch in the middle where the moon was being reflected. The whole thing seemed to hum with a magical energy, with fireflies and possibly fairies dancing all around it. I looked at the surroundings and realised that the hill went in a circle around the lake, so that all the water was contained in a great big ditch, like a sort of reverse moat.

Mesmerized, I took a shaky step forwards, beginning the descent down the hill. It was just as steep this side, so I bent my knees and went down sideways, keeping my hands on the ground as well.

I dropped my gaze from the lake to the wisp approaching it. It was now moving backwards, keeping it's bright, glowing eyes fixed on me and stretching out it's arms to me.

163

I hurried on downwards so that I could get closer to it.
The bank of the lake was about six feet from the bottom of
the hill, with little wavelets gently lapping at the ground.
The wisp floated gracefully just above the water's edge,
the glow casting a bright white patch over the ripples. I
slowly crept towards it, just taking a couple of steps for
now, wanting to get to it but trying not to disturb the
serenity of the scene.
Irissssss the wisp called me, more insistent than before. It's
voice sounded colder than ever, but it didn't matter. I
needed to catch it.
It began to drift out, towards the centre of the lake,
staring at me and calling even louder, it's voice becoming
almost venomous.
It drifted out further still, I knew I needed to follow it but
it was right over the lake. I stood on the shore, staring at it
and willing it to come back. I watched as it floated over to
the patch of moon, where it stopped and pierced me with
it's gaze. I felt myself being pulled towards it, like it had
me attached to it with some invisible chord.
IRISSSSS It was like the voices of a thousand wisps were
cutting through my ears, screaming at me and drawing in.
I couldn't take it anymore, I couldn't help it.
I ran.
Full speed, all thoughts of anything apart from getting to
wisp gone from my mind, I just ran.
Within the space of about two seconds, I got to the bank
of the lake, felt my head about to explode with all the wisp
voices, and saw the wisp disappear in a small puff of
smoke just as I took the biggest leap I could.
I was plunged into a cold like no other. The wisp's
hypnotic spell was instantly broken and I tried to scream

as I went down, but the freezing water immediately filled my mouth and froze up my vocal chords.

The frost bit at me and enveloped me in a deathly cold, inescapable prison. I tried to swim upwards, but my limbs would hardly move and I felt like I was being pulled violently down.

I went into panic mode more than ever before and felt like I was flailing around, but I was pretty much paralysed as I went steadily downwards.

I felt like screaming again when I got a sudden, sharp and awful pain in the side of my head, as if I'd just been shot. Then in my right leg, like it had been ripped out, then it suddenly went numb. Was there something in the water attacking me? Or maybe the cold and the pressure was just messing with my brain, or bringing back the damage in my head that Delta's blood had healed. I started to hear something nightmarish - a bloodcurdling, painful, ear-splitting scream.

Tripp's scream.

He sounded like he was being murdered and I tried harder than ever to go up, to escape, to survive. I was running out of oxygen and I began seeing things that weren't really there - great big black, feathery wings; blood pouring unstoppably out of a wound; an eye, a green eye, crying golden tears; a sword plunging into someone's torso; the sounds of gunshots everywhere; someone screaming as unidentifiable wild animals snarled and tore them apart; a human neck, held in the arms of someone from behind, being snapped. The sound of the snapping made me flinch and this time I really was able to scream. The sound of my scream filled the bitter lake like a lion's roar and in that moment, that terrifying moment, all I wanted to do was die.

To not be here anymore.

To not have to feel anything anymore.

I just wanted to go.

Struggling was getting me nowhere, I couldn't move.

I stopped screaming and began to shut off, allowing the pull of the water to take me. My hearing cut out completely, and I felt numb all over. My vision cleared the horrible images away, and started going black. I didn't shut my eyes, but they were stopping working.

I accepted my fate.

The heartbeat that had been racing so fast so much of today was slowing right down, taking heavy, laboured beats. Water from the lake flowed into my mouth and I could feel it going down and spilling into my lungs.

I thought about Tripp and hoped that he'd be okay. The last Reynolds. I hoped he managed to escape from this whole thing, and wouldn't feel too sad about my passing. There was nothing he could've done.

I missed him, and I knew he would miss me. We were a package deal, you rarely got one without the other. I mentally apologised to him, and told him that I loved him. My only regret as I began to fall asleep was that I couldn't say it in real life.

My heart slowed, my pulse getting fainter and my breathing restricting, my throat closing up.

I prayed that Delta would locate Tripp and Zen, and that they would all find somewhere safe to live, away from the evil people who wanted them dead.

With the little vision I had left, I held up my left hand and looked at it. I no longer felt any kind of pain, but I could see the red, that looked quite purplish down here, coming off and smoking upwards, almost mimicking the wisp. *Blood.*

Here lay Iris Christina Reynolds, sixteen years old, and sorry she couldn't tell her brother that she loved him one last time.

Chapter 21

I've never felt anything stranger than seeing my own corpse. I'm not sure when exactly I changed from being it to looking at it, but it felt both right and wrong at the same time.

This was *me*.

This was not a perspective from which anyone was supposed to view themselves, and yet I felt a sense of freedom. My point of view was still under the water, and the body was just a couple of feet away from me.

The white hat had come off, I don't know when, but now the bright pink hair was spread out in the water, like a lotus flower, finally in bloom. My arms and legs were static, with blood still leaking out of my left hand and neck, diffusing into the water.

I'm sorry. I half-said, half-thought as I stared at the body that used to be me.

I'd been quite pretty actually. I never really had any problems with how I looked, I didn't care that much, but I never felt like anything special. I'd just been me (and a bit Tripp). But now, looking at me from the perspective of someone else, I was a pretty girl. I obviously didn't look my best right now, I had just died and was underwater, but still.

I didn't feel any pain anymore, I didn't feel wet, I didn't feel anything physical. I didn't feel like I was there, I could just see the remnants of myself and felt sad but also at peace. I didn't need to worry or feel afraid anymore. I felt happy that I was done with life. Free.

Just as I was beginning to float further away from the body, off to who-knows-where, I felt something stopping me. I was suddenly tethered to the lifeless body below me. There was something creeping towards it, searching for it and longing to collect it. Some kind of claw. Attached to some kind of electric blue, reptilian arm. I felt a strange mixture of emotions. There was a hopefulness that I hadn't been expecting, but also a sort of disappointment that I maybe wasn't done after all.

Both a happiness and a sadness.

The claw gripped onto the black coat that the body was wearing and began to tug, pulling it up towards land. The body looked very limp, like a ragdoll, it made me feel all kinds of weird and distrubed to watch.

Suddenly the surface was broken and I saw my beloved Delta with huge, desperate eyes, picking up the body and gently setting it down on the dry ground.

Delta was snuffling and whimpering and making other distressed noises that hurt to hear, and his face looked more distraught than I'd ever seen any face look. He seemed to be crying, which I wasn't aware that dragons could do.

His tears were golden, which didn't seem right to me. Such a grand colour shouldn't appear on such an amazing, majestic creature when he had been emotionally reduced so much.

He sniffed all over the body, licked the face, trying to bring life back to it. He shed his tears so that they flowed and washed all over the body, and I felt myself being dragged back towards it. I wasn't being put back in it, but I was getting closer. I tried to resist coming back, tried to struggle and run away from the inevitable but I had no force.

No, I want to be free.

I tried in vain to be rid of this life.

As I looked back at the broken dragon, I stopped. I couldn't leave him.

Delta kept trying desperately to bring me back, crying all over the corpse and cutting himself again and again with his sharp claws, pouring the blood over the body and letting it fall into the open, drowned mouth.

Closer still I came back to myself and my dragon. I could hear him wailing again, a sound that was as bad and torturing to hear as the scream from Tripp that I'd heard in the lake. I wanted more than anything to reach out and comfort him to tell him that it was okay, that I wasn't hurting, but he couldn't see me. He could only see the empty shell of me, the thing that once was me.

He cried and bled harder, having to keep renewing the cuts on himself as they kept healing, and covering me in the curative liquids. It was so nearly working, I was so close to life again, but there was something stopping me from being able to inhabit the body. Delta could sense it too, some kind of invisible barrier. I couldn't tell what it was, nor could he and it was upsetting and frustrating him.

In an almost giving up gesture, but seemed more in mourning, he flopped his head onto me, falling hard onto my chest.

He didn't mean for it to happen, but that was the key.

A small ocean of water shot up out of my mouth and I sat bolt upright coughing and spluttering, suddenly back in my body. I felt like I'd just been struck by lightning, everything burned, the weightlessness disappeared and I had never felt heavier in my life.

But I was alive.

Unfortunately, I was also able to feel pain again. I was in agony all over, but especially in my head and chest. My hand and neck were still bleeding and stinging, though that feeling was fading pretty quickly thanks to the dragon blood leaching into the open wounds.

I sat up, in shock, breathing heavily and looking around, trying to stop the buzzing and screaming still ringing in my ears.

Realising I was back, Delta quickly lifted his head from me and stared at me for a second, before attacking me with love and affection and licks. I held onto him, crying and laughing at the same time, unable to believe that 1) I had just died 2) I had been okay with it and actively fought to keep it that way, and 3) My dragon had been able to bring me back to life.

Not only had he woken up and seen that I was gone, he'd been able to follow my scent and find where I was, even though I wasn't entirely sure that the lake was real and

not some mythical, wisp-made realm made purely for luring people to their death, then pulled me out and been so desperate to revive me, he'd cut himself and cried all over me until I was literally pulled back to life.
Delta brought me back to life.
I felt a surge of amazement and love, more powerful than I'd felt anything before or knew was possible and cried into him more. I was cold and wet and felt so weird in my body, but I was here, and I had a vaguely renewed sense of life. I'd been given a second chance by my dragon.
I wanted to thank him and tell him how incredible he was, but I couldn't speak. I was so overwhelmed, so freaked out by what had happened, I just held tightly onto him, sobbing along with him and wondering what the hell was wrong with me for following what was clearly a terrible idea to follow.
I tried to move my legs, but they ached so much. Especially the right one, the memory of how numb it went made me shiver. I winced in pain as it flared up while I tried to get up, and Delta started sniffing all over me, making sure I was okay.
I swallowed, trying not to be sick, and had to lie back down, holding onto my ears, to let the spinning and humming in my head calm down.
As I lay there, the pain started wearing off, but I felt like I could hear the laughter of the wisp, making fun of me for falling for it's tricks. I almost screamed, wanting to dispel the memory of it, and got up almost immediately. I was shaking, and had to hold onto Delta for support, desperate to get away. I glanced at the lake, and got a sharp pain in my eyes as the echoing image of the wisp flashed before

me. I turned away and screwed up my eyes, trying to get rid of it.

Delta sensed that it was time to go, he made me sit on top of him and used his teeth to pick up my rucksack from where he'd dumped it on the ground after taking it with him for me.

He took a couple of steps back and crouched low, positioning himself like a cat about to catch a mouse. He took a giant, flying leap up to the top of the hill, then gracefully jumped down the other side onto the relatively flat terrain.

He started running, gently but quickly, trying to get as far away from this cursed place as possible.

Once we got to a small clearing, he put me on the ground and wrapped himself around me tightly, but not so tight that I felt claustrophobic, then turned on his central-heating to the max and started the drying process. I knew that in this situation, I was really supposed to take my sodden clothes off so that I didn't get hypothermia from them, but I think my circumstances were a little different, with a dragon wrapped around me who was dedicating himself to warming me up and drying me off. He kept looking around, clearly not going to go to sleep, but his warmth and the gentle, constant beating of his heart made me tired. Hearing his heartbeat made me put a hand on my chest to feel mine. It felt peculiar now. It took me a minute to realise what exactly was different about it; it didn't feel like mine anymore.

It was matching Delta's. We were perfectly synchronised. I buried myself down within him, nowhere near sleep yet but never wanting to move from the safety of him.

"Thank you, Delta." I was finally able to whisper.

Chapter 22

Once again, I had no dreams, but falling asleep turned out
to be terrifying. I tossed and turned within the Delta-nest
for ages, trying to get to sleep but my body wouldn't let
me fully go. I was constantly almost-sleeping, but my head
was filled with thoughts of the wisp, the lake, the screams.
Dying.
What surprised me now, was how okay I'd been with it at
the time. I didn't fight it, I just let it happen.
I was disappointed in myself, and now the desperation to
not die was making sleep almost impossible. Tripp was
right, I was terrified that if I went to sleep, I might not
wake up ever again.
When I finally was able to start sleeping, I woke up twice
during the night, before I managed to pass out properly.
When I awoke during daylight, Delta was still wrapped
around me, warming me up as he had been through the
whole night.

There was no snow falling, but the frost was vicious and merciless, making me glad I'd put on both pairs of jeans. I felt more normal today, my head tingled slightly but apart from that, all seemed to be alive and well, and I immediately felt very awake, none of the usual morning drowsiness. I was suspicious of how okay I now felt, it seemed that I should be more shaken, but I was alright. As long as I didn't think too much of last night. Physically though, I was pretty much fine.

I looked up, trying to figure out what sort of time it might be. The sun was high in the sky, looking so falsely bright and cheerful. So it was around midday, I'd clearly slept better than I thought I could.

It was brighter and drier than it had been yesterday, actually quite comfortable considering everything that had happened, which seemed wrong.

As I sat up, Delta moved his head, looking at me with big, concerned green eyes. I stared at him and stroked his warm scales. He gave a sort of deep hum, the closest he ever came to actual words, and nuzzled his nose into my side.

"I'm okay." I said as I hugged him once more.

He came away when my stomach rumbled loudly against his ear, making him jump.

"Sorry, I'll eat something, then what do you say we go and find our brother and sister?" I said, scratching between his ears, pretending everything was fine. He nuzzled again in agreement.

Again I thought about how I'd love to know how much Delta really understood me.

I ate quickly, a tin of pineapple rings and the second half of a flapjack, which helped me feel even more myself, before getting up and putting my rucksack on, wondering how Tripp had spent last night.

I thought about changing some of my clothes to clean ones, but that would involve taking off layers and was way too cold for that.

My teeth felt horrible, having not been brushed in almost two full days. Tripp had both the toothbrushes though, so there wasn't really much I could do about it except swoosh lots of water around like mouthwash. I repeated this several times and tied my hair up, having lost the hat that had kept it out of the way. The last thing I did before setting off was take out the little tin of dragon scales and collect the few that Delta had shed during the night. He wasn't shedding much now that it was cold so there weren't too many to pick up, and I didn't want to leave any traces of him for anyone who might be looking for us.

My right knee didn't hurt as much as it had, but it ached and felt sort of mushy, I didn't like the idea of running on it. I poked it and winced at the feeling of a very deep bruise. Later, I'd take off my jeans and have a look at the technicolours.

Just as I began walking, I stopped and realised I had no idea which direction to go in. Tripp had come into the forest at about the same time as me, around the same place, but the wisp had taken me so far from where I began, and then Delta took me even further to get away from the lake.

Thinking about it, I hadn't actually seen Tripp enter the forest, I had just known that he was running for it like me. I pushed that worry down and agreed with myself that I would deal with it only if it became relevant. For now, I decided, Tripp was in the forest. He was safe, he had Zen looking after him, Delta and I would find them soon.

"Any ideas?" I looked at Delta. He seemed to grimace, but looked to the left and blew a few little smoke rings in that direction. "Left it is." I muttered as we started moving. Delta offered me a ride, but I felt bad having to keep relying on him, and I thought I should probably keep moving after what happened last night.

I was finding it so hard to let that sink in.

I died.

It didn't seem real, but I knew that it absolutely was. It made me feel slightly sick to think about, remembering the sight of my floating corpse. I didn't like that word, *corpse*, or any of the others like it; *body, cadaver, carcass,* they had all been just words before, but they felt disturbing now, after I'd seen myself in that way.

I didn't like thinking about this, it was horrible, so I did something quite stupid to distract myself.

"TRIPP!" I screamed, at the top of my lungs. A few birds in the tree above flew off and I apologised to them.

Delta whipped around and we both stared at each other, shocked at how loud I'd been, neither of us quite knew what to say.

I immediately regretted being so loud, reminding myself that James and Nina had been in the forest last night as well. I had no reason to believe that they had left. I'd just wanted to break myself out of those other awful thoughts, and I did the first thing that came to mind, but I clearly overdid it slightly.

"Oops." I muttered. "Um, shall we just carry on that wa-" I cut off upon hearing something in the distance.

A faint voice coming from far back in amongst the trees.

"Iris!" A voice I knew very well, calling my name.

I suddenly started jumping up with excitement. "Oh my god, he heard me!" I squealed.

Delta's expression turned from shocked and horrified to excited too. He'd been right, Tripp's voice had come from where Delta had been taking us. We both started moving again, faster now.

I yelled out again, and Tripp replied, closer this time. My heart lifted and I felt a huge rush of happiness and relief.

The sound of a dragon calling out came as well, but not from the same place as Tripp. Close, but off to one side. Zen had probably gone a-hunting. Delta and I didn't slow down, but we looked at each other and something passed between us as we ran. I nodded, his eyes narrowed and he put his head down, streamlining with the rest of his body. The last sight I saw of him was his sudden launch upwards, but the action of his camouflaging was so smooth it was like he took off and flew into a different dimension.

I set my vision straight ahead again and put on another burst of speed, now getting hot under all my layers.

The running had sent my knee into agony, but I didn't care. The pain was easily outweighed by the elation that my brother was around, and seemed to be okay.

He didn't sound in any kind of distress, he just sounded how I felt; excited and desperate to find each other.

"TRIPP!" I yelped as I went.

"IRIS!" He was a lot louder now, so close, and I could hear the smile in his voice that echoed mine.

I slowed down a little so that I could listen better, he was several metres away still, but not directly ahead of me, he was somewhere off to the side and I couldn't tell quite where.

"Where are you?" I yelled, coming to a stop to get my bearings.

That turned out to be my fatal mistake.

I slowly began to turn around, trying to detect where his voice was coming from, but I didn't register his reply as I was grabbed violently from behind.

For a microscopic split-second I thought it might be Tripp, tackling me as a greeting, but no, this was much bigger than Tripp, much more aggressive.

All the adrenaline within me changed it's purpose very, very quickly. I went from being excited to terrified in roughly the same amount of time it takes an electron to make one full circuit around the nucleus of an atom.

I began to scream and squirm, but James clamped a big hand over my mouth. It was unsettlingly warm, smelled strongly of cigarettes, and slammed hard into my face like he was slapping me. He probably meant it that way.

He leant down so that he could easily whisper into my ear. "You're gonna keep calling him as if nothing is wrong and make him get over here." I shook as he took something out of his pocket and I realised exactly what he was doing to enforce this order.

The barrel of a gun was held to the side of my head and I felt all the blood drain from me.

I started to hyperventilate and unwelcome tears made their entrance. I swear, I have never felt a terror like what I felt right there. Everything around me suddenly seemed so temporary and unreal.

At this point I wanted to pass out, to be rid of all this, as James took his hand away from my mouth and used it to start slipping the straps of my rucksack down my arms.

I tried to shriek Tripp's name again, but my vocal chords wouldn't work.

I felt the gun press harder into my skull and winced. What disturbed me most wasn't the fact that I had a gun pressing into my head, it was that the point where it rested was exactly where, down in the lake last night, I felt like I'd been shot. The *exact* same place. That couldn't have been a coincidence, surely?

"If you call him "Tristan", or anything else out of the ordinary that will let him know that something's not right, I *will* shoot you." James growled.

He was trying to mimic the cold, scary tone that Nina had mastered, but he lacked the effortlessness, he was trying too hard.

It was still petrifying though, and I didn't dare disobey him. He may not have said it in so much style, but it got the message across. I believed him.

"IRIS, WHERE ARE YOU?" Tripp called out again.

As the gun nudged me I felt like I heard a small *click* from it. Maybe it had been my imagination, but it kicked me into the yell that I needed.

"T-TRIPP!" I tried to make it sound as natural, as there-is-definitely-not-a-terrifying-man-holding-a-gun-to-my-head as possible.

James kept pulling my rucksack off me, and I put my arms back, complying and letting the bag slip off more easily. He pulled it off and threw it down to the ground. I felt a pang of sorrow at how easily he'd removed from me the one thing that had been with me constantly since we ran away.

Now that I didn't have the massive lump on my back, he pulled me in with his free arm and held me tight, restricting my movements and still pressing the gun into my head. I felt a bit faint but was determined to not let fear get the better of me again. I made myself keep standing, even though the knee that had been kicked by this very man was beginning to buckle since my legs had turned to jelly.

Tripp called me again, so close I felt like he was about to burst through the trees any second. I called back, doing my best to keep my voice from getting hysterical, but it wouldn't have mattered.

He did, in fact, burst through the trees at that moment. I was happy to see that he seemed unharmed, but his face fell as soon as he saw what was going on.

He'd been running, but he almost fell over, he stopped so quickly. He opened his mouth like he was about to say something, but no sound came out. He didn't know what he was supposed to say.

We made eye contact, like we do when having conversations via facial expressions, but there was nothing to say this time. We'd have asked each other, "are you okay?" but that seemed like a pointless exercise at the moment. Just one thing passed between us during this eye contact; fear, of the purest kind.

Chapter 23

"Take the backpack off." James commanded Tripp, keeping the gun pressed firmly on me.

Wordlessly, Tripp obeyed, slowly removing his rucksack and keeping his eyes fixed on mine.

I could see how scared he was; his eyes were about twice their normal size and he was shaking too. Like I said, he didn't look hurt, but it looked he'd fallen over at some point - there was a patch of mud on his face that it looked like he'd tried to get it off, but didn't have a mirror so the job was badly done.

He wasn't wearing his hat anymore either, and his hair was scruffy and wild. He had even darker circles under his bloodshot eyes and I guessed he'd also had trouble sleeping.

"Leave it on the ground, and take ten steps this way." James barked. He tightened his grip on me as if to emphasise what Tripp was risking if he disobeyed.

He didn't disobey; he slowly put his rucksack down and took the ten steps towards me, so that he was only a few feet away. He stood still, hands up in surrender, and swallowed hard. He looked up to the heavens as if in prayer, but I knew that he was actually looking for the dragons. I followed his gaze and looked up as much as I could, but that wasn't far, I had to strain my eyeballs. I couldn't see or hear them anywhere. Hopefully they'd see what was happening and know to stay away.

Please, Delta, keep far away and stay safe. I thought.

I knew that both of the dragons could easily take out Nina and James, no contest. But if they got seen, SCREB would be alerted, and then it wouldn't matter if the dragons got rid of our attackers, the company would know about them still being with us, and that was something that we needed to avoid at all costs.

My eyes and thoughts snapped back to Earth as James placed one of his feet on top of mine to anchor me, and removed the arm that had been wrapping around me. I would've breathed a sigh of relief, but somehow it didn't seem like the time just yet.

I could tell he was reaching in his pocket and tensed up even more, if that was possible. Tripp went stiff too, following the path of James's hand with his eyes. I tried to read his face when the hand re-emerged. He didn't seem shocked or horrified by whatever came out, just kept an intense stare above my head.

"Parr?" James said, keeping the gun in place, and I realised he was speaking into a walky-talky. Or maybe a phone. It was probably a phone.

"Yeah, I've got them both." He waited for a reply that I couldn't hear. It was definitely a phone.

Tripp and I looked at each other again.

"*I'm sorry.*" I mouthed. Hot, burning tears rolled their way down my face and kept coming in a steady flow.

Tripp shook his head, telling me not to feel bad.

"Yes...No...Not far, I'm pinging you the signal now."

James hung up and put the phone back in his pocket.

The signal.

I'd forgotten about that part of last night, but now it came back, taunting me with the fact that I still didn't know how they'd been tracking us.

James shifted the gun up slightly, adjusting his grip and I flinched. Tripp made to lurch towards me but was stopped short with six simple words.

"Move, and I pull the trigger." He said it slowly, enjoying the amount of power that he was currently wielding.

Tripp moved his foot back to where it had been and his hands up again, either side of his head. He gulped again and I could see him trying to think of a way in which this ended well.

"Is there anyone else, or just you two?" James asked aggressively, wrapping his arm around me again in a tight death-grip. I knew he was talking to Tripp, which was good, because I don't think I was capable of talking at that moment, just the odd shriek of terror.

It took Tripp a few seconds to find his voice too.

"Just- just us two." His voice was dangerously close to cracking.

"Where were you heading?" James continued.

"N-not sure." Tripp said, weakly. "Just...away." Tears began gently running down his cheeks and I saw before me, the little boy that he used to be, getting told off for something that didn't seem like his fault to us. The little boy who didn't want to be in trouble for something he hadn't been meaning to do.

"Please don't hurt her." He almost whispered, both of us crying softly. James chuckled sickeningly, relishing how weak and helpless we both were.

Tripp's hands had been gradually dropping as he stood watching, and we both jumped as James bellowed at him. "KEEP YOUR HANDS UP!!" From the volume, I thought for a split-second that he'd pulled the trigger and my end was once again nigh. I think my eardrums and my heart nearly exploded. My legs gave out and If I didn't have the arm wrapped tightly around me and holding me up, I would've collapsed. Tripp visibly died inside a little and put his hands back up, staring down at his feet and trying not to move too much.

"Alright, Bell, you're trying too hard and it's an embarrassment." Came Nina's voice as she appeared somewhere behind me.

"Why've you got ro ruin it?" James whined. "This is my first big mission!" He sounded like a child complaining about his mum humiliating him in front of his friends.

"Shut up." Nina said as she moved into my line of vision, walking around and coming face to face with me. She bent down a bit so that she was level with me and narrowed her eyes as she stared into mine. More into my soul, actually. She had a vague scent of perfume about her, and I shuddered as it reminded me of the one that my mother used to wear. She kept looking at me for a moment, like a deathly staring contest. I tried to hold her gaze strongly, to say with my eyes that I wasn't giving up, that they hadn't broken me, but the tears and the fact that I was shaking with fear didn't really give that impression. She had such a threatening aura, like a grenade with the pin half-out. She gave an evil smile, triumphant that I was now at her mercy again, that the tables had turned since I left her last night.

"Nearly got away." She said smugly, then punctuated it by slapping me hard across the cheek. Sharp pain prickled all over the surface of my cheek.

I bit my tongue to keep myself from letting out any sounds of distress. I would *not* give her the satisfaction.

I looked back at her and tried to give her a Paddington-style hard stare, despite the panic going on within me. She just smiled though - she knew she'd hurt me.

"I was gonna do that in a minute." James muttered, pressing the gun back into me. I didn't like how much he was taking out his annoyance on it, like when my hairdresser was going on a rant about her teenage son and cut my hair four inches shorter than I'd asked.

Nina ignored James and walked over to Tripp. He still had his hands up, and had been watching the scene unfold, his face growing angrier with every second that passed. Nina took his face in her hand, one of the typical villain-moves, and like I had, he tried to stare her down but was clearly crumbling inside.

"You two look so much like your mum did when we were your age." She mused. That made me feel even more uncomfortable. Knowing that this woman had known our mother for around forty years, maybe more, and was now hurting and tormenting her two children. Specifically, her two children who deeply resembled her.

Tripp looked like he wanted to spit in her face, but he knew that would result in my brains being blown out. Nina clearly had a very spit-at-able face.

She slapped Tripp, and he also made sure not to let on how much it hurt.

"You two clearly know how dangerous it is for us to have you out on the loose, so let's not beat around the bush." She announced as she moved behind Tripp, put both his hands behind his back and pulled a pair of handcuffs from her pocket. Tripp shut his still-crying eyes in defeat.

I breathed a tiny sigh of relief when the gun was taken away from my head, but as the hands were briefly taken away from me to put the gun away, I didn't have the stability to support myself and I melted into a pile on the ground.

James violently pulled me back up, making sure to hold onto me as I was too jellified to stand properly on my own. I could still feel the echo of where the gun had been pressed so firmly, but it was gone now.

My relief was short-lived though, as I felt my own wrists being cuffed too.

"You're coming back to our base. If you comply, you'll be put to work, treated with respect, earn a decent wage and be given accommodation on the premises." Nina continued. "Of course, you won't be allowed off-site without supervision because of how much you know; and history dictates that you two can't be trusted to be discreet. If you don't comply," She finished cuffing Tripp, then pulled and twisted his arms at awkwards angles, purely for her amusement. His face contorted, and he tried so hard not to let her know how much she was hurting him, but he was clearly in agony. "you'll be removed from the equation entirely, and no one will have to know more than is good for them." She concluded.

She just threatened to murder two children, then cover it up and make it look like an accident. Two children that belonged to some of her oldest friends, and she sounded almost excited about the prospect. Psychotic.

"Ow!" I said, not meaning to. Without warning, James had pulled and twisted at my newly-restricted arms too, yanking my shoulders down aggressively. Nina rolled her eyes as her move was copied, and picked up Tripp's rucksack, slinging one strap over her own shoulder. She stayed behind Tripp and used her free hand to hold onto both of his, and James did the same with me.

They began walking us out of the clearing and back into the dense forest, keeping us level with one another and in front of them.

Tripp and I looked at each other as we trudged on in depressed, defeated silence. We weren't actively crying anymore, but his eyes were red and swollen and filled with sorrow.

No conversation passed between us, just dread.

Chapter 24

We walked on for an uncomfortable half hour or so, the trees that had seemed so magical and beautiful before now laughing at us. They seemed to go on forever, relentlessly. No one spoke as we walked, which made it feel even longer, every crunch of twigs and leaves under our feet like the screams of all our hope being destroyed.

James' hands kept a tight hold on mine, so there was no chance of me breaking off and running away. Not that I would've tried.

Tripp and I kept checking the sky, hoping that we wouldn't see our dragons following us, praying that they'd seen us and known to keep hidden. We never did see them, but I never relaxed about it.

I stared down at my scuffed-up and muddy boots as we went. I'd never felt like such a failure in my life. I didn't know what to do next. We were so close to getting away; we'd found each other, and so had our dragons. The four of us were ready to get out of here and go somewhere else where we would be safe for at least another day, and right at the last minute, we got caught.

And it was my fault.

I yelled first and without thinking, I led our captors right to us by letting my impulses get the better of me.

I looked over to Tripp to try and catch his eye, I'm not sure why, maybe to try and say something, maybe just to feel the small comfort of knowing I wasn't alone, but he was staring intently down at his own boots. It wouldn't have been comfort though, would it? It would be a reminder that my stupidity had dragged him into this too.

The signal.

What had James meant?

At the edge of the forest, I have no idea where, there was a black car parked all on it's own. Some kind of SUV I think, though I don't really know much about cars so it could've been anything else and I wouldn't know.

The doors were opened for us and we were shoved into the back seats. Before having the seatbelts done up, we had blindfolds put on, which I felt was an unnecessary precaution, but there wasn't really much I could do.

As James tied it round my head, I desperately wanted to kick at him and run, but there was no point. He was a lot bigger than me and I had my hands secured behind my back. I was no threat to him, especially since Tripp had already kneed him where it hurt last night. He'd learned his lesson.

The drive was uncomfortable with my hands immobilized behind me, and made of even more uncomfortable silence, save for the confident and constant hum of the engine. It was getting creepy how much they just didn't talk. I almost would've felt more comforted if they were continually threatening us. Then at least we'd have some idea what they were actually planning to do to us. Right now, things were just eerily left for us to ponder.

The feeling of dread and failure kept growing inside me, and I slumped down against the car door, resigning from the world. From life. Maybe it would've been better if Delta had left me in the lake.

During the drive, I was surprised by how much I wasn't really freaking out anymore. Getting found and taken away was the thing I'd been most afraid of since we left, but now that it was happening I didn't feel as panicky. Just numb, given up. I'd passed beyond the point of stress or panic or fear, and was in that weird, calm region of acceptance.

I wanted to hug Tripp, or just reach out and hold his hand, but the closest thing that we would've been able to achieve with our hands bound and out seatbelts on would be bashing our heads together.

After who knows how long, the car finally came to a stop and the engine switched off. Too late, I realised what was going on and started moving, but my door opened while I was still leaning on it. If not for my seatbelt I would've blindly tumbled out into a heap. James cursed as he violently unbuckled the seat belt and pulled me out of the car. It hurt as he did this, but I didn't care anymore.

My feet hit the ground and crunched on gravel. The smell of wherever we were was full of fumes and nearly made me cough as I breathed in the polluted air. So we were somewhere industriel.

It was still unsettlingly quiet; in what I could make out of this setting, I would've expected machinery noises, but there was nothing. There were no birds making any sounds, just the occasional whistle of the wind, and even that felt apologetic for interrupting the deafening silence. It didn't remain silent for long though, as I got pushed forwards and had to start walking. I heard the car doors slam, and the other sets of feet on the other side - Tripp and Nina.

I walked for what seemed like about twenty feet, but that's literally a shot in the dark, it could've been anything from ten feet to fifty and I wouldn't really be able to tell without my vision.

It was colder here though, I knew that much. Not just in temperature, but in atmosphere, in soul. The air felt cruel and unforgiving.

My feet were heavy, and I may or may not have but definitely did make my footsteps heavier and louder than they needed to be. It didn't mean or do anything, but I wanted to do something, *anything*, that wasn't being controlled by my evil puppet-master.

We came to a stop and I could feel the presence of a looming building just in front of us. There were a few beeps of a code being put into a keypad, and a door opened.

We were shoved inside, where the air warmed up a bit, but still felt unfriendly.

If this was like the other SCREB bases we'd been to before, we just entered a building that looked completely inconspicuous to the public, even if it was out in the middle of nowhere. It would've looked like some electricity management building for that area or something, I don't know. The one near home posed as a pharmaceuticals development centre, so no one who didn't work there gave it a second glance, let alone tried to enter. Then, underneath whatever the chosen building was - Tripp and I always referred to it as The Imposter - was an enormous factory. High-tech labs and state-of-the-art equipment, all operating underground where only the government and those that worked there knew about it. And us. That was their problem.

We walked through what felt like a corridor, and the feeling began returning to my arms. The pins and needles I felt as I walked was the worst I've ever felt, and this wasn't helped by the big hands holding tightly onto my forearms.

There were a few more beeps of another keypad, and this time it had voice recognition.

"Nina Parr."

"James Bell."

There were probably other security measures that I wasn't aware of, I'm pretty sure there's usually a retina-scan, and a finger-print one.

I was shoved forwards again and nearly died coming to the top of a staircase with no warning. Luckily, I was pulled back and so didn't fall to my death, but my legs were now shaking even more as I descended.

"Idiot." James muttered as he yanked me up from falling.

Down the stairs and two cold lifts we went deeper underground, still blindfolded, still being shoved and pulled about as if we were nothing more than clothes mannequins. I say "we", but of course I couldn't see how Tripp's experience was going, though based on context, I'm guessing not marvellous.

Getting out of the final lift, James kicked my knee again, in the back this time, but the same knee as last night. Again, my whole leg buckled and I would've fallen if he hadn't held me up. The pain was even worse this time, and I couldn't help crying out in pain, but I managed to stop myself almost as soon as I started. I didn't want them to know how much they were hurting us, but I could feel James's amusement.

"Overdoing it again." Nina chided, I'm pretty sure I could hear her rolling her eyes.

I was made to start walking again, limping and putting as little weight as I could on the right leg, but still wincing every other step I took.

We didn't walk for that long though, before we turned into a room and were shoved down onto the floor. My blindfold was removed and I had to start blinking rapidly, adjusting to the light that was a lot brighter than I was expecting.

James looked pleased with himself, and Nina looked annoyed at James for being so pleased with himself. Needless to say, there looked to be a pretty big age gap between the two of them.

"Just get out." Nina commanded James, as he pulled a key out of his pocket and threw it upwards. It hung in the air and flipped around several times before he caught it triumphantly, looking even more annoyingly pleased with himself. She took the key off him, and just before she shut the big metal door she stared death into both of us and said, simply, "Try to escape, there will be consequences." Before she shut the door assertively and the lock clicked into place.

Chapter 25

As soon as they were gone we moved and did the closest thing to a hug that we could manage.

"Are you okay?" We both asked, almost in tears from relief at being reunited and not dead.

Tripp was shivering a lot, and we tried to wrap around each other like we did when we were little in winter, but it wasn't very doable without hands.

"What happened to you?" I asked. We huddled together as best we could for warmth, and I felt the numb feeling that had been with me for all the time that we were coming here wearing off.

"I was looking for you in the forest, and Zen found me pretty quickly, and then we were walking but I tripped-don't." he said quickly as I couldn't help sniggering. He was smiling too though, him tripping over anything had become such a source of humour to us when we were little. Silly I know, but it still made me smile.

He continued talking, quickly, trying to get it all out as soon as possible. "I tripped over a tree root or something and fell down a massive hill. I think I twisted my neck a bit weirdly while I was falling, it was hurting afterwards and now it just constantly feels like it needs to click." He moved his head, trying to get the click from his neck, but nothing happened. "And I guess there was something sharp too, I got caught on something on the way down and there was this massive cut on my cheek." I looked at him, and realised the patch of mud wasn't mud, but dried blood. Now that I was able to look at him properly, I could see the faint trace of a long, jagged scar up his cheek. It wasn't one of those straight-lines ones like in movies after a sword fight, this was like a lightning bolt, splitting off in several small branches up the right side of his face. Something had clearly torn right through his flesh and I winced just looking at the already-faded scar.

"How-?"

"Zen gave me some of her blood." He slowed his words and smiled sadly. "My face was basically ripped in half, and I was bleeding. A lot. So she cut herself, just like Delta did."

"Oh my god. Are you okay? Is she okay?" I asked, amazed at what a good job of closing and healing the cut Zen had done.

I moved my head around and he turned his face a little so that I could get a better look at the mark. It went from just shy of the corner of his mouth, up to his ear, with little lines splitting off from it like veins. It wasn't that vibrant, but it had obviously come from an unbearably awful cut. Tripp nodded. "It hurt like hell, but it's okay now." He nodded, and leant his head on my shoulder. "Zen's fine.

She made me rest. I think she was saying that we'd go find you guys in the morning."

"You kind of did." I said, leaning my head on top of his. He laughed half-heartedly, and we sat, taking in our surroundings for the first time.

We were in a small room, and there was a security camera up in the top corner with a red flashing light on it. That looked to be the only thing that was working and unforgotten in the whole room. A dusty desk with an old computer monitor that looked like it was from the eighties stood opposite us, with a couple of sad looking chairs either side of it. There was a dead pot-plant in the other corner, and an old red wire sticking out of the wall, with a broken end, the little fibrous copper wires poking out. We were clearly in an abandoned office that wasn't built for keeping children locked up in, and I wondered if this was the first time they'd felt the need to take prisoners. I hoped so.

"What happened to you?" Tripp asked. I stared ahead for a second and gulped, thinking over the events of last night.

"I was ready to curl up in a ball and die-"

"Don't do that." He interjected. I nearly laughed at the irony.

"But then Delta found me. So we had just started walking to look for you, but then Nina and James appeared, so Delta hid me underneath him."

"Were you okay? Did they see you?" Tripp suddenly sounded urgent and worried.

"No, no they couldn't see us. We were both fine, but they got so close. So then Delta made me go to sleep, and I guessed that he was saying we'd look for you in the morning too, and I had a really hard time getting to sleep,

197

and then I saw..." I took a shaky breath, as Tripp looked at me in anticipation. "A wisp." I said.

He gasped slightly.

"Are you serious?" He furrowed his brow in concern and I nodded. "Please tell me you didn't follow it?" He didn't sound accusing, just scared for my sake. I looked at him apologetically and he sighed.

"I couldn't help it. In hindsight, I realise it was a *terrible* idea. I forgot how dangerous they can be. I thought of Willo. I forgot everything bad, just saw a pretty fairy-type thing and felt like I had to follow it."

"*You* would. Where did it lead you?"

I looked down, not quite sure how to say what had happened with the wisp. It seemed too weird to talk about, so unreal.

"It took me to this massive lake within the forest. Actually, for a lake it wasn't that big. For a pond it could be considered massive. Just a large body of water." I procrastinated saying what happened. Why was I so reluctant to say it? It's not like Tripp could be mad at me for *accidentally dying*. I think I was just afraid to admit it to myself out loud. I could say it in my head, but if I said it out loud, it became true, and I wasn't ready for that.

Tripp smiled, amused by my ramblings, and I went on.

"It made me jump in. I don't know why. I knew it was a bad idea, I just couldn't stop myself. It hypnotised me, or cast a spell on me or- or *something*." I said, quickly. I didn't like to admit it, but I was trying to convince myself that that was the case; that I hadn't just been *that* stupid.

"Jeez. You okay? Were you able to swim alright?" Tripp asked. I shook my head and swallowed, preparing to say

what I had to say. Tripp tilted his head, waiting for what
came next.

"I think I died." I said, plain and simple. Tripp didn't
move, just stared at me.

"What?"

"No, I don't *think*." I looked up and met his eyes. "I died."
I let it hang in the air. "I drowned. But partly, I just...gave
up." I felt a single tear roll down my cheek as I felt that
same, ominous cold envelop me as it had in the water.
Tripp opened his mouth, not fully understanding, but not
sure what to say.

"I saw my own corpse floating in the water." I could barely
say it aloud.

"But- but then how- how- what?" Tripp stuttered.

"Delta. He pulled my body out of the water, and cried on
me." I noticed I was now saying 'me'. I hadn't thought of
the body as 'me' at the time. It had been just that; a body.
Tripp stared at me in disbelief. "He *cried*?"

"Golden tears. I couldn't believe it either." I nodded. Tripp
looked down and gulped, digesting everything I'd just
said.

"Are you sure? You were- you were...dead?" he almost
whispered 'dead', as if it were a rude word he'd just
learned and wasn't sure how allowed he was to say it. Even
after I'd been so blatant and open about it, we both still
felt uneasy with the word.

I nodded again. "Certain."

"Are you, you know, okay?" He asked, still in shock.

I looked away. "I think so. I felt a bit weird when I- when I
came back, sort of not quite real. But I'm okay now. I feel
normal. I think." I tried to sound sure of myself, but that

had never been one of my strong points. I *did* feel normal, but I felt like I shouldn't, so it felt wrong to say that I did.

"You died." Tripp said quietly, half to me, half to himself. It wasn't a question, it was a statement he was trying to accept. He sounded so broken as he said it, a lot more broken than I felt about it, and I realised why.

At the start of this week, we'd found out our parents were dead, and that had crushed us. Now, imagine I'd just found out that my brother had also died suddenly. Even if he was back now, he'd still, at least for a time, left me as the only living Reynolds. Our family had dramatically been quartered within a week. I wouldn't be able to cope if I lost him as well.

"It's okay." I said, trying to sound reassuring. "I'm fine now, I promise. I'm alive. I was only- only *gone* for a little while."

He just kept staring at me, tears brimming in his eyes.

"You died." He repeated, his voice cracking at the end.

"I'm back though." I whispered. I didn't mean for it to come out as a whisper, but I couldn't stop it.

"I wasn't there, I couldn't help you." He was also whispering now. That broke my heart, seeing how small and helpless he was seeing himself.

"It's not your fault." We were both crying now. Tripp leant onto me, giving me an armless hug that would've probably been the tightest he'd ever given, had it been an actual hug. Even like this though, he was giving a good hug. I still got the warm, safe feeling that I always got from him.

"Just promise you won't ever do it again." He said gently.

"I promise, if you never do it ever." I agreed as he nodded. I promise we don't normally cry this much. It had been a rough week.

Chapter 26

We half-slept for a while, maybe a couple of hours. I
forgot to look at Tripp's watch when we got in the room. I
grew steadily hungrier as time passed though, having not
eaten much.

All our flapjacks had been stolen from us, and probably
wouldn't be returned. If nothing else about this situation
was, the deprivation of flapjacks was definitely abuse.

I knew we should be staying up and trying to think of a
way to escape, or just figure out what they might be
planning to do with us, but we were both exhausted.

Not sleep-deprived, I may not have slept well but I'd slept
enough. We were just tired of life at this point, and sleep
was a nice and easy - albeit temporary - escape.

Finally, we were awoken by the door opening suddenly,
and Nina poking her judgmental head through, give us a
blank expression, that somehow still felt like a bit of a
death-stare.

We both looked up at her and didn't say anything, but hoped she was coming to let us out or bring us food or something. We tried to look unbroken at her, still have fire left in our eyes, but I don't think it worked. She smiled in pity, we looked pathetic to her. Like abandoned wolf cubs, out in the cold, with barely a chance of survival on their own, and at the mercy of a hunter.

She didn't say anything to us, just tossed a couple of plastic packets at us before shutting and locking the door again.

We stared down at the packets to see what they were and sighed in disappointment.

Chicken and Mayonnaise Sandwiches.

Well that was just insulting. We were hungry, but not that hungry. We would never be *that* hungry.

"They're either mocking us or testing us." I said, staring down at the fluffy bread.

"Or they just don't care." Tripp said, monotonous.

"Fair point." I kicked the sandwiches away, out of my sight and wondered whether or not I could be bothered to get up. Not for anything in particular, just to move. I was slouched over and felt really sluggish at the moment. I didn't like it, but I also didn't see any point in getting up.

"Time?" I asked. Tripp kicked away his sandwiches too and turned around for me to look at his watch.

I raised my eyebrows in surprise. "Bloody hell, it's twenty-to seven."

"God," Tripp was stunned too. "we've been here for about four hours."

I sat up straighter, hardly able to believe it had been that long. Hearing how late it was clearly motivated Tripp, as he gently pushed me off him and stood up, stretching as much as he could without his arms. I looked up at him, wondering if he had any form of plan.

"Let's look around. There might be something that can help us." He said. He would've been holding out a hand to help me up, but that wasn't really an option right now.

"Like what?" I asked, very aware of the working security camera on the wall.

"I don't know. I just want to move. Maybe there's a stray blueprint of the building, or a pair of chain cutters." He sounded desperate. I looked up at him, half wanting to get up and look around too even though I knew we wouldn't find anything. He knew that too, but he didn't want to admit it.

I chewed my lip, wondering whether or not it would be safe, and shook my head. "We're being watched." I used my head to point upwards at the camera. Tripp looked at it, then back at me.

"So? What are they gonna do?" He moved his head again, trying to get the click in his neck.

"Nina said there would be consequences." I shifted uneasily.

"Like what, Iris?" He raised his voice, suddenly snapping and I flinched, not expecting him to get like this. "What the hell are they gonna do? Hold a gun to one of our heads? Oh wait, they've already done that." I realised with relief the rage was being directed at SCREB, not me.

"They've completely destroyed our lives in the space of less than a week, it's their fault that Mum and Dad are gone and we're now being held as prisoners having done nothing wrong except exist! What could they do now to mess us up further, kill us? That would honestly be a bit of a relief from what's happening now, so if they want to kill

203

us then maybe we should let them." He finished his tirade by twitching his head and neck at a hideous angle, trying to get the click to punctuate his words but still nothing came of it.

I didn't say anything, just looked down, hoping he didn't mean that. I know that at the time I had welcomed death, but now, even amongst all that was happening, I realised how much I don't want it yet. I wanted to get out, find the dragons and find safety, and not let SCREB win.

I felt Tripp look at me, suddenly going quiet and realising what he'd just said.

"Sorry." He said, quietly and coming closer to me. "I- I didn't mean it, I just-"

"It's okay." I looked up and met his gaze. "I get it. Let's go find some stray blueprints." We smiled at each other, a mutual, unspoken agreement to try not to die, and not accept death if it was offered as an alternative to living like this.

I stood up and stretched out, my spine clicking satisfyingly as I twisted. Tripp was very impressed with my clicking vertebrae.

We walked over to the desk, which had an inch-thick layer of dust on top of it. Down the side of the desk was a column of three drawers, and down the side of the drawers was a patch of green furry mold.

I turned around and grabbed the handle of the top drawer behind to open it, as Tripp leaned over me and looked inside.

"Nothing." He sounded disappointed but not surprised. We repeated the same process for the next two empty drawers, except the third one had a large dead spider in it.

All the while, I kept looking at the camera, hoping and praying that we weren't being observed right now. My heart rate was going up just at the prospect of it.

I'm sure Tripp would've had us look some more, but just then, the door opened again, and James and Nina stepped in. We stared at them, and they stared back. It was obvious what we had been doing, there was no trying to pretend we were innocent. They'd probably been watching through the camera anyway.

I dreaded to think what might happen next. I mean, technically, we weren't trying to escape, just violating privacy and directly rebelling against a very large and powerful company. Absolutely awful and corrupt company, but still very powerful and easily able to overpower the two of us.

"Your ride is here." James said.

What? Tripp and I looked at each other. Was that it? Were we just being collected without being punished for our misbehaviour.

I looked back at James, who was coming towards us, blindfold in hand. Nina was close behind him, and Tripp and I tried to back away, but there was nowhere to go, we were quite literally cornered. James grabbed me roughly by the shoulder, and tore me away from my brother. I tried to put all my weight back, make it harder for him to take me, and Tripp and I would've grabbed onto one another if we'd been able to, but I was carelessly ripped away like a cow calf from it's distraught mother. Well, maybe not as bad as that.

I wanted to kick him, wanted to rebel, but I was afraid of what might happen to either me or Tripp. It was clear that these people had figured out that we're each other's biggest weaknesses, and they were perfectly comfortable abusing that knowledge.

My blindfold was put tightly back on, and after James checked that my handcuffs were still secure, I presumed I got the go-ahead, as I started being shoved out of the room. I heard Tripp and Nina following behind, and as we left our little abandoned office, I felt the air get warmer. The floor out here was slippery and I had to really grip with my feet to avoid slipping over, being rushed as quickly and aggressively as I was. James was no longer guiding me by holding onto my hands or arms, he just had one hand placed firmly and assertively around the back of my neck. Ready to tighten the grip if anything was amiss. They didn't give any indication as to where they were taking us, but I guessed back to the base near home, where all the records and information on us and our parents were.

I hadn't heard anyone else speak while we were here, or the usual sounds of machinery and work, so I assumed this was one of the smaller bases.

These were dotted around the country, much more frequent than the big ones, so that they could be used as holding space. The hunters and trackers would go out and catch their unicorn or whatever they were going after, then bring it back to one of these. They would sedate the unicorn properly and make it safe to travel with, then get it into a big truck or something and take it to one of the big research facilities like the one our parents worked in. I didn't know all the locations of the small ones, but I knew they were everywhere, so that a hunter was never too far from one to get their animals there. They were hidden in plain sight, disguised as all sorts of things so that the magical animals were never safe.

My knee hurt as I walked, and I got a similar numb feeling throughout me to the one I'd gotten when we were being taken here. We'd been caught, we'd failed but I didn't really care anymore. I did feel the smallest degree of hope though, walking back up the stairs and the lifts, towards the exit. I know that was silly, we weren't coming anywhere close to being free, but at least we were leaving here. Plus, I knew my way around some parts of the one at home, maybe familiarity could be our weapon if I was right and we were being taken there. We'd have a better chance at getting out of the one that we knew.

As we got out, that same horrible fumey smell greeted me and this time I did cough as I breathed. Breathing that in on an empty stomach made me feel really sick.

The sound ringing in my ears as we walked made my stomach drop. I'd expected us to be going in the car again, but the sound explained why we'd been waiting here for so long, rather than just gone straight on the road. They'd have had to contact people, let them know the situation and have this sent over.

A helicopter.

I'd heard them a few times at home when we were on visits to SCREB. Just over a year ago, we observed a pegasus being brought in from one.

A beautiful pegasus whose wings had been severed. Her golden blood dripped down her sides like tears, tarnishing her flawless white hide. She was screaming as the people walked her in, hitting her with horse whips. I didn't know any living creature could make a noise like

that, her cries tore apart the layers of my mind and her face contorted in pain like I had never seen before.
Like no one should ever see or feel.

Tripp and I watched on in horror, unable to do anything or believe that these people were okay with what they were doing. We were hardly able to speak all day after that, just couldn't get the horrifying images out of our minds. Our parents scolded us for being so upset by this. The pegasus didn't matter so we shouldn't care about it. When this didn't work, they told us not to worry, the pegasus wasn't really in that much pain, they were just loud animals by nature. I was insulted that they'd told us that, when we were about ten years too old to believe it. Back in the present, I tried not to think about it, but the noise of the helicopter made the scene play out in my head all over again, haunting me. Quite Pavlovian really.

Nina.

That was why I recognised Nina. She had been the one leading the pegasus from the helicopter into the building. It struck me suddenly as I thought back, that was why I already had such a deep-rooted hatred and fear towards her.

I got a lot colder as we drew nearer, and the sound of the propellers filled my ears painfully. I tried to resist going in, leant back and made it as awkward as possible, but I was shoved in and landed in a heap on the trembling floor of the helicopter. Tripp was thrown on top of me and the door slammed shut, shaking the whole vehicle. I started panicking; we may have been inside a giant protective shell now, but last time I flew it hadn't gone well and I wasn't keen to do it again. Especially in the context of being a prisoner.

Tripp got up off me and we sat up, going back to back and feeling for each other's hands to make sure we were both okay.

"I'm gonna lie back." Tripp whispered. "Try and get my blind fold off." He moved away from me slightly, and leaned back, lying down so that his head met my hands behind me. I poked him on the nose by accident, and moved my hands up to the thick piece of fabric covering his eyes. It was tied on tightly, cutting into his face. I gently moved it up his forehead and slid it off, but poked him in the eye as we were jolted around. We were taking off.

"Sorry!" I said quickly, as a wave of guilt flooded me.

"Don't worry, just get down so I can get yours off." Tripp said quickly, he didn't seem fazed. I lay down so that he could reach me and he carefully removed my blindfold.

I blinked a few times, but it wasn't such a dramatic adjustment this time. It was dark outside, and the lights set into the roof were dim and gentle.

I sat up and Tripp and I looked at each other, wondering what the hell to do next. We were prisoners of the sky now, which meant we had much fewer options.

The movement of the helicopter made us sway and fall over again, as we reached out to grab each other on instinct, but this just resulted in straining our wrists and crashing into one another.

It was still cold, and I was glad I still had on both pairs of jeans. Thinking that reminded me that our rucksacks had been stolen from us. We were now wearing everything we possessed.

We scooted to the edges and used the walls to help us
stand up and get our balance. The darkened windows were
big, almost spanned the entire back of the helicopter.
There was a solid wall inside, separating us from Nina and
James. That was good, it meant they couldn't see us.
Unless there was a camera back here but I put that
thought to the back of my mind. This helicopter was
specially built for carrying large and potentially dangerous
animals, which was why the wall was there. That way, if
the sedated animal suddenly awoke, the pilot wouldn't get
ripped to shreds.
I took a turn around and looked outside at the world
below. I had to take a step back and a sharp breath in. We
were *very* high up.
This shouldn't bother me, but after flying the way I had I
couldn't stand looking down and seeing the huge distance
between us and the ground.
"You okay?" Tripp turned around from the opposite
window to look at me. I nodded and swallowed, clenching
my fists and making myself look back outside. It had
begun to rain, gradually getting heavier, and I sensed that
a storm was coming.
There were lots of trees, we were still above the forest, and
dotted around the edges I could make out lots of villages. I
wondered if one of them was Meaden.
I realised that I was holding my breath as I stared down,
clenching every muscle in my body and forcing myself not
to move, to keep looking.
Thank goodness I did, because I suddenly saw a flash of
white darting underneath the helicopter. For a split
second I thought lightning, but then, with a second flash,
this time of blue, I gasped and realised what it was.

"Dragons." Tripp and I both muttered at the same time. Zen and Delta had kept themselves hidden but followed us. The tiny glimmer of hope began to return inside me. The rain continued getting heavier, pounding down and distorting the view from the already dark windows, but the rapid flashes of white and blue going in and out from underneath us were clear as day. I prayed that they were camouflaging their undersides from the world below, just showing their colours on top so that we could see them. I was glad to see they were keeping very low, and well back from the front of the helicopter so that they could only be seen by us. Tripp and I turned around to face each other, grinning but also wondering what to do. A horrible thought struck me.

"If they follow us all the way home, they're gonna get captured." My smile instantly disappeared. Tripp's turned into an expression of deep thought.

He looked back out the window, staring down at the dragons shooting around for us.

"We have to get them to stop following. Can we tell them to stay here? We'll let them know when it's safe, just get them to stop?" I asked urgently, coming over to look out the same window as Tripp. He was silent for a few more seconds, frowning and looking down, scanning the area.

"No." He said slowly. I got a feeling of dread as I recognised something in his tone. "We're gonna jump."

211

Chapter 27

I stared at him, waiting for him to laugh at his joke, but he was deadly serious. I looked out the window, and then back at him.

"You're crazy." I said.

"I know. But it's our best chance to escape." He looked out at Zen and Delta.

"We'll die. We will *definitely* die." I backed away from the window.

"The dragons will catch us." He pressed, eyes wide and insistent. I shook my head, anxiety growing in my stomach at how eager and certain he was. He came closer to me and I knew he would've been putting his hands on my shoulders if he'd been able to.

"Iris," He said, gently. "I know you're scared, and you have every right to be, but if they take us, if they get us back to their base, everything gets worse. They'll make us work for them, torturing animals, and if we refuse, they'll torture us. They'll use us as threats against one another, like in the forest." His eyes were pleading, his voice desperate. "If we get out now, we can get away from them and they won't have power over us anymore. And you were right, if Zen and Delta follow us, they'll be in trouble too. We're still above the forest, so we've got somewhere to hide as soon as we're out. We can escape, but only if we go *now*." He finished. I swallowed, knowing he was right, but scared through to my bones of jumping out of a moving helicopter. Against every instinct, I nodded.

"Yeah?" He asked.

"Yeah." I said, stepping towards the window. This happened to be the side that was also the door. Our obstacle now, was opening it. But with violence or cunning - that was the question.

We looked down at what seemed to be the lock mechanism. Not knowing anything about the engineering of helicopters, it was a bit hard for either of us to know what to do. And we had no hands to work with.

"I think we're going to have to smash it." Tripp said. I grimaced, not liking the idea of breaking the wall of a flying vehicle in the rain, even if we were about to leap out of it to our deaths.

"Come on," He grinned. "We're getting great at smashing windows." I laughed half-heartedly, and tried to compress the restless feelings of dread within me.

"Oh crap." Tripp cursed. I looked back out the window and saw what he meant. We weren't over the forest anymore, we'd passed it and were now going over towns and fields, our reptiles still frantically circling underneath. "Umm...that's okay. This is England, there'll be another forest to fly over." I said, trying to reassure both of us.

Tripp nodded and started looking all over the wall. His
eyes lit up towards the back.

"Air holes." He said with glee.

"Fantastic, we won't suffocate after all." I said. He raised
his eyebrows and smiled at me.

"We can call us one of those two," He gestured outside
with his head. "get them to break the lock from out there."
I looked at him. "You really think that'll work? I know
they're intelligent, but-"

"Let's just give it a try." He said. I didn't argue. If we
could get out without having to smash the window, that
was definitely a plus. He got right up to the slits in the
glass at the back and called out.

"Zen!" Good choice. She may have been one of the laziest
creatures I'd ever met at times, but she had impeccable
aim and was better at precision than Delta. I looked at the
wall separating us from the cockpit, nervous that Tripp
might be heard, but the wind and rain should obscure his
voice from human ears.

He called again, and this time, Zen's silvery white head
popped up in front of him, making sure to keep well back
from the view of the pilots.

"Good girl!" Tripp beamed at her. "Zen, baby, I need you
to do something really important for me." Zen's ears
perked up, making little splashes in the raindrops falling
on her head. "You see that box thing on the side there?"
He looked at it as much as he could, pressing himself right
up against the glass. Zen followed his gaze and her eyes
locked onto it. "I need you to take it off. But you need to
be careful about it, don't just-" He broke off as with one
graceful swoop of her claw, Zen had the bulky lock off and
falling to the ground. Tripp and I stared at her, amazed at

how smooth that had been. "Alright, that was perfect. Thank you, Zen." He said in awe.

Zen chirped, pleased with herself and looked back to Tripp, awaiting further instructions.

"You and Delta, get ready to catch us, we're gonna jump out to you." She seemed to nod and dove back down.

Tripp turned back to me. "We have to move quickly. They probably received an alert, if they didn't notice the lock by themselves." We both went back to the door, which was now rickety and threatening to open on it's own. I resisted the urge to keep as far away from it as I could.

Tripp turned around and grabbed onto the handle behind him. He took one more look at me, trying to be encouraging, before he ripped it open.

Wind and rain poured in and Tripp damn near fell out there and then, but he managed to hold on and steady himself. He looked out and took in a breath, trying not to freak out for my sake.

I too looked down and felt my legs turn back to jelly, backing away instinctively. Tripp beckoned me back over with his head. I sank to the floor and made myself shuffle over towards him on my knees, the right one throbbing in pain. Tripp got down too so that we were on the same level, looking into my eyes and trying to make both of us brave.

The rain peppered my face like little bullets, and the wind made it hard to keep my eyes open. I looked out again and had to shut them, holding my breath for a second to keep from screaming.

"I can't do it, Tripp!" I yelled, trying to get my voice above the level of the weather. The edge was too close, I felt like it was inching towards me, ready to drop me.

215

"Yes you can!" Tripp shouted back, blinking rapidly to combat both the rain and the prospect of hurtling to the ground from a great height.

I shook my head and shut my eyes tight, trying not to be such a wimp, but there was no pretending I was able to do this. I hated myself for being so pathetic, especially when Tripp was being so courageous. If I hadn't hit my head, if flying had been fine, I'd still be frightened but I might be able to do this.

"You can, Iris! You can because you *have* to!" Tripp yelled. My heart was beating so fast it could've matched the propellers above us. I stared at him, hyperventilating with the world around me spinning. I hesitated too long. Tripp knew I wasn't going to be able to stop hesitating.

"I'm sorry!" He yelled as he stuck out his leg and shoved me over the edge.

I swear to God, everything I did this week was 'the scariest thing that's ever happened to me'. This was much worse than dying. I screamed loudly, but heard nothing through the rush of the wind and rain. Above me, Tripp leaped out and began flying downwards too. The helicopter got smaller and smaller alarmingly fast as I descended.

I felt my stomach turn and flashed back to that first time I flew after hitting my head. The wind and rain and cold attacked me and my head started spinning, I almost felt like I wasn't in my body anymore. My eyes were shutting involuntarily, images flashing through my head as I lost all control of myself.

Barely able to breathe, I screeched, thinking I'd hit the ground as I suddenly crashed into something hard and momentarily stopped falling. Realising it was Delta, I tried desperately to hold on with my arms, but they didn't move and I just managed to strain my shoulders and slid off his wet, slippery back.

I heard him roar in distress as I started spiralling down again, this time facing the ground and became certain I was about to die. I saw trees below me, getting closer and closer, as if they were growing up to me.

My hearing went. Not because everything was too loud, I just became deaf. I blinked several times and realised I was blacking out as Earth got nearer and nearer. No, I couldn't do this again. I couldn't be the girl who kept crying and fainting.

"NO!" I screamed at myself in desperation. I felt something grab me from behind with sharp claws. My shoulders were held in an iron grip and the trees suddenly weren't moving so fast.

I stopped screaming and started taking short shallow breaths quickly. I shut my eyes on purpose now, but my hearing was back, somewhere above me Tripp was screaming, and although my body felt more liquid than solid, I was fully conscious.

My head was pounding, but I was able to almost ignore it and tried to focus on my breathing. Delta had me now. I may not have felt it, but I knew I was safe.

We exploded through the treetops in a shower of leaves and rain, and got closer to the forest floor, quickly but not like a bullet anymore. I hit the ground hard, Delta not being the best at smooth landings in times of stress, but he's working on it and it's not his fault.

As he released me from his claws I fell onto my side and strained my shoulder, but I was mostly okay. Apart from the fact that I couldn't move and was a trembling mess on the ground.

I was essentially a puddle now.

I heard the screams of my brother get closer, then the burst of the treetops, then a thud as he landed clumsily a few metres away. Neither of us said anything, we just lay there in the rain, breathing, shaking and marvelling at the fact that we were alive and no longer in the grasp of those who wanted us dead.

I kept my eyes tight shut and clenched my stomach, desperate to get the ground to stop spinning underneath me. Delta sniffed at me, trying to make sure I was okay, but I couldn't find it in myself to even grunt and let him know I was alive. He could tell though, he sat down next to me to wait for one of us to regain the ability to move.

Chapter 28

The storm got worse as the night grew even darker, and I got completely soaked before I even attempted to move. I needed to keep down on the ground, to make sure it stayed there.

I was still shivering, but I finally managed to sit up. My head hurt and I threw up on the ground next to me, feeling worse than I ever had before. The rain beat down on me and the cold made my face hurt, but we were at least being shielded from the wind by the trees now. It had gotten completely pitch dark, but the dragons were giving off a bright glow so that I could still see. I looked over to Tripp, lying sprawled on his side on the ground like a splat. He was still breathing heavily, his cuffed hands out behind him and gripping onto the ground to keep it there. I slowly moved over to him on my knees, unable to stand up yet, and let myself flop down next to him so that I could look at his face. The scar where his face had been ripped open was flaring up, red and intense.

"You okay?" I asked. My voice came out a lot more shakily than I'd anticipated. Eyes still shut, he swallowed and nodded, before trying to sit up. He gasped in pain as he moved his legs.

"What? What's wrong?" I asked frantically. He shifted his left leg around, looking down at it and trying to move the foot but winced and had to stop.

"Zen dropped me and I landed badly. I think- I think I've broken my ankle." he said, defeated.

"Oh, Jesus. What do you need me to do?" I asked, trying not to panic. It wasn't anything fatal, but at the moment Tripp's brain was the closest thing we had to medical supplies.

"Mate, I'm not sure you can do anything without your hands." He groaned. I'd forgotten that part. I hoped neither of the dragons offered up their blood, it wasn't fair to keep sapping it from them, and we didn't know how much we'd be able to take without overdosing. Dragon blood is a very unknown territory, the only thing known about it for humans is that it sometimes heals. But no one knew how much was safe to take, or what the consequences could be, or whether or not it would actually work every time. Plus, as a vegan, I didn't feel great about using animal blood for anything, even if they were giving it to us willingly.

Perhaps the dragons could be of use right now in a different way though. I looked over at Delta. His glow was fading, he'd fallen asleep while I was lying down and hadn't noticed me get up. Zen was watching us though, with concern in her big blue eyes. I didn't know if this was a good idea, but it had to be worth a try. I shuffled over to her and she stared at me, wondering what to do.

"Zen, if I give you my wrists," I only twigged the potential
for disaster in what I was about to do as I said it out loud,
but it was the only thing I could think of. "do you think
you could really carefully break the chain?" I asked. She
perked up and Tripp looked at me with wide eyes.

"Rainbow, that's not-"

"You just threw me out of a moving helicopter, let me
have this one." I cut him off. He shut up and nodded as I
turned around and held my arms out for Zen. I shut my
eyes nervously, hoping I wasn't about to lose my hands.
I jumped as there was a small thunder clap and my heart
started racing again. The rain came down heavier and I
took a deep breath, bracing for Zen to strike me.

She didn't though, I guess her method was easier for her.
I felt the cool metal on my wrists warming up and realised
she was using fire to heat the chain up so that I could
separate my hands. The heat grew and I started to worry
that it would burn me completely.

"Zen, careful." Tripp said, trying to keep his voice level.
My wrists began to sear and I tried to pull them apart, but
they wouldn't go yet.

"Come on, Zen!" I exclaimed, trying not to panic but very
much panicking. It got too hot, like lasers were going
through my wrists and I screeched as I ripped my arms
apart with a force I didn't know I had. There was a loud
clank as the chain flew apart and I held my arms out to the
cold rain.

It felt good to have them back. I rolled my shoulders a few
times and stretched my arms right out. The metal
bracelets of the handcuffs were still attached, and would
be for the foreseeable future, but that didn't matter.

I went back to Tripp, still on my knees but much faster now that I had my arms to help.

He stared at me, impressed that that had worked and not really hurt me. I didn't mention how much the skin on my wrists was burning, that wasn't important.

"Okay, what do I do?" I asked, feeling less like jelly now. My head was hurting less and I felt almost back to normal. That being said, I hadn't felt 'normal' since we ran away, so who knew what that meant anymore?

"Uh...I need something to act as a splint." He said, looking around and trying not to move his leg too much. I nodded and stood up cautiously. Still a bit wobbly, but okay.

I started scouring the ground, looking for bigger, strong sticks that I could tie around his leg. The rain and the darkness made it hard to make anything out very well as I got further away from Zen's light, and Tripp tried to move a bit to help, but he cried out in pain as his foot rolled in.

"Don't move." I said. "Just lie down, I'll find some sticks." He nodded reluctantly and put his head back down, trying not to show how much he was hurting. I ran over to a big tree nearby and looked down over the roots. It was hard to see them clearly, but there were much bigger sticks round here, fallen branches surrounding the trunk. These ones were a little drier too, thanks to their mumma tree acting as an umbrella, as much as she could without her leaves. Now I just had to find a straight one for Tripp. Ironic.

I jumped as I heard him whimper in pain, but looked over and saw Zen working on his handcuffs.

"Anything there?" He called to me.

I got down and moved around the base of the tree, using my hands to help me search. I almost screamed in surprise when I felt some kind of cold, wet snake wrap around my neck, but it was just my sodden hair falling down. I quickly flicked it out of the way and continued looking around the tree.

"Yes!" I squeaked as I found a long, straight-ish stick, a couple of inches in diameter. I grabbed it and ran back over to him. The stick would be long enough to hold his leg on both sides, but I needed to snap it in half. I put it on the floor and held one end down with my foot while I wrenched the other end up. The wood wasn't as soaked as the sticks out in the open, but it was still soggy and slippery, which just made it easier to break. There was no loud snap as it broke which was disappointing, but there was a great crunch as one half came away in a splintery mess.

"Just tie it on?" I asked as I knelt down by Tripp's feet and pulled off my scarf.

"Yeah, make it tight so that I can't roll over it. Protect the ligaments." He instructed, sitting up and leaning back on his newly freed hands. I held one half of the stick on each side of his leg and foot, trying to keep them flat as I wrapped the scarf around and pulled it tight. Tripp winced a little but nodded for me to keep going and I tied it on as tightly as I could. He handed me his scarf to add another layer, and once it was all tied on I took a moment to check all over it. It wasn't very well done, but rain was making everything awkward and harder to manipulate. It would do for now anyway. It would have to do for now.

"How's that?" I asked as he looked down at his leg. His face was on the brink of extreme pain, but he held it together and inspected my handywork.

"That should be okay, thank you." He said, blinking through the pain.

"What else? Does it need heat? Ice?" I asked, feeling angry that our rucksacks had been taken from us. If nothing else, we'd at least have painkillers to try and soothe him.

"Ice." He said, breathing hard. "For the love of God not heat." I cursed the weather for not snowing anymore, looking around for any patches of frost. There was nothing around that I could see would be of any use, but Zen seemed to have an idea. She had been trying to get my attention but be quiet at the same time so that she didn't wake Delta. She was frantically looking between me and him to indicate that I should go to him. I hoped she was right.

"Brilliant!" I said. I leaped up and went over to feel his skin. He hadn't gone to sleep with his internal fire going, he hadn't even thought about it. He'd just been lying down and happened to nod off.

I carefully took the end of his coiled up tail and moved it over to where Tripp was lying in agony. It just reached his foot, and I gently wrapped the end around the scarves. Tripp breathed a small sigh of relief as the cold, scaly skin mimicked ice on him. We jumped as there was a flash of lightning somewhere far off that lit up our spot for a split second.

"Thank you, Iris." He said, having to shout now to be heard over the storm. We both screamed as there was another, louder thunder clap.

"Is there anything else?" I shrieked, looking around as if a magical antidote would suddenly start growing from the ground.

Tripp shook his head, eyes shut. "Just elevation. Then that's about all we can do for now." He was in so much pain that he was trying not to let on.

I adjusted his foot so that Delta's tail was going more underneath it and it raised up, properly elevated. As I did this, it got too much for Tripp to not let on and he screamed out in pain. A scream that filled the trees and the rain and the clouds and was about more than just his ankle. The scream I'd heard in the lake.

"I'm so sorry!" I cried as I finished shifting his leg around and set it in position.

"It's okay. Thank you." He said, actually crying now. I moved up to his top half and lay down next to him. He held onto my hand and squeezed, just crying to himself now. I wrapped my free arm around him and held on, trying to shield him from the horrors of the world around us.

"You're gonna be okay." I whispered as he held onto me like he would never let go. We didn't need to sleep, but we had to stay like this for a while. He was in no state to move, and he definitely wasn't letting go of me any time soon.

Zen wrapped herself around us to try and provide some warmth, and opened out her wings above us as a shield from the storm. The rain was loud on top of her scales, but it wasn't going on us anymore. A huge roar of thunder made us both jump again and huddle closer together, hoping it would stop. We just lay there in our dragon-nest, awake and waiting for daytime to save us.

I felt like we were back under the car on that very first night of all of this. That felt like a lifetime ago now.

225

Chapter 29

After the sounds of thunder and rain finally died down, I reached up and moved Zen's wing a little so that I could see the outside world. Her warmth had been a God-send, and she carefully made sure that none of her warm skin came into direct contact with Tripp's ankle so that it didn't get warmed up.

Somewhere through the night, he'd drifted off, still holding on to me. The pain had gotten too much I guess. I'd been awake the whole time and heard his pathetic whimpers during his sleep while his foot tried to twitch but couldn't do it properly in the splint and just aggravated his ankle.

The damp new day was just beginning as the cold, deceitful sunshine crept through the gaps in the trees. The darkness still lingered, but it was gradually being shifted. My stomach growled and I thought of flapjacks, then got sad when I remembered that all our stuff had been taken from us. So we had no food and no way of knowing when or if we might next come across some. Even if we found another town, almost all our money had been in the rucksacks so we were screwed. We had nothing.

I looked up at the sky, at what or whoever might be in charge of all of this.

"Why?" I asked, my voice coming out as a croak. I daren't ask 'Why us?' because, why not us? Just why at all? Why did any of this need to happen to anyone?

Out of the blue, Zen started hissing and spitting. She got up quickly and stood in front of me and the now half-waking up Tripp, before I was able to see what was upsetting her. Delta got up and did the same, the two of them forming a protective barrier in front of us.

"What? What's wrong?" I asked them as my heart picked up speed, but they just put their wings out to shield us further.

Tripp looked up, panicking and tried to sit. He'd been jolted into full consciousness but for a second forgot about his ankle as he hastened to move.

"Oh god." He groaned as I tentatively sat him up against the defensive dragons. They were now growling and hunching over, like cats ready to pounce. This was the first time I felt genuinely afraid of them, I'd never seen them like this.

My heart pounding, I sat down against them next to Tripp and squeezed his hand.

"Woah, it's okay." Came a voice from the other side of the dragons. A man's voice, calm and soothing. The growling got a little quieter and footsteps drew nearer. I held my breath, afraid of what might happen if an outsider told everyone that he's seen real dragons in the woods.

"You two are so beautiful." Came the man's voice again. The growling got quieter still and I felt the attack-stances relax. Tripp and I looked at each other, confused. This guy didn't seem that surprised. Like he hadn't been expecting to just randomly stumble into a pair of dragons, but it wasn't a shock to him that said dragons existed.

"What's happening?" Tripp whispered. He hoped I'd have known the answer, having been awake when this all happened.

"I don't know." I said, unhelpfully.

There were a couple more footsteps, slow and careful. The growling got slightly louder, then slightly quieter.

"It's okay. I'm not going to hurt you." The man said. He spoke slowly, trying not to upset anyone. He carried on talking to them gently, telling them everything was fine and he didn't want to harm them until the growling went down. In fact, it turned to purring and I guessed that they allowed the man to stroke their noses.

Why was he not surprised about dragons? Why was he being so calm and collected about this?

"What are you two doing out here?" He asked. Now he seemed confused. Only now.

Slowly, keeping us hidden from the view of our visitor, Delta and Zen maneuvered their long necks to look back at us. Delta looked me in the eyes, and for the first time since we left home, he didn't look scared or worried.

There was a gleam in his eye that I'd never seen before. A wave of trust washed through me and I sensed that he was telling me that things were going to be okay. This feeling was slightly tainted after trusting the wisp so much, but I knew Delta. If he believed, I believed.

The dragons looked back at the man and then slowly began to step apart in perfect unison. I turned around quickly so that I was facing the man, and Tripp turned around slowly so that he didn't dislodge his ankle. The man standing before us had dark skin and black dreadlocks tied up out of the way and covering the tops of his ears. He wore black trousers and deep red tunic-style jacket, with a large brown bag slung over his shoulder and big brown boots. He looked at us with equal parts confusion and concern. His eyes were warm and friendly, and the feeling of trust and assurance that Delta had given me strengthened as he looked at us. The thing that seemed a little odd to me was that his gaze kept flicking to my hair. Not like he liked it or didn't like it, like he simply couldn't believe it. I didn't know what the protocol was for a situation like this.

I opened my mouth to try and speak, but in an instant, his eyes switched from my head to Tripp's scarfed-up foot and he took a step closer.

"Are you okay?" He asked. He seemed to genuinely care.

"Uh-" Tripp said, then realised how impolite we were both being. "I think I broke my ankle. It hurts. Really badly." He finished. I shivered in the cold morning air, wishing Zen was still wrapped around us. The man stepped closer and knelt down. We both recoiled slightly, but out of instinct from being approached by a stranger, rather than any kind of fear of this guy. He looked down at my messy splint/scarf modern art piece, then back at Tripp's face.

"I'm so sorry, I wish I'd brought something with me, I wasn't really expecting to run into anyone this early." He said, regretfully, looking through his bag.

"Don't worry." Tripp said, still confused as to what was going on. Was he an angel sent to help?

"Oh, I'm Gideon, by the way." Said the man, holding out a hand. Tripp took it tentatively and gave it a shake. His expression turned from confused to impressed and amazed.

"Tristan." He said. That handshake must have been dynamite if he introduced himself with his full first name. Gideon moved over to me and offered his hand again. I took it and was genuinely blown away by the level of his handshake. It was incredible. It felt so professional and I absolutely understood why Tripp was now Tristan.

"Iris." I said with a mixture of awe and uncertainty. Perhaps we shouldn't have given a strange man in the woods our real names because his handshake impressed us. It was a really good handshake though.

"Nice to meet you both." Gideon said with a friendly smile. It didn't seem like a creep giving a false friendly smile, it seemed genuinely warm and caring, like a dad. I hoped I was right and not wildly misreading the situation.

"You too." We said in unison.

"How did you manage to do that?" Gideon asked gesturing at Tripp's ankle.

"Tripped." He said weakly.

"Into a ditch." I added, to try and make the story a bit more believable. Gideon made a sympathetic face.

"That's unfortunate. Really, I'm so sorry this happened today. Usually I at least have something with me to dull the pain, but today you've caught me without anything of use." He sounded so annoyed with himself, you'd think we were good friends.

"Honestly, it's okay." Tripp said. "You had no way of knowing."

"Still, the *one* time I come unprepared and I find someone who actually needs help." He whacked himself on the forehead in frustration. Tripp and I looked at each other, not sure what to make of Gideon. Everything about him seemed so genuine, but - I think understandably - we both had trust issues at the moment.

"Are- are you a doctor then?" I asked. He looked at me and his eyes quickly flicked from my face to my hair to my ears, then back to my face.

"An alchemist by trade, but my eldest son is on his way to becoming a healer, and my wife works in the medical side of herbalism, which I've dabbled in since meeting her." This statement absolutely convinced me that he was not an angel, but a wizard. He must be. *Alchemist, healer, herbalism.* The only other explanation was that he was hardcore into fantasy, to the the degree that it had become a slightly out of hand LARP. I really hoped it was the former.

Tripp and I made slightly nervous eye-contact again, while Gideon re-fastened his bag.

Delta began to saunter back over, trying to act cool, and sat down behind me and Tripp.

"They're wonderful creatures, aren't they?" Gideon said, looking up and staring at Delta with wide eyes.

"Yeah, they're amazing." I replied, adjusting myself to sit more comfortably.

"How did you come to find them?" He asked. Once again, Tripp and I made eye contact, for just a tiny bit too long this time.

"If you don't mind my asking." Gideon said. "It's just that they're so rare around these parts. It must be about thirty years since I've seen one in real life." He turned his attention to Zen, who was sitting just to the side and watching intently.

"We, um, we found them when they were babies. While we were out hiking a few years ago. They were drifting down in a stream because they couldn't swim yet, so we got them out. Then they didn't want to leave our sides." I said. As I started that fake explanation, I didn't know where it was going to finish, and I kept telling myself to stop before I dug too deep a verbal hole, but the words made themselves heard.

Tripp nodded in agreement. "We'd never seen dragons before and haven't seen them since." That was our truth now.

"Remarkable." Gideon muttered. Not in the way that implied he didn't believe us, in the way that he was truly amazed at what he'd just learned.

"And, are they safe out here? In this place?" He looked concerned. I suddenly felt slightly defensive. That felt like something Nina would say, if she was going undercover to capture our dragons. Maybe this guy really was concerned about their welfare. Maybe, as well as being an alchemist, he had a weekend job of gathering magical and supernatural animals for safety so that the evil humans couldn't get them, but I was still nervous.

"It's only that at weekends, I scout around here, finding any magical animals and trying to get them to safety." Gideon declared. Oh. I stared in disbelief; I hadn't expected to be so right.

"They're fine." I said, trying not to be rude but not really sure what was the right response.

"Perfectly safe." Tripp interjected. "We're with them all the time that they're out in the open, and even then it's in places like this where people hardly ever go, and other than that they go off and hide themselves away from the world." We both nodded earnestly.

Gideon smiled, seemingly satisfied with that answer. "Well that's good to hear." He looked up at the sky, which was now getting to that blue shade with just a tiny hint of purple in it as the day creeps in even further. "Well," He said happily. "I was about to go and find something to eat, you four are welcome to join me should you wish. I know my way around here fairly well, and you seem like nice people." he smiled warmly. He too seemed like a decent fellow, and we were really hungry, what else did we have to do?

Chapter 30

Together, Gideon and I helped Tripp up onto Zen's back as she crouched down to make it easier. He tried not to let on how much pain he was in, but his face was too contorted in anguish for it to be a secret.

He held on for stability and Zen stood up while Delta sauntered behind, keeping watch from the back of the procession. Gideon looked impressed at how tame they were, and I wondered what his past experience with dragons had been like.

I was more than a bit nervous about going with him on a whim, but if he knew where to go, that was more than we knew. We had Zen and Delta anyway, they would keep us safe if there were any signs of attack. I just hoped that 'something to eat' didn't involve the hunting and killing of rabbits or squirrels or something.

"So," Gideon began as we started walking through the damp twigs and leaves that carpeted the ground. "are you

from round here?" He didn't seem to be prying, just
making conversation.

"No. We're from-" I started to say, but then realised I had
no idea where we were to say how far away we were from,
and although so far he'd been kind and welcoming, I
didn't really want to tell him exactly where we lived.
"-somewhere else." I finished, weakly. Tripp looked at me
with an expression that sort of said *'Really?'* and I
shrugged apologetically, not pretending that my answer
had been any good. It seemed to satisfy Gideon though.
"How nice that you've been able to come here with your
dragons." He smiled.

"You're from round here?" Tripp asked, amused by
Gideon's unquestioning acceptance of my vagueness.
"Yes, I've lived nearby my whole life. I've never stumbled
upon adventurers with their own dragons though." He
said. We laughed nervously, though I liked how he
referred to us as 'adventurers'. Upon the mention of the
dragons, Delta made a noise that sort of like a small roar,
but just to get attention rather than be threatening.

"I'm so sorry, I've been so rude. Do they have names?"
Gideon asked, mortified at how impolite he felt he'd been.
"It's okay, don't worry." I said. "That's Delta." I pointed
behind us at him and he made another, more satisfied
kind of noise.

"And this is Zen." Tripp said, patting her on the back and
she bared her fangs in what was her version of a friendly
grin.

"Nice to meet you, Delta and Zen." Gideon said happily.
"How old are they?" He studied Zen as they walked on
next to each other.

"Four." I said definitively, then remembered that our story consisted of us finding dragons, not eggs.

"We think." Tripp jumped in to fix the story. "We found them four years ago, and they were very young and small at the time."

I silently berated myself for almost letting it slip. I don't think it would be that bad if he knew that we'd found them as eggs and raised them, but then we'd have to explain about SCREB, and I'd already accidentally said that we rescued them from drowning.

"Oh they're still very young then." He said, slightly surprised at how young they were.

"Yeah, still babies." I agreed while I shrugged to myself. I had no idea how quickly dragons matured or at what point they stopped being considered 'very young'. I knew they could live for a very long time, but due to the lack of modern knowledge surrounding them, I didn't know if that meant three hundred or three thousand years. I just knew that they would outlive me and Tripp, and we hadn't told them that so as to not upset them. They were still babies to us though.

"You know, my wife, Sandrine, found what we thought was a dragon egg, it must be about eight years ago now. We kept it warm for several weeks waiting for it to hatch." Gideon said, a gleam of joy in his eyes. "When it eventually did, it turned out to be a caladrius!" He laughed and I tried to join out of politeness, but I had no idea what he was talking about.

"A what?" Tripp asked.

"Sorry, of course, they're not so well-known nowadays." Gideon said kindly. "It's a bird that has the power to diagnose death, or to heal." As he spoke, his words vaguely rang a bell. Maybe I'd read about it somewhere, or maybe it had been mentioned in one of the lectures our parents made us attend, but I felt unsurprised at his bird story.

"He'll look at a sick person, and if the sickness is incurable and fatal, he'll turn his head away in shame. But if it is curable, he absorbs the illness and his white feathers turn grey. Then he flies up into the sky and dispells the illness into the sun." I looked over at him, aghast. That part didn't ring a bell.

"Is he okay?" I asked. "Do they live after that?" I asked. Gideon chuckled. "He's fine, his feathers turn back to white and he comes back down demanding food, like nothing ever happened." He said. I wondered if they weren't so common nowadays because of people like our parents.

"That's amazing." Tripp said in awe.

"It is, isn't it? Usually they only live with royalty, but the one that Sandrine found was abandoned, and after he hatched, he refused to leave, his name is Silus."

We carried on walking as the day got lighter but not warmer, talking about dragons and caladriuses. I wondered where Gideon could be from if he was so familiar with dragons and his occupation was alchemy. He never said, and I didn't want to ask, in case it led to him asking us more about ourselves, so we just stuck to the safe subject of mythical creatures.

We came to a stop in a clearing with several apple trees surrounding it. My stomach started growling and my mouth drooling slightly upon seeing them.

There weren't half as many as there would've been in the warmer months, but they were the sweet, yellowy kind that get cut up into wedges when you're poorly. In the middle of the clearing, was a fallen tree that looked like it was to be used as a bench. It was very wet, but it would've been quite nice during cool summer days when the sun is setting and the breeze is gentle and the worries are non-existent. Even in the aftermath of the storm it was beautiful here. The grey air made me nostalgic, but I'm not sure what for.

"This is where my sons and I go when they come with me." Gideon said as he took off his bag and laid it down on the ground.

"It's lovely here." I said as I stood up on the log to look around, then quickly hopped down and ran over to the nearest tree. There was a low hanging branch with four apples on it, and I grabbed all of them. I ran back to Zen and handed two of the apples to Tripp.

"Thank you." he said, though it got lost as he immediately took a huge bite. I bit into my own with a satisfying crunch and I don't think an apple has ever tasted better.

"Hungry?" Gideon asked as he too plucked an apple off the tree and took a bite too. It was rhetorical, but we both nodded enthusiastically. He sat down on the log in the middle, not caring that it was sodden, and watched Delta slinking around and sniffing at the trees.

"Is he alright?" he asked.

"Hm?" I turned to see what Delta was up to, an embarrassing amount of apple in my mouth. "Oh-" I swallowed hard, and then regretted that I hadn't chewed more. "He loves the smell of apples. Won't eat them, but sniffs them uncontrollably. He's a bit odd." I said, watching the great reptile snuffling like a bunny around every tree that he could. It made me happy to see him like that, it was like he was a baby again, figuring out what everything was and not worried about anything. He was a lot clumsier back then, always tripping over his own feet and tail, but whenever there were apples around now he returned to that carefree little hatchling that he used to be. I smiled thinking about that time. "Zen's the same with pears." I added.

Tripp nodded in agreement. "She gets really confused by them. We're not sure why."

We laughed as Zen perked up and looked around at the mention of pears. With her movement, Tripp winced as his leg was dislodged from where it had been lying out across her in rest. She sank back down as she realised she'd hurt him and bowed her head in sorrow.

"It's okay, it's not your fault." Tripp said, stroking her neck and trying to convince her that he was fine. I could see how much pain he was in though, from how he stiffened and his voice wasn't quite full.

"How is it?" I asked. He looked at me and tried to smile, but his eyes were dead.

"It's okay." Was all he was able to say.

"Have you taken a look at it? Since the actual break?" Gideon asked, moving closer.

"No. It was too dark to have seen anything properly last night, and too cold to take off his shoes and socks." I said, trying to justify it. I felt a stab of guilt and stupidity for not looking at it as soon as it happened. That would've been a good idea.

"I can't say I blame you for that, but you've no idea what state it's in." Gideon reinforced both my defence and my regret at the same time.

"Fair point. I probably should've thought about that."
Tripp said, remembering that he was supposed to be a
doctor. He dropped his fresh apple core to the ground and
handed me the other, full apple to hold. Balanced on Zen's
back, he carefully swung his leg over so that he was sitting
side-saddle. He leant down to start undoing the scarves
but immediately pulled back up.
"Nope!" He cried out in pain. I dropped the apples and
grabbed onto his hand so that he didn't fall off as he
sprung upwards so suddenly.
"Thank you." He said as I started untying the scarves
myself. I did it as carefully as I could, but I could hear in
his breathing that it hurt. The makeshift-splints fell off
either side of his leg when the scarves came away, leaving
little sticky bits of bark and moss stuck to the leg of his
jeans.
"Do you need help?" Gideon asked. I knew he was just
being nice, but I wanted to talk with Tripp alone if
possible.
"Actually, could you please see if there are anymore sticks
that we can use to re-splint it in a minute? These won't be
that good while they're still so wet." I asked. Gideon
nodded and disappeared a little way into the trees,
scouring the ground for anything dry.
Slowly and gently, I began undoing the laces on Tripp's
muddy, scuffed up boot. These had been nice, relatively
new boots when we left.
"Do you think we can trust him?" I whispered as we both
leaned our heads in together.
"I don't know. He seems fine, and he's helped us rather
than hurt us. Plus, that handshake." He whispered back. I
truly wanted to trust him, so that had some we actually

could trust, but I knew that might be reckless. But that handshake.

"Yes! possibly the best I've ever felt. These two are pretty chill, and they're very good at reading people usually." I pointed out.

"Yeah, and he's clearly from somewhere that dragons, or mythical creatures at least, are a normality." Tripp continued the list of pros.

"Do you think he's a wizard?" I asked.

Tripp thought for a minute, then nodded. "Something along those lines at least. Ow!" He said as I finished with the lace and started shifting the shoe.

"Sorry!" I stopped what I was doing and held everything still for a moment.

"Don't worry. Keep going." Tripp said, before continuing. "If he's a wizard, that's great, but does he think we are too? He didn't question us having dragons and being humans, but if it's normal, or at least used to be normal, for him, it might look like we're magical."

"Well with hair like this who wouldn't think I'm magical?" I grinned. Tripp mock-slapped me but was smiling too.

"He seems to want to help us. And he's got a family, including a son who wants to be a doctor too." I mused as I tilted the boot up to get it over his heel. It came off and he was left with a damp grey sock.

"Our parents had a family including a son who wants to be a doctor but I can't see them being so trustworthy around anyone with unrestrained dragons." He pointed out. That was fair, but I got a much warmer feeling off Gideon than our parents.

That was a horrible thing to realise.

"True, but they also wouldn't have led the people and dragons to an apple grove and offered to help while telling stories about a magical healing herron." I said.

"Also true." Tripp conceded. We didn't say anymore on the subject, we were both too horrified to carry on as I finished taking the sock off.

His whole ankle was swollen up and bruised into an Aurora Borealis of blues and purples and blacks.

"Jesus Christ." We both said in unison, staring at it. It was like a car crash; it was horrific to look at and made me feel slightly sickened, but we were unable to tear our eyes away from it. It seemed to also be pulsing lightly, but that could've been my imagination.

"Umm..." I stuttered, trying to figure out what the procedure was for this kind of thing when our medical supplies were zilch. Tripp was now breathing heavily, trying to keep calm about this misshapen potato that was attached to his leg.

"Don't worry," I said, worrying a lot. "it's not as bad as it looks."

"How the hell can you possibly know that?!" He shrieked.

"Because that's what you've always told me when I've hurt myself!" We were getting hysterical looking at it, and I dreaded to think how it must've felt.

Zen looked back at Tripp, craning her long swan-like neck so that she could just about see what was going on on her back. Delta stopped sniffing at the apples and came over to see what was wrong. They both started making noises of distress which just made everything seem worse.

"Calm down, guys, it's okay!" I raised my voice to try and be heard over the panicking dragons, like a mother trying to keep her kids calm after they've seen a spider.

"What's wrong?" Came Gideon's voice as he rushed over to us, dropping a small armful of sticks.

"Oh." His eyes widened and his face dropped when he saw Tripp's bulbous ankle. "Keep it elevated, how bad is the pain?" He asked, putting a hand on Zen to calm her down so that she would stop moving so much and Tripp could regain his balance on her. He had been rendered pretty much speechless after looking at it for so long but he managed to get out the words, "B-bad. Very bad!" As he tried to adjust himself to keep the foot up on Zen's neck.

"Don't look at it!" I commanded. I don't know if that would've helped any, but he began staring up at the sky instead.

Gideon looked at the ankle, studying the bruising and frowning.

"Thank griffins I found what I did." He said, half to himself.

"What?" I asked frantically.

"Lenimen leaves. They grow very quickly when dragons are nearby." Out of his jacket pocket, he pulled a small bunch of long, deep purple leaves, shaped like eucalyptus.

"That seems way too convenient to be true!" I screeched, assuming they were some kind of antidote, but I'd never heard of a leaf that only grows for dragons. Tripp was now fully lying down and groaning in pain.

"I know." Gideon said, smiling slightly maniacally as he waved a couple of the leaves in front of Zen's face. Like a primal instinct built within her, she breathed a tiny flame over the leaves, singeing the tips.

Before I could react, Gideon stuffed the leaves into Tripp's open mouth. I almost screamed upon seeing someone shove an unknown and potentially poisonous substance

into my brother's mouth. Was this the moment that
Gideon revealed himself to have been undercover and just
waiting for the chance to kill us? Was this the moment
that we truly learned to appreciate the danger of
premature trust?

Tripp started to chew the leaves, unaware of what had just
been said and probably assuming they were something we
were familiar with.

I held onto his hand, too late to stop anything, as he
swallowed and coughed a couple of times. Trembling, I
waited for something to happen, unsure whether to be
angry that we'd put blind faith into possibly a murderer,
or elated that he'd helped so much despite only knowing
us for about an hour.

Tripp began to sit up slowly, eyes shut so that he couldn't
see his ankle.

He seemed okay.

He didn't seem to be hurting anymore. I stared, not sure
what to say.

"It won't heal it completely." Gideon said behind me. "But
it will ease the pain and make the swelling go down, while
the healing process speeds up." His words threw a comfy
blanket over the panic, and even in the seconds went by I
watched the bruises fade to a couple of shades lighter. It
was miraculous, I didn't know how to react as I watched
it. It was like a timelapse video of the healing process, but
in real time.

Now I was one hundred percent sure that Gideon was a
wizard of some kind. The speed with which he moved
with the leaves, you could tell he worked with ingredients.
Even if he himself wasn't an herbalist, he clearly had
knowledge on the subject.

Tripp bent his knee, pulling his ankle in closer to him, and had a look, staring at it in amazement.

"How does it feel?" I asked tentatively.

"Still hurts a bit, but it's just an ache now." He said, I'd never heard him so happy to be aching.

We both turned to Gideon in total awe. He smiled warmly at us, pleased that we were so impressed.

"Thank you." Tripp said earnestly, not sure what else to say to such a miracle-worker.

"Glad I could help." Gideon nodded at him.

Chapter 31

Several hours later, we were beginning to learn the truth.
Tripp - with his new, dry splint - and I on the ground,
leaning back against our dragons, stuffed with apples and
blackberries and staring at Gideon, who sat with his back
up against the log.
He wasn't telling everything, that much was clear, but nor
were we and we were still pretty much strangers, so I
couldn't blame him. But Tripp was able to move without
being in agonising pain and no one had tried to kill or
hurt anyone, so I was warming up to the idea of trusting
him much more. Maybe that was stupid, but stupid hadn't
stopped me before, so why should now?
He didn't tell us what he was, but I was still sure he was a
wizard. He said he was aware that mythical creatures were
nothing more than that - mythical, to most people, but he
knew it was safe to talk about them with us because we
had dragons protecting us. Dragons were especially rare
now.

"A long long time ago, they were everywhere." He said. "My grandfather used to tell me stories of them from when he was a boy." He had a glint of bittersweet nostalgia in his eyes. He looked down, remembering. "He had a pet one, much much smaller than these two, a little hunting one really, but it died when I was about ten." He gave a sad little smile, reminiscing about times gone by. I felt like we should say something consoling, but we sat, transfixed by his words, even though they were sad. He had a way of talking that held attention without demanding it. "Even then, dragons were starting to become rare. He was known around town as 'the old dragon man' and that was the last time I saw one. The last time a lot of people saw one." He finished. He looked up, smiling again. "Sorry, I didn't mean to make things sad." He said.

"No, it's okay. I'm so sorry about the dragon." I said, trying to think of something more meaningful and less generic to say. The way he said the last part, that dragon had clearly meant a lot to him. He looked at ours with the same childlike wonder that Tripp and I had when we first came to have them.

"What was it's name?" Tripp asked.

Gideon smiled sadly again. "Spike" He laughed a little, thinking back on the name. "He was about this big." He held his hands about two feet apart, then a foot off the ground. From what I understood about dragons, that was very small.

"Ever since then, I've been on a personal quest to find dragons again, but never did until now." That sentiment weighed on me. The sorrow and desperation that must've been felt in thirty years of trying to find one, to know that they still exist.

I had a horrible thought in my mind, a horrible suspicion that I knew why the dragons had been disappearing. SCREB had existed pretty much as long as humans themselves. Of course the name and the methods had been different and evolved over the years, and there had been times throughout history when they weren't so prominent. But through all of time, the principal had remained the same; get rid of magical beings. In the last two-hundred years or so, the mission had also become research and experimentation. However, only in the last seventy to eighty years had they developed the technology to do such damage to so many creatures, who kept themselves hidden from humans as much as they could. The technology to, say, almost wipeout an entire species.

I swallowed hard thinking about that. I hadn't realised how rare dragons were, I figured I just hadn't seen any others because we lived in a normal town. Maybe it was because there just weren't any others.

"But," Gideon said, shaking me out of my thoughts. "I found two today, and a pair of new friends, so this has turned out to be a wonderful day." He smiled at us, but it wasn't the sad smile anymore, he was truly pleased to have met us. This made me truly pleased to have met him, and blessed him with the gift of meeting dragons at long last. I liked that he was also considering us friends. I wanted to consider him a friend too, he was the kind of person who was easy to want to be friends with.

I think I really did trust and believe that he wasn't someone undercover, or anyone else who wanted to harm us now. The dragons' comfort with being around him played a big part in that, and it's hard not to want to be friends with someone who had a handshake as professional as his.

"I'm glad we got to let you meet dragons again." Tripp said, smiling.

The whole rest of the day passed surprisingly quickly. We got back on the move, but didn't find any mythical creatures. While we moved, Tripp kept riding on Zen and Gideon told us about Spike, in exchange we told him about Zen and Delta as babies. How sneaky we had to be to keep them a secret from our parents, but we didn't tell him the real reason that we had to keep them secret. We said that it was simply because we were worried that our parents would take them away, or tell people who would take them away. It was just safer if they didn't know. That part was true.

Twilight came and we were in another, smaller clearing with more brambles surrounding it. Gideon and I gathered sticks and stones and built a small fire, while Tripp ate blackberries on top of Zen. I felt a heavy half-sadness weighing on me as we built the fire. Gideon didn't have any camping equipment with him. He'd leave us within the next few hours, and we'd be without a guide again. I liked him and wanted to keep hanging out with him, if only to have someone who knew the area and could show us where all the apples were. More than that, we'd be stuck with nothing real to do anymore. Our lives had become running from SCREB, but today we'd been able to forget that and make a new friend who we could talk about dragons to. We'd been able to be us, not just the runaways.

We'd told him that we were just out exploring with our dragons, since we didn't get much of a chance to do so at home. I think he could tell we were lying, or at least not telling the whole truth, but he didn't pry. He thought we had a home to go back to, a safe place to be.

I found it strange how he kept glancing at my hair, seeming to be in great thought. Maybe dyeing hair was just very uncommon where he was from?

I wondered what his family was up to, going about their normal business and knowing that their father was coming back tonight. His children had living parents.

"Can you please help me down?" Tripp asked as Delta gently lit the fire. I held his left hand and put my arm around him as he slid off Zen's back to make sure his foot didn't bump on the ground. Together, we sat down on the almost-dry ground with our backs against Zen and looked into the fire. It gave a kind of warmth that I was starving for and looked so magical right now, against the pink and orange sky. It made me think of the first time Mum and Dad took us camping when we were eight. That was one of my favourite memories.

"How does it feel?" Gideon asked, sitting down a few feet from us, facing into the fire but turning his head to look at us. Tripp looked down at his ankle, still wrapped up tightly in our scarves.

"It's fine if I keep it still." He finally said.

"That's good, isn't it?" I asked. Tripp nodded and threw a twig into the fire.

"Where do they go?" We looked up as Gideon broke the melancholy silence. "Your Zen and Delta, when you're at home?" He looked truly concerned for their wellbeing.

250

Tripp and I exchanged a nervous look, and suddenly the fire was not warm, but too hot.

"We don't know." Tripp admitted.

"They fly away." I continued.

"And come back when we summon them." He finished. Gideon stared at Delta, in awe of his bright blue coat.

"Are they safe? Really? If they're just flying around who knows where, aren't they at risk of being hunted?" He asked. Not trying to call us out for bad parenting, just wondering if the dragons really were okay.

"That's what we've always been afraid of." Tripp said, slightly ashamed. "We know they're not truly safe, but we don't know of anywhere that they would be."

"We just hope and pray that they'll come when we call them, and trust that they're able to look after themselves." I said, grimly.

"We don't really have another choice." Tripp punctuated. There was another silence, but this one was less empty. Gideon nodded, understanding our dilemma.

"What if there was somewhere that guaranteed safety?" He asked. Tripp and I leaned forward, listening intently, wondering if we could be right. Was he really a wizard? Could he possibly be from a secret world that was hidden from humans and full of magic? It sounded too fairytale and typical to be true, but a secret magical world was something that Tripp and I had always believed in. It was where we liked to pretend that Delta and Zen went even though we were almost certain they just flew to some remote area and lived their dragon-lives doing dragon-things until we called them.

"What do you mean?" Tripp asked, a little nervous.

Gideon looked down and swallowed, pondering how much to say.

"What if- what if there were a village nearby, that humans can't get to?" My heart beat faster with excitement at his every word. "A village where magic is everywhere and creatures roam free and aren't in any danger?" he stared at us, in the fire light he looked like a knight from a fantasy story, offering a pair of peasants a quest.

"Are you serious?" Tripp asked slowly. My mouth hung open, staring with wide eyes as the full weight of this revelation dropped onto me like a ton of bricks.

Gideon nodded, not a speck of humour on his face.

"I understand that you love them and don't want to part with them, but for their sake, I want to put the offer out." He smiled warmly.

"If no humans are there, then-" Tripp started to ask but he broke off as Gideon smiled again and moved the hair on one side of his head to reveal a pointed ear.

An elf ear.

Again, we stared in disbelief and at the same time absolute belief and elation.

We were right. I had been so convinced of this my whole life, I didn't really feel the need to question it, I just felt an extreme sense of excitement about learning that it was true. It was true. I believed Gideon absolutely, I just *knew* that he was telling the truth.

"So," I said slowly, realising what this meant in relation to what he'd said. "you think that we should send our dragons to live with you." I didn't like the idea of saying goodbye to them, even if it was or their own good.

"While they're not with you, but I'm certain we'd be able to find a way for you to see each other again." Gideon said, trying not to upset us. This gave me a small bit of hope. "You two could come and see them in the village." He said thoughtfully. I got the sense he'd been sitting on the idea of telling us all of this for a while, but had to be certain and was still trying to make sure that it wasn't a mistake.

"But, you said humans can't get there." Tripp said, confused.

Gideon shook his head. "Only magical creatures can open the way, but if we wanted to, we could bring humans in. It's rare, but not unheard of for humans to come and live with the elves."

I got more bubbles of excitement inside me, knowing exactly what I wanted but not sure if it was okay that I wanted it. Gideon seemed to be hinting at it, but I didn't want to outright ask in case that was rude. Was he asking what I wanted him to be asking?

"From your hair, I thought you were an elf at first but I wouldn't be opposed to the idea of you two, visiting. Or even living among the elves."

If he was serious, and telling the truth, we could tell him our real story.

Could we really go and stay with elves?

Safe from humans, magical creatures roam free. It sounded perfect.

I'm sure it would've been, but the gunshot prevented us from finding out.

Chapter 32

With a singular, horrifying *BANG*, Gideon was down.
Tripp and I screamed and rushed over to him.
He lay on his back, staring up at the purple sky and
gasping for breath as blood spurted out of his side like a
waterfall. I looked around in a panicky haze, trying to see
where the bullet had come from, but I saw nothing. I
could hear something in the distance though.
A vehicle approaching us.
"What do we do?!" I screamed, looking back down at the
bleeding Gideon. His eyes were wide and blood was
beginning to come out of his nose.
"Pressure!" Tripp yelled, tearing one of the scarves off his
ankle and pressing it onto the wound. The blood crawled
up it, dying the grey an ominous red.
"San..." Gideon tried to get words out. I held onto his hand
and he gripped me tightly, looking into my eyes while
tears leaked out of his amber ones. They were so bright,
like honey with light pouring through it.

"You're gonna be fine." I said desperately, trying to make any one of us believe it.

He shook his head. "Book." he said weakly.

"Book?" Tripp and I said together, quickly. I looked down at the scarf and regretted it. You would never have known that it wasn't red to start with.

I was vaguely aware of Zen and Delta charging in the direction of the vehicle sound, roaring and going into battle-mode. I heard screams, but not of fear, of surprise. Gideon grabbed both mine and Tripp's wrists and held them desperately. With great effort, he took one huge breath in that sounded like his lungs were collapsing. "Get the book...to Sandrine." He managed to get out.

"Okay, we- we will." I cried, not knowing what he meant, but I suddenly thought of something as he was fading. Out of the pocket of his jacket, I pulled the four remaining Lenimen leaves. With hands shaking like mad, I handed two to Tripp. He took them quickly and tried to put them under the scarves, holding them on the wound. I folded my two in half and tried to get them into his mouth, but he started coughing before I could. A load of blood came up as he coughed and looked back up to the sky. The pain in his face matched that of the pegasus we'd seen last year.

"NO!" Tripp cried out as Gideon began to shut his eyes. His hands had gone dangerously still. Almost everything about him was still, but his mouth was still moving ever so slightly. Tripp and I both leant in to hear him.

"Thank you for letting me see dragons again." He whispered, a single tear trickling down his cheek.

That was it.

He just stopped. Blood kept flowing out of him, but he was gone now, gone to be with the stars.

Tripp and I sobbed as I stared into his blank, half-shut eyes, frozen in the wonder of seeing dragons, but tainted by the pain.

"No." Tripp said again, much quieter now, as he kept the scarf pressed onto the wound, as though it could change anything. "NO!" He got hysterical. He'd just lost his first patient. A tiny arrow of desperate, forced hope struck me. I didn't really believe in it though. Gideon was no more.

"Dragon tears." I suggested, slightly hysterically. Tripp looked up, hoping so much that it could work.

"Yes!" He said, not quite convincingly. "Where are-" He looked around, but stopped short when we both tuned back into the sounds of whatever was going on behind the cover of the trees. There were screams and roars and machinery. Nina had clearly brought great reinforcements. We looked at each other in panic.

"I'm sorry." We both cried to Gideon several times as we had to get up and go to the dragons. I hated to leave him, but there was nothing we could do. As we passed it, I swooped my arm down and grabbed Gideon's brown bag from the ground and ran with it, hoping and praying that it had the book in it, so that we could somehow get it back to Sandrine.

We didn't run nearly as quickly as we usually did, because Tripp had to lean on me on his left side and could only take small steps. We took too long. It sounds cruel, but I couldn't help thinking how much quicker I'd be if I'd left him and gone alone.

The sight that greeted us made me want to just die and leave everything behind again. There was a huge, black van with it's back open and engine running. The kind of size that could hold two dragons. There were six people, including Nina and James, wrangling with the dragons. How the hell they'd managed to do it I don't know, but the people had somehow gotten muzzles onto their snouts, preventing them from breathing fire.

James and another guy were trying to tighten some kind of lasso device around Zen's neck, while two others were trying with Delta. The two great beasts were flailing and fighting it, but I think the lassos were giving them electric shocks. Crouching at the back of the van, Nina and one other person were loading up a pair of huge guns. I felt my blood burn and my brain nearly explode at the sight of people trying to take advantage of our dragons.

"STOP!" I screeched at the top of my lungs. Of course they didn't, but I did draw attention to us. Time slowed down and sped up at the same time as heads turned towards us. I felt Tripp tense next to me and curse me for making everyone look at us. If we could both move fine, it wouldn't have been so suicidal, but I'd just made us into targets.

It turned out to be a good thing though; Delta, who was closer, wailed as much as he could through his muzzle, like a whale crying out in distress. He tore away from his captors while they were distracted and bounded towards us. His eyes were bright and frantic, wider than I'd ever seen them and pupils fully dilated.

As soon as he reached us he crouched and I shoved Tripp up onto him. Tripp screamed as his ankle was moved, but we didn't have time to care.

As people ran at us, I saw Zen breakaway from her lasso and immediately took off upwards. That was good, Delta could hold the two of us no problem.

I heard a gun fire and Tripp and I screamed as a bullet flew through the air in between our heads as I finished getting him on Delta. As if there wasn't enough, this gave me extra adrenaline and I clambered onto Delta behind Tripp faster than I've ever moved before.

"GO!" I shouted as people got even closer. Five people were approaching. Nina stayed behind with her huge gun, but that wasn't the one that had shot at us. I don't know how but I knew that for sure. She wasn't paying any attention to us, just her gun.

Too late, I realised what was going to happen.

I wrapped my arms tight around Tripp's waist and buried my head in the hood of his coat to try and make myself less aware that we were about to take flight again. Maybe if I couldn't see, my head would be alright this time.

Delta took off, the wind rushed all round, people yelled at us, a gun fired twice and a dragon wailed. It was Zen, but she kept flying, I heard her wings flapping several feet in front of us.

Three more gunshots.

She wailed again, and suddenly her wings went silent.

"NO!" Tripp sounded more distressed than I'd ever heard him as I took my head out of his hood and saw to my absolute horror, Zen falling out of the sky.

Down, down, down she went, with the bright red tufts of several tranquiliser darts visible in her skin as she turned over in her descent. Even at such a distance while she fell, I could see the purest form of fear in her eyes. They were too bright not to see, with the dark growing around us.

Delta and I screamed too as we watched her go down, but he knew that if he took a dive directly downwards, Tripp and I would fall and this time have no one to catch us.

Instead of a direct swoop down, he turned in a tight spiral towards the ground. Zen disappeared below the trees and Delta tried to speed up, but the wind was against him and started buffeting him about as he corkscrewed down.

As we held on, screaming, I had to shut my eyes. I could feel my head going bad, but I fought the pain and dizziness, trying to focus on *down*.

Delta managed to regain control but he'd strayed from the spot where Zen went down and was frantically searching around as the trees got closer and closer. Somewhere off to our left, another two tranquilisers emerged and hit him in the side. He shrieked and lost control again as the dart hiccupped the rhythm he'd just gotten with the wind. He started falling faster now, really falling, not gliding down. Tripp and I held on for dear life, coming so close to falling off so many times.

Delta stuck his wings out desperately, trying to make the landing smoother. We crashed through the trees and Delta *just* managed to keep upright enough to land on his front so that Tripp and I were not hurt.

The second we were on the ground I leapt off him, ignoring my pounding head, and pulled out the darts from his side. A single drop of Indigo blood came out of each wound and dripped delicately to the ground.

I moved to his front and examined the muzzle. It was made of black, harsh wire that bent and moulded around his mouth and nose perfectly. With horror, I realised it was actually being held on by pins surrounding the edge, stabbing into his skin like a corkboard. I cursed the people that did this to him and gently removed each pin before throwing the muzzle as far away as I possibly could, screaming in frustration as I lobbed it into the forest. I put my arms around him and held onto him, before looking up to see how Tripp was. He was not in a good state.

Hyperventilating, crying with bright red eyes, trying to put his ankle in a position that came anywhere close to comfortable.

"We- we have to go- go find Zen." He stuttered. I nodded and wiped away my tears but more replaced them as visions of Gideon's dying face flashed through my mind, haunting my memories. The handcuffs were still attached to me, and it was like I could still feel him gripping onto my wrists.

I looked back at Delta, who's eyes were half-shut. I stroked him on the nose as golden tears fell from his eyes. Last week I wasn't aware that dragons were even capable of crying, now I'd seen one do it twice in three days.

I didn't think he'd go to sleep, he was clearly fighting it, and Zen had at least three in her while she was falling, still conscious.

"As soon as Delta's okay, we'll go." I said, trying to sound more confident and braver than I was. Tripp shook his head quickly.

"We have to go. *Now.*" He sounded so weak and helpless as he kept trying to find a good position for his foot, but just succeeded in jolting it and he cried out in pain. It was more than this this time though. He just let out a scream to the world. The sound broke my heart and took me back to the cold lake again.

I moved back to him and held out my arms. He sank into me and held on, sobbing into my shoulder as I tried not to cry myself.

"I know, and we will. But we don't know where they're taking her," I tried to channel the way he would speak to me if I were in his state. "and Delta can't track her scent while he's like this."
I gently moved him down to the ground so that he wouldn't have to support himself and he melted. This was the worst I'd ever seen him.
He was broken.

Chapter 33

Half an hour or so later, night was fully upon us but
Delta's drowsiness had worn off at last. I re-splinted Tripp
with the one scarf we had left and tried to be strong and
not cry, but I couldn't get Gideon's dead eyes out of my
head.

I wondered what his family was up to, going about their
normal business and believing that their father was
coming back tonight. His children were half-orphans.

And it was our fault that their father was dead.

"Is he okay now?" Tripp asked, looking to Delta, wanting
to go and find Zen as soon as possible, but not wanting to
be unkind and make Delta go before he was able.

I looked to Delta's head, his eyes were bright again. Sad
and scared, but bright and burning with determination to
get his sister back.

"Yeah." I said, surprised at how level my voice came out.

"I'll help you up and we'll get going." I said, putting an
arm around Tripp to stand up with him.

My knee still hurt, and having to run around supporting Tripp hadn't helped, but he was in a much worse state. I shoved him up onto Delta's back and got on behind him, before Delta stood up and began to walk, not quite strong enough to fly yet.

He went quickly, so I could see how agitated he was. He was sniffing all over the ground, trying to find the way that she'd been taken and settled on a direction that didn't seem particularly wrong.

I looked up at the stars as we walked. They were so bright, like there was something to be happy about. Or sad about. They looked like they could've been tears, cried across a dark face over centuries of watching tragedy and heartbreak playout in the world below.

I felt like crying still, but I realised I just couldn't anymore. I'd run out of tears and now just felt numb again. There were still ghost tears all over my face, but I could tell I wasn't going to be able to really cry for a while.

We moved on in silence, part out of sadness, part fear. Nights hadn't been pleasant since we left home, but this one felt more ominous than ever.

Every sound made us flinch, even if it was just Delta stepping on a twig. I held on tight to Tripp and he held on tight to Delta, clinging together like castaways on a raft.

The cold got worse as time went on, but no snow came. We were probably too far south for that now.

South.

"They're taking her home." I realised. I said it quietly, but in the darkness of the night, it could probably be heard a mile off.

As much as he was able to on the back of a moving dragon, Tripp turned around and looked at me with sad puppy eyes.

"She's bait." I added, looking down

He shrank down slightly. "So they've set us a trap. And we have no other choice but to walk right into it." He sounded despondent. I too sank as he said it, knowing that there was no way around it. They'd set us the perfect trap in an evil scheme.

"Delta," I leaned forward and spoke gently to him, wishing that there was some other way we could get Zen. "we're gonna go back home." That time it felt really weird to call it 'home'. I felt so alienated from it.

As time went on, we got tired. Hunger began to creep back in and I got thirsty. The apples had been juicy, but not filling in the long run, and the cold was getting to my throat as I breathed. We went for what seemed like forever, but the forest stretched on, never ending and laughing at us for trying to find our way out.

We came to a stream, running slightly downhill and splashing a little too loudly for comfort. Not that there would be anyone around, but I still wished it were quieter. Delta sat down when he got next to the stream and took a long drink.

"You okay, buddy?" Tripp asked, patting Delta as he continued to gulp.

"Oh god, he hasn't eaten at all today." I realised. I thought we were hungry, but Delta had been walking around all day without anything at all to eat.

"We can take a break." Tripp said reluctantly. "Give him a chance to find some food."

I slid off of Delta and tensed as a load of twigs snapped loudly when I landed. I reached up and took hold of Tripp, supporting him as he got down and placing him gently on the ground.

He'd given up crying and gone numb too, he stared straight ahead once he was down, into the void.

I walked to Delta's head and he stopped drinking as he heard me approach. His eyes were wide and worried, I tried to give him a smile but I knew it didn't reach my whole face, so he wouldn't believe it. I stroked his nose and knelt down next to him.

"You okay? I'm sorry about today, Delta. I'm so sorry." Again I felt like I should and wanted to cry, but just couldn't anymore. Delta wailed slightly, like he was asking if Zen was gonna be okay.

"We'll keep going to find her soon, but you should find something to eat." I told him. I hated saying it, knowing what the 'something' would end up being, but I knew it was what he had to eat.

He nuzzled me and I hugged him, before he got up and slipped into the darkness of the trees.

Suddenly the night felt a lot more dangerous, and we were more vulnerable. I could hardly see anything, it was so dark now that Delta's glow was getting further away, but the moon was bright and my vision had been getting quicker at adjusting to the dark. It had had to.

I looked back to Tripp, who was sitting up and still just staring ahead at nothing in particular. I moved over and sat next to him, staring at the same nothing.

"You okay?" I asked. I knew it was stupid, I knew the answer, but I wanted to ask.

"No." He said, shaking his head. His voice was fragile and unsteady, with just that one word. "Are you?" He looked at me, his eyes were no longer the bright marbles that they usually were.

"Not really." I shook my head too. I felt like a huge weight was resting on me again. I could hear Gideon's voice still in my head, and whisperings of unknown voices telling me that it was our fault, as if I didn't already know that and hate myself for it.

"It was our fault." Tripp said as if reading my mind. I didn't know how to respond. There was nothing more to say, that was the truth and there was no changing that. We were responsible for a man's death.

"You got his bag, didn't you?" Tripp said eventually, breaking the painful silence. We both looked down at my side where the bag lay on the ground, strapped over my shoulder.

"Has it got the book in it?" He asked, staring down at it.

"I forgot about that." I said, slightly ashamed.

I unfastened the toggles holding the bag shut and put my hand inside. Sure enough, my fingers closed around the hard cover of a book. I pulled it out and tried to inspect it. The black cover was made of something leathery, but it didn't have the leather-scent, so hopefully it wasn't. There were swirly designs and patterns all over the cover that I could just about make out, with flowers and leaves forming from the lines. I guessed it was something to do with herbology, if it was for Sandrine the Herbalist.

"How are we gonna get it to her?" I asked. I desperately wanted to get it to her and fulfill the dying wish of someone who'd helped us, but I had no idea how to go about that.

"Once we've got Zen, we'll come back here and…" He trailed off as he realised he wasn't sure where to go from there.

"Burn that bridge when we come to it." We said in unison.

"What's inside?" Tripp asked, taking a closer look at the flowers etched into the cover.

"I feel like we shouldn't open it." I said, twiddling with the long green ribbon, tied in a bow and holding the book shut. "It wasn't meant for us to have, and he wouldn't have told us about it if he was able to give it to her himself."

"Good point." Tripp conceded. He ran a finger over the cover, feeling the etchings and trying to see with his hands.

Suddenly, out of the dark silence, came a loud *Squawk!* Immediately my heart rate skyrocketed and I wanted to leap up and run in the opposite direction.

Tripp and I both looked up and stared at the trees to our right, where the sound had come from. It sounded like a bird, but not any that I'd ever heard before. It was more husky, more wild, like said bird had been gargling gravel. Slowly, I stood up, suddenly on higher-alert than ever, leaning forwards as my pulse sped up and I felt my legs prepare to run. I was scared, but somehow I began to slowly move forwards, still leaning to try and see what had made the noise. I got another, impending sense of doom and wondered why the hell I was walking directly towards it.

"Rainbow, don't." Tripp whispered as I crept slowly towards the trees.

"I'm just having a look." I said back, as if that justified it. The squawk came again and I jumped, it was closer now and the sound pierced the night like a needle.

I stood still at the second squawk, but kept leaning and squinting, desperate to see what was making the noise. A bead of sweat trickled down the back of my neck as I heard the rustling of footsteps approaching. What the hell could it be? The footsteps definitely weren't something huge and menacing, they were small and scrappy, like a little dog might make while sniffing around and tracking a scent.

The footsteps stopped and all went very quiet. Surely this meant that my heartbeat would become audible at any second. I just stood, frozen in place with quivering legs, waiting for the beast to reveal itself and eat me.

Squawk!

I nearly collapsed at this last one, my legs got so shaky which made my knee hurt again, which made me question even more why I'd actually walked this way in the first place.

"Come on, let's go." I said quickly, turning around and rapidly moving back to Tripp, regretting ever going towards the sound.

The rustling footsteps started again, and as the creature drew nearer, Tripp quickly slipped Gideon's book back into the open bag, hanging off my shoulder, and put his arm around me as I got to him. We were about to stand up together, when the source of the noise burst out for us to see, with another, more frantic *squawk*. Looking at it, I tilted my head and didn't feel so afraid.

The animal standing before me was one of the strangest I'd ever seen; it was like a dragon that had been crossed with a velociraptor, a chicken and a sheep.

Fear turned to confusion, trying to figure out what this thing was. Don't get me wrong, it was hilarious to look at and I loved it dearly as soon as I saw it but it wasn't anything I recognised.

The body itself was dragon-like, but it walked up on it's hind legs like a dinosaur. No feet, but cloven hooves that seemed to go with the ram-horns on it's scaly head. Scaly apart from the massive beak that went with it's little feathery wigs that looked too small to fly with. The whole thing was no bigger than a King Charles Spaniel, and it looked around everywhere, bobbing it's head erratically. It's massive, bulbous eyes were like a dragon's; glowing yellow with black slits for pupils.

It kept hopping around, flapping it's little wings and occasionally squawking. If things weren't so bleak and awful right now, I might've laughed at it. It didn't seem to be in any distress, just a particularly crazy breed of creature. It gave off a glow like a lot of magical creatures seemed too, making it much easier to see and make out all the different animal parts.

"What is it?" I marvelled as the thing stumbled over to the water and had a drink. The two of us sat back down just to observe the funny little thing.

"I have no idea." Tripp pondered, slightly amused. This was genuinely the funniest animal I'd ever seen.

I wondered if it was perhaps some experimental-hybrid that was made by SCREB had escaped somehow. I didn't know for sure if they did that kind of thing, but I'd be in no way surprised. I could think of no logical reason why they'd wanted to patchwork this particular collection of beings together, so maybe it was a real creature that just kept itself hidden up until now. Tripp and I jumped again as it turned around and squawked at us, then looked at me directly in the eyes.

Chapter 34

I got a sudden bad feeling as the creature stared at me. It tilted it's head, inspecting my soul as it held my gaze. The greenish light it gave off made it feel even more eerie, like an alien movie. The longer it stared, the more the bad feeling within me intensified as I grabbed onto Tripp's hand.

"Is there any chance you can walk?" I asked, thinking of how much the Lenimen leaves had helped, how he'd been able to move a lot better since taking them.

"Maybe." He said, looking down at his ankle and moving it around a little, without flinching. "Not much, but a bit. Why?" He could clearly sense my bad feelings of doom.

"I think something bad is about to happen." I said, slowly rising and keeping my eyes fixed on the now silent, petrified creature. "I'm not sure why I think that, but I have a very bad feeling." I said, not very helpfully. I helped Tripp up and were about to start inching our way in the direction that Delta had gone went the dragon-chicken went mental.

It started squawking at the top of it's lungs and jumping around like it was made of springs that had suddenly uncoiled. It started coming towards us and spitting at the ground, hitting everything in a six-foot radius. The spit was violent yellow-green and as it hit the ground, all the twigs and leaves began to sizzle and fizz as smoke rose up from them.

"Oh God it spits acid!" Tripp shrieked as we leaped apart in order to avoid the horrible green on the ground.

I tripped on a tree root and fell to the floor while the animal came squawking and jumping my way. I started to scramble to my feet, but quicker than I could move it was already spitting at my hands.

The pain was indescribable. My fingers felt like they were being ripped forcefully off, the flesh bubbling and boiling and hotter than the sun. The green liquid was thick and viscous, clinging on to me and burning no matter how much I tried to flick it off my hands.

I screamed as it tore through my skin, creeping up towards my wrists and destroying my gloves. The handcuffs began to heat up, singeing my wrists and I tugged at them in a pathetic attempt to get them off.

I wanted my hands to just disappear if it meant the pain would stop, and I began clawing at each of them in turn with my own fingernails, making the pain worse, but unable to stop myself.

"Get to the water!" I heard Tripp yell. Of course! Without even looking where the creature was, I got up, still crying with pain and ran to the stream.

The second I got to it, I plunged my hands in and again, pain engulfed them, but a different kind of pain now. Like they were being burned from the inside out this time, rather than the other way around. I tried not to keep screaming, but it was just too much. I looked down and although the light was further away now, I could see the water bubbling and boiling where my hands were. Even if I couldn't see it well, the sound of the sizzling and steaming was horrible to hear. I held my hands down under the water though, and after increasing dramatically, the pain started to subside.

I was about to breath out and start to relax, but I heard Tripp screaming behind, and was once again transported horribly back to the lake with the wisp.

I quickly stood and looked back, not daring to look at my still-painful hands. Tripp was down, trying to move away, as green liquid was being spat at his leg.

"NO!" I yelped as I ran clumsily over. I grabbed a stick on my way and nearly dropped it as the rough bark rubbed against my palms and sent a fresh wave of pain flaring up through to my wrists.

I held onto it and desperately prodded the creature in the side. It turned it's attention to my stick and stared at it with it's massive, rounded eyes. It clicked it's oversized beak a few times, then launched itself at the end of the stick, gripping onto it and attacking it with it's surprisingly sharp bill. I shrieked as it jumped up, thinking it was coming for me but it was only interested in the stick now. I threw it a few feet away and the creature followed it, spitting acid at it and completely ignoring me and Tripp now.

Tripp was still screaming and crying at his leg, so I quickly turned back and grabbed him under the knees and armpits. I lifted him and started running, carrying him like a baby to the stream and trying not to fall over. He wasn't heavy, but I wasn't strong.

I felt my arms and back straining and we both screamed as everything hurt and I finally collapsed, dropping him into the stream.

He started screaming even more when the water started boiling all around his legs and looked like he was about to pass out, but was clearly resisting the urge. In a few more seconds, everything calmed down and for a moment we just held onto each other without saying anything, in shock over what had just happened. That seemed to have been happening quite a lot recently.

Upon hearing another loud *squawk*, we both flinched and looked up at the creature, but it was just playing with the stick, paying us no attention and acting like nothing had happened.

"What the hell is that?" We shrieked in unison. We stared at each other, still stunned and both silently answering the question; *I have no idea.*

Breathing heavily, Tripp began to clamber out of the stream and I helped him up using my elbows, trying to keep my hurting hands out of the way and not touching anything apart from the frozen night air. They didn't feel like they were actively being burned anymore, but they still had an unrelenting burning sensation. Does that make sense?

Before we could do anything else, Delta bounded into sight, his gentle blue glow quickly intensifying and making everything a lot more visible. He looked distraught again, he'd clearly heard our screams and worried that we were dying.

He only looked at us for a second, then whipped his head up to look at the hybrid animal playing with it's stick like a six year-old surrounded by building blocks.

"Delta-" I started addressing him but he leaped up to the little creature and started hissing at it. He seemed to know what it was, or at least how dangerous it was.

He stood still and square, poised to attack, as the hybrid, who seemed to have about four brain cells, matched the stance of the dragon who was at least twenty times his size and stared up. Call it brave or stupid, but the creature spat up at Delta in a shot of flourescent green.

Delta blinked as the acid fizzed for about five seconds, then dripped delicately down his nose and onto the ground.

He began to growl.

The hybrid squawked.

Tripp and I watched, glued to the scene like a gladiator fight about to get good.

The hybrid spat and squawked at Delta again, before jumping up and flapping it's little chicken wings. Delta pawed at the ground, getting ready to destroy.

"Don't hurt it!" I squeaked. Delta turned his head to me ever so slightly, so that the hybrid was still held in his gaze, but he was giving some of his attention to me. I shook my head gently. I know it just seriously hurt me and my brother, but I didn't believe it intended to. I think it was just an animal obeying it's animal instincts. Whatever the case, it wasn't right to hurt it if we didn't have to, and we didn't. We definitely didn't.

Delta didn't look happy about it, but he turned his full attention back onto the hybrid and stopped pawing at the ground. He let out one huge, terrifying roar, the likes of which I'd only heard once before, during a visit to the factory when we walked past one of the experiment rooms. I'd never heard anything like it from Delta though, he'd never shown himself do something so aggressive and again, I felt afraid of him. It wasn't a feeling I liked having towards my dragon.

The hybrid got the message and hopped off, squawking and flapping along on it's merry way.

"Thank you, Delta." I said, trying to keep my voice from shaking.

He looked at me and almost nodded, then went back to glaring towards where the creature disappeared.

He walked a few feet in that direction and stood with all his feet wide apart like a wolf, and his fangs bared.

His tail whipped around violently and he growled gently in warning. I knew nothing with even half a brain cell would come this way with him guarding us, so I turned my attention back to my brother.

Tripp managed to stand up, keeping his weight very much on his right foot, but still he stood. We both looked down at his left leg.

The scarf and sticks that were his splint had been annihilated, and most of the jean-leg had been singed out of existence.

His pale, skinny leg shivered in the cold, burned and blistered, with the blackened edges of the denim flapping around as if still trying to keep him warm.

I remembered my current jean situation and thanked my past self so much for my response to getting cold. All of our spare clothes had been taken, but they left us with what we were wearing.

"You're definitely going to freeze to death." I said, slipping my boots off so that I could remove the outer pair of jeans.

"You don't say." Tripp said, staring down at his red, raw and sore knee before looking back up at me. "What is happening?!" He looked confused as I gingerly unzipped my jeans, being as careful as I could and trying to touch them as little as possible, and began pulling them down. I couldn't help but laugh a little at his shocked face, until the jeans were low enough for him to see that there was a second pair underneath.

"Why, Iris? Why two pairs of jeans?" He asked.

"Because I'm a superhero." I said, pulling the ankles off and suddenly feeling the chill as I threw the jeans at Tripp's face.

I prodded both the back and the front of my knee and then regretted it. It was still a bit mushy and instantly felt like it had been stabbed with a frozen knife.

"That's weirdly fortunate, thank you." Tripp said, staring at the jeans as if I'd just handed him a treasure map.

"You need help getting changed? Because of-" I started pointing at his ankle.

"No, I got this, I'm not that weak." He said, sitting himself down to make it easier.

"You are a bit." I replied as I turned around and started walking up to Delta.

I approached slowly and cautiously, trying not to make any sudden movements.

He was still snarling and threatening anything that might dare come this way. He was trying to protect me, but I felt such a fear that I'd never gotten from him before, and that I didn't like at all. I thought I'd been afraid of him when he first saw Gideon. I thought he'd been viscous and abnormally aggressive then, but that was nothing compared to how he was with the hybrid creature.

"Delta?" I said gently, a few feet away from him. His growling quietened down a little and he flicked a glaring eye at me. I took a deep breath and a few more steps towards him. I felt like I was walking towards a rabid dog that could lash out at me at any second.

"It's okay." My voice shook. I held out a hand as I continued gradually getting closer to him. "It's gone now. We're fine." I spoke slowly, trying to keep my voice soft. He seemed to relax a little, his limbs didn't seem so tense and his growling almost stopped completely.

So slowly and so carefully, I put my hand on his nose and almost had to pull it away, his skin was burning hot. I could feel the blisters on my palm burning up, I gritted my teeth and held it there though. This was the only way to make him relax sometimes.

"Everybody's okay." I swallowed my insincere words. "We're gonna go find Zen."

Delta's eyes softened and he got quiet as I began to stroke him. He got out of his attack stance and went back to the concerned, gentle creature I'd known for the last four years.

I frowned as he changed, such a contrast from the beast he'd just become.

He started purring and nuzzling me lovingly, as if nothing had happened.

"Everybody's okay." I repeated, muttering it just to myself this time. Trying to make it true.

Chapter 35

"These fit me surprisingly well." Tripp said behind me.
Delta and I both turned to look at him to see that my jeans
looked fine and normal on him, as if they were boy's jeans.
They were the baggier of my pairs, as opposed to the usual
stupidly-skinny-with-ridiculously-small-ankles kind that
you find in the girls' section, so he looked pretty
comfortable in them.
"Hm. Well done." I said, slightly impressed that he'd
managed to get them on alone with his bad leg and ankle.
Clearly the Lenimen leaves were working wonders for
him. Thinking of the Lenimen leaves made the image of
the dying Gideon flash through my mind again, and I
forced myself to shake the thought away before it could
get to me too much.
Instead, I focused on how badly my hands stung. It now
felt like I'd put them on the hotplate of a stove that was up
on full blast.

I did that once. I was about five and helping my mother cook something on the back burners, while Dad and Tripp were out. We didn't realise that I'd accidentally switched on the front burners instead. She'd left the room for about thirty seconds to answer the phone, having instructed me to not to touch anything, but I had decided to be helpful, so I stood up on a stool to mix whatever was in the pans on the back. I leaned over to get a better view of the pans, and put my hands right on the switched on hotplates, singeing them badly. I screamed and cried and Mum came rushing back in and ran my hands under the cold tap for ages, before applying some kind of salve and bandaging them up. They were so blistered and painful for the next week, I could hardly do anything.

Now, eleven years later, I looked down at those same blistered and bright red hands. Bigger and shaking now, more worn out, but still the same hands. Still the same, familiar pain. Staring down at them, I felt another twinge of nostalgia within me and almost smiled a little, remembering the horrible pain of that day, but also the being looked after and getting to sit in my parent's bed with Mum while we watched *Dancing On Ice* together, as Dad and Tripp baked flapjacks for us.

What a simple time that was. They were the same hands, but they belonged to a different person now.

The blisters looked like an alien nesting ground in the blue light of Delta, softer again now that he wasn't in defence mode.

"Oh my God, your pockets are basically non-existent!" Tripp exclaimed, breaking me out of my reminiscence. I smiled at him, amused by his revelation.

"I know, I told you."

"Yeah, but I didn't think it was this bad!" He seemed genuinely shocked. I smirked at him, smug with how right I was, even if it was because of a great unfairness.

"How does your leg feel?" I asked as Delta and I walked closer to Tripp.

"Absolutely bloody awful." He said and I realised, as we approached him and Delta's light made him more visible, that he was leaning back on a tree and still putting zero weight on his left foot.

He didn't seem too put out though, he was distracted and amused by the tininess of the pockets on my jeans and seeing how far he could fit his hands inside. Not far.

I smiled again at his childlike wonder and I turned to Delta to check that he was okay. I could smell on his breath that he'd eaten, and he looked eager to get going in order to find Zen. He nosed my hands to make me hold them up and he started licking them, trying to make them better. I smiled down at him, even though his saliva just made the stinging worse. Only a tiny bit though.

"Thank you." I said, stroking him on the nose again with my forearm.

He seemed perfectly back to normal now, and I could almost forget the terrifying monster that he'd become, that seemed like how I always used to imagine dragons.

"What's this?" I heard Tripp ask. He sounded confused, and looked it too when I turned to see what he meant. He held something small in the palm of his hand, still leaning on the tree, but frowning down at whatever he was holding. I stepped closer to see what it was.

"What the hell is this, Iris?" His voice sounded a lot sharper now, accusing me of something. I got a horribly anxious feeling in my stomach as he held his hand out for me to see what he was talking about.

"Oh no." I looked down and started to feel hot and a little faint, anything even resembling positivity evaporating. My heart and stomach both dropped and I felt my brain short-circuiting trying to handle the guilt that suddenly devoured me.

My breaths became short and quick, and I swallowed hard before daring to speak again.

"It's my...my SIM card." I couldn't bear to look up and meet his eyes, so I just continued staring at the little plastic and metallic chip in his hand that I'd taken out of my phone forever ago and forgotten about.

"As in, the one that's registered in your name, and that was issued to you for free by SCREB?" His voice was low and dangerously calm. I almost stopped breathing, unable to believe how enormously I'd screwed up.

What is wrong with me? I screamed inside my head over and over, wishing that the ground would just swallow me up.

"Tripp-"

"The one that they could access with no problem and could use as a tracking device?" His voice got louder and he stood up straighter, making me take a step back.

"Tripp, I'm so-"

"The one that's the reason they kept finding us, that Gideon is dead and that ZEN IS GONE?!" He properly yelled now. A kind of anger that I had never, ever heard from him, and that terrified me. I took another step back as he completely stopped leaning on the tree, and stood on both his feet equally.

281

I'd never felt scared of Tripp before, only ever the opposite. We'd been each other's protectors through our whole lives, but I'd done a terrible, terrible thing.

"Tripp, I'm sorry. I'm so, so sorry." I began to plead. It wouldn't make any difference, the damage had been done, it was my fault.

"For the love of God, Iris! WHAT THE FUCK IS WRONG WITH YOU?!" He shouted, and finally I dared to look at his face. A mixture of distraught and ballistic. His wide eyes were red from both tears and anger, he was absolutely seething.

He looked like Dad. He scared me.

I wanted to die again, or to fix everything, or to go back in time and stop all of this from ever happening, or send Tripp and Delta on the way to retrieve Zen and leave me here to rot in case I messed up again.

"I'm so sorry! I didn't mean to!" I screeched, crying at what an awful thing I'd done. I felt the guilt physically wrap and tighten around me, restricting my breathing.

Tripp was at a loss for words now, just staring at me in disbelief. The scar on his cheek had turned white and vibrant, and looked even more like a lightning bolt.

"I'm sorry, I'm so sorry." I continued, over and over again. He took a step forward, raising his hand, and I took one back, afraid he might hit me. I'd understand why if he did, but surely he wouldn't? Not Tripp? He wasn't like that. Nothing like this had ever happened to us before though. He'd never been thrown into such a rage by his idiot twin sister before.

I shrank back and braced for impact as his hand went further up, quicker and ready to strike.

He didn't though, instead, he threw the evil SIM card as far as he possibly could behind me.

"Why?" His voice shook. "Why did you even have that? Why would you take it?!" He shouted.

I took another, nervous step back and flinched as I backed into something warm. It was Delta, catching me protectively. I suddenly got even more scared that Delta might lash out at Tripp. He never had in the past, but I'd just seen a side of him that I didn't know existed, and that was in order to protect the two of us. But If Tripp seemed to be threatening me, Delta's claimed one, I didn't know what he might do and didn't want to find out.

"I-" My voice was shaking too, but out of fear and guilt rather than anger. "I was gonna put it in a bin somewhere before we left. To keep my phone as separate as possible, in case they could use it to track us, to lead them away from us. But I forgot." My words began to crumble towards the end as Tripp buried his face in his hands in astonishment at my sheer idiocy. Again, he couldn't think of anything to say, he was just shocked at how utterly stupid I'd been.

"I'm so sorry!" I said it over and over again, but it would never feel like enough. It would never be enough.

"I really can't believe you did that." He took his hands from his eyes and stared again at me with a mad glint that our parents used to get and had always put the fear of God into me. This time was no exception. His voice had gotten calm again, but not in a good way.

"Come on, we'll go find her. Let's go and-" I started spewing the words out, not sure what else there was to say.

"Stop." Tripp commanded, cutting me off. The sound was definitive, leaving no room for argument. I felt the rest of my words crash in my mouth as they were suddenly unable to escape.

He stared at me for a couple more seconds, before turning around and walking. I got worried he was about to stomp off into the woods and leave me for dead, even if it was what I deserved, but he turned back to me halfway to the stream.

"WHAT IS THE MATTER WITH YOU?!" He screamed with fire in his eyes and hatred in his voice.

I flinched as he yelled but I couldn't reply or follow him. I just stood against Delta, shivering and crying for so many reasons.

So much for not being able to cry anymore.

Tripp turned around furiously and stomped down to the stream and knelt in front of it.

I wanted to follow him and try to say something, but I knew that was simply a terrible idea. I'd just have to wait here, living with the worst thing I'd ever done and waiting for him to come back.

He splashed water onto his face a few times, then sat with his hands in the water, staring down and breathing heavily. I stayed several feet away and wished again that I could disappear. Not go somewhere else, just stop existing altogether.

As I watched Tripp in anguish, he slumped over, angry and crying, staring into the water. He made a violent sideways motion with his head, and finally, his neck clicked.

Chapter 36

"Can you fly?" Tripp's voice was dead. I turned around
from looking at the stars upon hearing him and wasn't
sure what to say. I'd made the biggest mistake of my life
and wanted to keep apologising, but what would that do?
Just get annoying and not solve anything.

"I think so." I swallowed, hoping the words sounded more
convincing than they felt.

"Well can you or not?" Tripp asked, sharply. In truth, no, I
didn't think I'd be able to fly all the way to where we
needed to go without my head getting bad again, but I
couldn't say that. Looking into Tripp's hurt and angry
eyes, I just couldn't do it.

I pushed down the doubt inside me and replaced it with
fake determination.

"Yes." I said, nodding and pretending I meant it.

He seemed to buy it - or didn't really care - and walked the
few steps over to where Delta was sitting down and
watching the two of us. He was limping badly and I

wanted to help him, but I knew he'd reject it and just get angrier.

He knelt down, keeping all his weight on his right leg, and scratched Delta between the ears.

"You okay to take us home, while it's still dark?" He asked softly. For that one sentence, his voice went back to normal. For that one moment both Delta and Tripp were the gentle, loving creatures I knew, not the sinister bundles of aggression I'd seen tonight.

Delta chirped and stood up but kept his legs bent so that he was lower to the ground and Tripp could clamber atop him more easily.

Once he was on, he didn't look at me, just stared up into the sky. Again, I cursed myself internally and screamed in my head, asking what the hell was the matter with me?

I swung my leg over the back of Delta and loosely held onto Tripp in front of me. I didn't want to, and I felt him completely tense up, but he reluctantly let me hold on, knowing that I had nothing else to hold.

I took a deep, shaky breath, preparing for the flight. *It'll be fine.* I told myself. I'd flown a few times since hitting my head, and I may not have been fine, but I'd gotten better every time. This would be no exception, just a longer flight.

Tripp leaned forward a bit and held onto Delta's neck, ready to go.

I would've preferred it if I'd been on the front, since Delta was my dragon. I didn't mind it at all when Tripp's ankle was still really bad and we just had to leave as soon as possible, but now that there was a choice, I would've liked to be in front, so that I could hold onto his neck.

It didn't really matter, I knew that, but I couldn't help feeling a slight twinge of annoyance at Tripp's assumption that he was to go in front now. I didn't dare say anything though, he was angry enough as it was, and after what I'd done, I wasn't exactly in a position to get picky and demand a different seat.

It didn't matter.

I was still concerned about flying as we took off, for Delta's sake as much as my own. He seemed to have made a full recovery from the tranquiliser darts, but we hadn't asked him to fly yet in case he wasn't up to it. He didn't seem worried about it though, just anxious to find his sister, so I assumed he must be feeling back to normal. Lashing out at the hybrid had probably adrenaline-filled him enough to make any trace of the tranquiliser dissipate into nothing.

So the only thing to worry about was my head. And the possibility of Tripp pushing me off and sending me hurtling to my death at great speed, but that was unlikely. Hopefully.

The take off was smooth in reality, but in my mind it was rocky and unstable. I resisted tightening my grip around my brother, which probably wasn't a good idea from my safety's point of view, but it was so tense between us already, I didn't want to make things worse.

I still didn't want to look around at our surroundings, for fear that I might go into panic mode. Instead, I kept my eyes either clamped shut, or staring intently at the inside of Tripp's hood. I didn't dare put my head on his back like I normally would, I could feel his hatred for me radiating off him like electricity. He was practically sparking with me being in such close proximity.

The night became colder and quieter up in the air, and the chill bit cruelly away at the raw skin on my hands.

As we moved along, every tiny jolt sending my heart rate through the roof and making my stomach churn, I felt more unstable and unsafe than I'd ever felt while flying. Even the first time I'd ever done it had been less scary than this.

The weight on my shoulders felt heavier than ever, and I knew that it wouldn't go away until we had Zen back. Even then, it wouldn't disappear, maybe just lighten a tiny bit. I would never stop feeling guilty about this, the weight would be there for the rest of my life. Forever haunting me and reminding me of what an idiot I'd been. I wondered if Tripp would ever forgive me. I wanted him to, but I didn't think he should. I would never forgive myself, that was certain, and I'd understand if he never did. I'd be surprised if he did.

I wondered if Delta would.

That hurt just as much as the thought of Tripp not doing it. Delta hadn't seemed angry at me, but I wondered if he would if he wasn't so good-natured. Or if he fully understood what was going on. He was intelligent, but I was sure he didn't know about SIM cards. I'd never needed to explain them to him, so chances were he didn't really know the full extent of how much it was my fault. He just knew that Zen had been taken and we needed to get her back, before she got experimented on, or tortured, or-

Nope. Not doing that.

My inner voice cut over my other inner voice. Zen would be fine. We'd find her and rescue her and she would be fine and alive.

I had no idea how we were planning to rescue her, and I don't think Tripp did either, we hadn't really talked about it. I think we were just going to wing it once we got there, but right now we had to focus on actually getting there, then deal with the slight technicalities of what the hell we were going to do later.

The Dragon Twins Volume 1

Chapter 37

It felt so weird returning home.
Delta got very cautious approaching the town, and rightly
so, but it was still dark so we were okay. He scoured
around, making sure we weren't going to be seen by
anyone, and landed on the beach. This early in the
morning and this late in the year, we were in no danger of
being seen by passersby other than drunks who wouldn't
pay attention or remember us.
We had him drop us here, rather than by the SCREB base,
so that he was a safe distance away. If he took us right
there, then it was almost certain that he would be detected
and follow a similar fate to Zen. We'd be able to get new
supplies from our house while we were here too, assuming
we could get inside.
After we got off him, he nuzzled me and wailed anxiously,
making sure to keep quiet though.

"We'll be okay." I said softly, scratching between his ears and trying to reassure him. Tripp stood by - watching, cold and impatient.

Delta turned slightly and flung his tail towards me, stopping just before he whipped me in the stomach. It gently curled around, and several of the scales peeled up at one end, like wobbly teeth.

"Thank you." I said as I gently removed the loose scales and put them in my pocket, ready to use next time we needed to summon him.

He gently nuzzled Tripp too, who was perfectly nice and gentle with Delta, scratching and stroking and telling him everything would be okay.

Delta eyed me nervously, rubbed his nose against me one last time, and took off almost directly upwards. Like a bullet, he was suddenly gone.

My head was hurting, but not too much. It should pass soon. I was cold, tired and hungry, but none of those feelings came close to being as strong as the guilt and shame that reignited in me when I turned and looked at Tripp. His face was a storm of misery, anger, exhaustion, and dread. He avoided looking at me, shunning me like I wasn't there. Instead, he stared out at the sea, rough and choppy. It made the air even colder and windier, churning up the already tense atmosphere.

After Delta was gone, Tripp still ignored me, but turned around and started walking up the beach, towards the road. He took big steps and I had to hurry to catch up with him, nearly falling over on the uneven sand as I ran.

When I got to him, he didn't acknowledge me, but he also didn't speed up and make it harder for me to walk with him, which I appreciated. I wanted to reach out and give him a hug, or to say something that would make things better, but the only thing that could possibly make things better was getting Zen back.

Up the steps from the sand, we walked across the road through the eerily empty park as the wind whispered haunting melodies, warning us of something bad.

I looked down as we walked. I walked, he limped, but was trying not to show it and definitely would not accept my help if I offered it. But, he was walking on it, which he wouldn't be able to do for several weeks had he not taken the Lenimen Leaves.

You killed a man.

My conscience taunted me as I thought about those leaves. Those leaves were a life-saver, and our way of thanking the kind man who'd shown them to us?

Death. Perfect.

"What time is it?" I said quickly, to stop my mind and thoughts from going too far down that rabbit hole.

Tripp looked at his watch, then looked straight ahead as he kept walking.

"Twenty-to-three." He said, emotionless. I nodded, not sure what to do with the information, but glad I had it.

"Thanks." I said. He ignored me and carried on walking.

I carefully put my hands in my coat pockets to shield them from the cold, but they still hurt. I could feel the blisters coming up more, ready to burst if I wasn't careful, and the cold metal of the handcuffs chafed against my burnt wrists, making them even more sore and itchy.

I wondered how Tripp's leg was. Clearly not good, but maybe the leaves had lingered in his system for the acid attack so that it wasn't as bad as it could be. I doubted

he'd be able to walk, however stubborn he was, if the acid
had done it's full damage.

His limp got worse as we walked, but we were nearly at
our house. Walking through these dark, empty streets
made me feel almost like nothing was wrong. It was a
walk I'd taken hundreds of times before, coming back
home from the cinema, or the park, or the beach, Tripp
and I had walked here with our parents when we were
young and with each other for the last few years. This
street, filled with arcades and cafés and tattoo parlours
was part of my home and it felt so painfully familiar
walking on this pavement. But it also felt distant now,
painted with a thin coat of longing for a different time.
When our parents were alive and Tripp didn't hate me and
there wasn't an evil government corporation after us.

As we walked past it, I stared into the window of the café I
worked in. All the outside furniture was stacked up inside,
ready to be put out again in about five hours. I'd done that
so many times - I'd been doing it just a week ago. In fact, I
was scheduled for a shift today. My boss and co-workers
probably guessed from the news that I wasn't going to be
making it in to work. If only they knew how very close I
was.

Over the train tracks we walked, and for once I didn't run
ahead out of an irrational fear that the barriers either side
would come down, trapping us so that the train could hit.
There would be no trains round here at this time.

I looked out ahead to where the rails disappeared from
view - we'd been using them to escape earlier this week,
and now we'd come crawling back in desperation.

We crossed the deserted road, passing a harmless druggie
who paid us no attention, and turned the corner. This was

the first time I'd seen the pub on the corner empty. We never went inside, it had a reputation as being the roughest pub in the town, but I'd never seen it without at least three half-drunk men sat outside, smoking and glaring at passersby.

We turned the corner onto our road, and I felt strangely reluctant to step onto it. It didn't feel quite right anymore. We both paused before taking any steps forward. Neither of us said anything, we just stood for a few seconds and looked at the familiar, filthy street. When we finally did start walking, I started to get more nervous. I wanted to reach out and grab Tripp's hand, but that didn't really seem like an option right now.

Don't worry, there hasn't been a murder on this road in at least three years. A little voice in my head tried to be reassuring. *Which means it's about due for another one.* Another, less reassuring voice argued back.

I looked nervously at Tripp, not truly afraid that he would do anything, but the second voice unnerved me.

It was true, not a single murder had taken place at the end of our road in about three years, and before that there had only been four in our lives, and only one face-stabbing. Good to be home.

I'd always felt a little nervous walking down here in the dark, but that was because of what happened to other people. I myself had never actually had a bad experience down here at night, and nor had any of my family.

The smell as we walked made me gag, and my empty stomach churned uncomfortably. At this end, next to the pub, was a deli-meat takeaway. It was right on the edge, so walking parallel to the back-half of it was unavoidable to get to our house.

Thirty feet away from home.

There was a load of green broken glass on the pavement, in a puddle of some kind of alcohol, all visible and shining under the bright yellow light of the lamp post above.

Twenty feet from home.

There was one of the worst-parked cars I'd ever seen round here. The back tyre was up on the pavement, the front at least a foot away. One of the worst, not *the* worst.

Ten feet from home.

Massive pile of dog-crap. Standard.

Next door's garden was overgrown and unkempt. We never spoke to our neighbour this side, she scared us. Always wearing entirely camo print, huge hoop earrings, and often stood outside smoking, next to her terrifyingly loud alsatian. Whenever we saw her she would glare at us and sometimes make rude comments about the way we looked. Most nights she blasted awful rap music from her stereo on full-volume, starting at about half-past eleven at night. My bedroom wall was the other side of her wall, so I often couldn't get to sleep at night because of her.

We stopped and stared at our house before opening the gate and walking up the path.

All over the front step outside the door, were cards, candles and bunches of flowers. I looked at them in astonishment, unaware of how popular we were.

Although, there were a hell of a lot of people around here that joined in with this kind of thing because it was trendy.

Tripp shoved open the gate and walked up the five-foot path towards the door.

"Sickening." He muttered as he waded through the small sea of pretend sympathy. I half agreed with him.

As he reached the door, I hoped and prayed that it would be unlocked. I saw no reason it shouldn't be - we locked it Monday night, but it was broken into the same night and I doubted that they would take the care to lock it again after they left.

The handle seemed to be stiff, but it opened. As Tripp went in, I stayed behind and had a quick look at all that had been laid out for us. There was an A4 photo of the two of us and our parents, several tacky, cliché-looking cards that said tacky, cliché things like 'gone but not forgotten' and 'gone from our sight but never from our hearts' that were meant well, but felt forced. What really got my attention though, was a bunch of iris flowers, wrapped in a rainbow flag. Taped onto it was a photo from the summer, of Tripp giving me a piggyback, both of us grinning like idiots. The photo was glued onto a piece of white card that had been signed by all of our friends and on the bottom, underneath the photo were the words 'come home soon' written in cursive.

I grimaced as I looked at it.

Staring at this shrine made me feel slightly sick and I thought of the lake again, when I was actually dead. That made me feel a bit faint and unstable, so I stopped looking at all the unnecessary stuff that had been left for us. As if it would actually change anything.

I quickly hopped over it all and tripped over the threshold as I did so, automatically putting out my hands out to catch myself and immediately regretting it. I smashed into the floor and bit my tongue to stop myself from yelling out in pain as at least two blisters burst and the rest flared up in pain.

The impact brought tears to my eyes but I held them back, annoyed at myself for the sheer volume of tears that I'd shed this week.

I got up, shaking my hands like it would make them less painful, then gently shut the door so as to not alert any neighbours that we were here.

I couldn't see Tripp anywhere, but I could hear activity coming from our parents bedroom.

I began to walk towards it, peering into the open living room door as I passed. Everything looked like it was still there, but a lot was out of place; the place had clearly been searched. I didn't go into the room, it felt too weird. I was an imposter in my own home.

I moved on and stood in the doorway of our parents room, looking down at Tripp. He was kneeling on the floor, with the big red rug flung off to one side. The floor safe that we weren't supposed to go near was exposed, and he was just opening the lid. The way he crouched over it, he reminded me of Gollum, staring down at the stash.

Chapter 38

"We shouldn't take that." I said, watching him and knowing it wouldn't make a difference. Not sure if I was right, or if I was just being difficult and ridiculous, but this felt so wrong, even if our parents were gone.
Tripp sighed in exasperation, stopping momentarily. "And why not?" He looked up, glaring and meeting my eyes for the first time since he yelled at me.
"It's not ours." I said weakly, realising how much I sounded like I was being awkward on purpose, but I hated the idea of taking this.
"It's our parents', and guess what? They're dead." His voice became icy and patronising. "This is our inheritance, we can do whatever the hell we want with it."
He looked back down and started picking up the wads of fifty-pound notes. I moved closer, eyeing them nervously. He was right, but it still felt like stealing.
"They never gave it to us." I muttered. This wasn't another attempt to stop him, it wasn't even really spoken to him.

Just a quiet declaration to myself, laced with regret and guilt.

"And now they're never gonna have the option." He counted the money and handed me some, unable to carry all of it himself.

I held it cautiously, as if it might burst into flames at any moment, counting how many wads I had.

Twenty.

Each of fifty notes if I remembered correctly.

"A hundred grand?" I asked, looking up at Tripp holding the other half in his arms.

"Should be." He said, checking through and counting how many bundles he had.

"So, the plan is that we just go to SCREB and offer them a load of cash in exchange for Zen?" I asked, not wanting to be pessimistic, but I was skeptical.

"That's about the size of it."

"Do you really think that's gonna work?" I tried to look into his eyes, but he avoided mine.

"I don't know, Iris." His voice got sharp and threatening again. "But have you got any other ideas?" He left the question hanging in the air, mocking me.

"No. Sorry." I said, defeated.

We both got up and I kicked the lid of the floor safe shut, then used my feet to move the rug back into place, just in case anything happened. In case anyone unwelcome turned up. Without speaking, we hurried upstairs to our bedrooms.

The way I walked into my room, you'd think I was walking into a morgue. It wasn't that cold, but I shivered as I entered.

I looked around at what had once been a perfect blend of nineties grunge, boho and modern that I'd made my sanctuary, but was now the after-effect of a break-in. My retro movie posters were half-detached, Buttercup and Westley hanging on by only one corner, while Magenta and Riff-Raff's faces were being covered by the falling half of their poster, leaving only Frank-N-Furter's mad gaze visible.

The fairy lights that had been strung from corner to corner had fallen down at one end and hung sadly like a dead vine. The powder-blue paint that coated three walls and had always seemed such a happy colour was now a symbol of my sorrow, and the fourth wall, covered in city-skyline wallpaper just made me want to run away from everything all over again.

The window that I'd left open had been shut, and most of the stuff on my desk and shelves was on the floor.

I stepped through the crime-scene looking carnage and dropped the money onto my bed. I wanted to look around more at my things; my photos, books, origami portfolio, but I needed to be quick. And it would start to hurt if I looked too closely at the things that weren't quite mine anymore.

As I walked to my wardrobe, miserably stepping over my fallen dream-catcher and broken-stringed violin, I saw my camera on the floor. Smashed to buggery. This sent a violent surge of fury through me; that camera was one of the best ones available and had been my sixteenth birthday present back in February, ready to start studying Photography this September. It had come with me every day to college and given me some of my best work.

The Lost Dragon

I felt like screaming when I saw it lying there in pieces,
but there was nothing I could do.

I swallowed, took a deep breath, and looked away from it,
vowing that amongst other things, SCREB would pay for
the destruction of this.

I opened up the wardrobe, pretending that the camera
wasn't there, and grabbed my backpack. It wasn't as big or
sturdy as the rucksack that I'd started with, but it would
do the job. I unzipped it and tipped it up to empty it, but
nothing came out. I looked inside and everything was
gone. It had been emptied for me. I let out a small, useless
cry of frustration. Not that I needed anything that had
been in there, but I so hated the thought of those people
going through all my stuff and emptying what wasn't
theirs to empty, taking what was mine.

I stood up and threw the backpack onto my bed, no longer
sad but angry. I stomped over and stuffed the money into
it, pausing briefly to listen when I heard a sound coming
from somewhere else in the house.

It was only the shower. I hadn't been planning on having
one, and had assumed that Tripp wasn't either, but then I
remembered it was about three in the morning so we
would have several hours to kill before being able to get
on a train.

Perhaps I would have time to look around after all. As if
this wasn't the room I knew most in the world, as if
looking around would make me find anything that I didn't
already know was here, even if it was heartlessly broken.

On the bed was still my dismantled mobile phone. I stared
at it in anger, both at it and at myself.

In an act of self-hatred, I picked up the phone and threw it
as hard as I possibly could across the room. It hit the wall

301

and fell to the floor in several more pieces than it had previously been.

I sat, bitterly staring at the spot where it had hit the blue wall. Just above that spot was a round mirror in a frame with the moon-cycle painted all around it. I hadn't seen my reflection in a couple of days. She didn't look as nice as usual. I slowly stood up and walked towards the mirror. I looked different.

Not only tired and uncared for, but like a different soul was living in my body. My bloodshot eyes were darker and stormier, sunken into their sockets like rotting fruit. My skin was paler but rough, with spots and little cuts and scabs all over. The bits of hair that had fallen out of the hair tie, while still pretty bright pink, had gone limp and dead.

I hated this. I tore myself away from the mirror, from seeing everything that had gone wrong with my face as if it were the most important thing to be worrying about. I pulled my boots off to give my feet some time to breath, and ran downstairs to grab some food. My running was a lost slower than usual, and my eyelids were a lot heavier, but I was hungry and this was an opportunity to stock up for travelling again, hopefully this time to keep.

As I gathered canned-goods, packets of dry food and bottles of water, I felt that same fear as I did just after the phone-call that changed everything. It was just a different type of urgent now; we had to get to Zen before she got seriously hurt, if it wasn't already too late, but we couldn't do that until the trains started.

I sat down at the table, eating a banana and took Gideon's bag off. I'd hardly thought about it, even though it had been strapped on me since I picked it up in the forest.

It felt sort of wrong to be carrying it around, like some gruesome hunting trophy, but if we ever found a way to get to Sandrine, I had to give it to her.

I put it on the table and undid the toggles to see what was inside.

The book was still there, but I didn't open it; along with a small hessian bag of coins that I didn't recognise; a reel of golden thread; a few different bottles of dried herbs; a small knife with a cover on the blade made of the same leathery material as the book; and a gemstone of some kind. It was about the size of a tennis ball, but a slightly misshapen oval. The surface was smooth and cold, bright indigo and it looked like inside, in the core, there was a clump of gold and pink bubbles. I stared at it in amazement, it was so beautiful and felt heavy in my hands, but seemed to hum with some kind of energy, like it was magical. I reminded myself that it actually probably *was* magical and inspected it all over.

Did it do anything? Was it just something to look pretty? I didn't recognise it as any of the stones I'd seen during the hours I used to spend looking at the stones in our auntie's jewellery shop, bored out of my mind while she and Mum talked. I got pretty good at identifying stones from that, but I couldn't name this one. It reminded me of blue opal, but that wasn't quite it.

"What's that?"

I whipped around at the sound of Tripp's voice, almost dropping the stone on the floor, but I managed to catch it mid-air and nearly had a heart attack in doing so.

Tripp stood, staring and frowning. His hair was wet and he was in a fresh, clean set of clothes, including his own pair of jeans. I hadn't realised how dirty his face had been until I was seeing it clean, he suddenly looked a lot less meth-addict-ish. The lightning bolt scar on his cheek was still there, still white and sharp. If anything, it looked deeper now.

His voice still sounded irritable, and his eyes were still angry, which made me feel sheepish when I answered. "I'm not sure. It was in Gideon's bag." I held it out for him to see. He quickly took it, not looking at me, and began inspecting it. He looked puzzled, and I guessed he was going through the same thought-process about almost recognising it that I had just gone through.

"I think it's magical." I said, taking a bite of my banana as I watched him ponder it. He didn't respond to me, just kept turning the stone over and over in his hands, looking at every last inch.

He handed it back to me without a word, before grabbing a banana for himself and disappearing back upstairs.

I sighed, wishing he didn't hate me and at the same time hating myself.

I carefully put all the items back onto the bag, being extra cautious with the stone as it suddenly seemed awfully fragile. I don't know if the stone would've smashed had I dropped it properly, but now that I knew it was there I definitely didn't want to find out.

I took the bag with me back upstairs, and dumped it onto my bed. I didn't take much notice of my surroundings this time, knowing that it would just upset me.

I went and had a shower, probably taking too long because I was actually able to wash my hair with shampoo and conditioner this time. It was so tangled and knotted, it must've taken at least thrice as long as usual. I lamented the small loss of pink dye from my hair and cursed James and Nina for the handcuffs that were still acting as irritating bracelets, with the little chains continually tickling my neck as I washed my hair and making me jump.

My hands were in an awful state and although the water seemed to be helping, I had to be really quick applying the shampoo to my head so that it didn't inflame the blisters. My knee stung where I'd been kicked as the hot water hit it, and I made myself look at it. I felt like throwing up when I saw it. The bruise was the deepest, darkest purple I'd ever seen on a human, with flecks of dark brown and green. There was a mysterious yellow substance leaking out of both the back and the front, in both the places that James had kicked me. It didn't come back when I washed it away though, so I counted that as a win.

I took a deep breath before bending down to get a closer look. The yellow pus had been coming out of deep cuts that I hadn't known were there, but were partially scabbed-over and had clearly been there for a few days. I tried not to panic, but it was hard, looking at the worst thing I'd ever seen on my body. The fact that the cuts had gone completely unnoticed unnerved me, but I blamed it on being so cold that my nerves hadn't fully realised. How the cuts got there in the first place made me uneasy too, James must've had a blade hidden in his shoe.

When I reluctantly got out, back into the cold, unforgiving bathroom I hastily grabbed some tea tree oil from the medicine cabinet and doused my knee in it. It stung slightly, but the good kind of sting. I hoped it was the good sting anyway. I then wrapped it in a wound-dressing pad of cotton and bandage, then looked at my reflection again.

I still looked kind of beaten up, but at least I was now clean. I now only looked about a quarter-dead, instead of half-dead. My eyes were a little less red, but still not bright or shiny, they'd become sad and dull.

I didn't look in the mirror for long, just took a can of deodorant, a pair of unopened toothbrushes and a tube of toothpaste, then went back to my room and put on a clean T-shirt and jeans. This time with an extra jumper and hoodie, so that I had five layers rather than three.

As I got dressed, now calmer and not filled with adrenaline, my eyelids got heavier and unwilling to stay open, my movements sluggish. I tried to look at the clock on my bedside table, but it lay on the floor with the face smashed and the hands stationary. I didn't feel angry about it anymore; maybe it was the sleep deprivation, or maybe I was starting to give up again, but I didn't care.

I put on my dark green coat this time, bidding the black one farewell in favour of the clean and dry one, and a different pair of boots. I stuffed a few extra clothing items into my bag and got a strong sense of déjà vu.

As a pathetic replacement for the sleeping bags that had been lost, I rolled up a blanket and held it together with the buckle-up strap holder that my yoga mat usually lived in, then threaded the holder through the straps on my backpack so that I wouldn't have to carry it and it just hung behind me.

We may not have been in such a hurry to get away from people coming after us, but I knew we should get out as soon as possible, lest any neighbours wake up and notice the activity going on in our house. I hadn't switched on my big ceiling light, just the small lamp on my desk, but my room was at the front of the house so if the guy across the road got up at half-four like usual, he'd be able to see that a light was on and we could be in trouble.

The last things I got before leaving were a new grey set of hat, scarf and gloves to replace the ones I'd lost. Where we were going, whatever the plan turned out to be, they already knew who I was, but I at least wanted to be able to keep my hair hidden from the public, as my most distinctive feature.

Finally I put on both my backpack and Gideon's bag, switched off my lamp and went downstairs, hoping that I hadn't drawn any attention to us.

Tripp was in the ransacked living room, dressed in his coat and boots and ready to go, checking through his own backpack to make sure he had everything. He'd had the same idea as me, and had a dark purple blanket tied up with rope hanging on his backpack straps. He didn't look at me as I came in.

He too was wearing a different pair of boots, but he still had on his navy blue duffle coat - he would never part with his Paddington coat.

I stared at him nervously, guilt crashing down on me all over again as I saw his stern expression softened with a single tear rolling down his cheek as he put a butternut squash into his bag. Zen loved butternut squash.

"I'm so sorry." I said, meaning it perhaps more than I ever had before. He was being torn apart worrying about Zen, not knowing if she was being hurt or tortured, or if she was even still alive. Apart from each other, our dragons were our best friends, and he'd raised her since she was an egg.

He looked at me with broken eyes, but didn't say anything. He didn't look enraged anymore, just sad.

Sadder than I'd ever seen him, almost ready to give up on everything.

He went back to his packing, but threw me something. I caught it with a catch that, if were in good moods, we both would've applauded. I looked down at what it was, and felt all other kinds of guilt and sorrow towards my brother. It was a jumbo-sized sandwich bag, stuffed to bursting with sandwiches, completely filled with cucumber, tomatoes and hummus.

"Thank you." I said, my voice sounding pitifully close to tears. I looked back up at him, astonished that he'd actually done this for me.

He didn't respond, didn't look at me, but he gave a very gentle nod, almost as if he was forgiving me. Almost.

He shouldn't, as much as I wanted him to, it wouldn't be right if he did. He'd have been saying that what I did was okay, and it definitely wasn't, so in a way I was glad that he didn't forgive me. I was also glad he'd calmed down though and didn't seem to want to kill me anymore.

I hung my head shamefully as I put the sandwiches into Gideon's bag strapped to my side. I hadn't put anything else in this bag, using it only to carry what was already in it, but they wouldn't fit into my backpack.

Tripp finished getting his possessions together and put on his own scarf and gloves.

As he walked towards the door, I noticed his limp was still bad and incredibly pronounced. I followed behind him and switched off the light as we left the room.

We stepped outside into the icy air, and I felt my stomach tighten with dread at being outside again. I worried that someone would see us and either A) Not recognise us, think we had been breaking in to the house and call the police to take us away or B) Recognise us and call the police to take us away. Neither option was good.

A group of drunks walked across the other side of the road, singing a wildly out of tune rendition of *Bad Romance*, but they were the only living beings around, and they paid no attention to us, so we were okay.

As I quietly shut the door and leapt over the pile of flowers and cards, much more successfully this time, I started shivering and my breaths became visible in the cold.

I followed Tripp down the path and onto the pavement, where we started walking towards the train station. I would've liked to stay in the house for longer, and I suspected that he would too, but we needed to be out of there before the street started waking up.

It was painful on my knee, but I walked a bit faster to catch up with Tripp, who was limping really badly now. The Lenimen leaves had done wonders for him to be walking two days after breaking his ankle, but they were clearly not a complete miracle-cure.

Without saying anything, I put his arm over my shoulders and took some of his weight. As much as I think he wanted to, he didn't object. In fact, he put more weight on me and his face eased up ever so slightly, reluctantly accepting that he couldn't do this on his own.

Chapter 39

The train station doors were shut and locked, and the
ticket machine was out of order, but the benches were
deserted and under shelter. It did nothing to warm us up,
but it gave us a place to wait out the time before the train
got here.
The tension was still there, but Tripp at least allowed me
to help him walk and sit down. Neither of us spoke as we
sat, alone and afraid, waiting in the dark.
I wanted to talk, but I didn't know what to say. Instead, we
just stared and waited. Stared at the street ahead of us that
hadn't had a murder in at least three years, at the
twenty-four hour newsagent at the end that we never went
in becuse the people in there hated children, and seemed
to count anyone below the age of twenty five as children.
It was strange seeing such a usually busy part of town so
empty. Not a single car went by on the road in front of us.
The only time I'd seen it this empty was almost a week

ago, when we were in this same place, now running away
for a dragon's life rather than our own.

I looked to my right at Tripp, to see that his eyes were
already shut and he'd fallen asleep sitting up. I felt like
doing the same, but I blinked several times and made
myself stay awake. He deserved a rest and I didn't want us
both to be unconscious.

I looked down at his left foot. It was twitching a little,
nowhere near as much as it usually did, but at least it
could now move.

Bored, hungry, and trying to distract myself from the cold
and the growing fear of the night, I took out a sandwich
and took a bite.

It was *so* good. It was just a normal sandwich, there was
nothing special about it, but I was so hungry and had
pretty much just been living on travelling food for a week.

As I ate, I kept blinking and adjusting my position, trying
to keep my brain working to avoid going to sleep. It
wasn't as easy as I would've liked, my eyes shut a couple of
times and had to mentally yell at myself to get them open
again.

As time went on, stopping myself from going to sleep got
both easier and harder. I got more and more tired, and just
sitting down in the cold meant that my body wanted to go
into shutdown mode, but every time I shut my eyes the
vision of Gideon's got clearer and clearer.

Filled with pain and sorrow, the light fading quickly.

I kept shaking my head, trying to think of anything else
but the picture wouldn't leave. I heard him trying to
breathe, gasping for air and telling us to get the book to
Sandrine.

Over and over again the scene played in my head, the feeling growing worse every time.

A man with a wife and children who believed he was alive had been killed and it was our fault.

No, not our fault. *My* fault.

I wanted to scream. I felt like my head was going to implode. Without fully deciding to do so, I suddenly sprang up onto my feet, unable to bear sitting in those thoughts any longer.

My fault.

I was breathing too quickly, my face was stinging. Maybe from the cold, maybe from tears.

I killed a man.

If I hadn't been so stupid he would still be alive and Zen would still be here and Tripp would be okay.

He's dead because of me.

I stumbled forward towards the road, hyperventilating as Gideon kept dying in my mind's eye. I felt the need to scream so badly, but somehow no sound would come out.

I keep screwing up.

I kept moving forwards with no goal in mind. With nothing in mind apart from the haunting memory that I couldn't escape.

Things would be better if I wasn't around.

I wasn't really in control of my own actions, I just felt myself moving towards the road without objection.

Tripp hates me.

I put my hands over my ears as I moved, trying to block out the voice in my head that wouldn't leave me alone. My voice.

It's my fault.

Far off in the distance, I heard the noise of a singular, solitary car in the distance. Moving closer. As I kept stumbling onwards, the sound of the car got nearer and the voice in my head got louder, the vision more and more real.

Tripp would be better off without me.

Yes, maybe the voice was right. So much of what had gone wrong was because of me, maybe it would be better if I just stopped being here. I got closer to the curb as the car engine got louder.

Gideon's dead because of me.

For a second I stared into nothingness as the car got nearer, wondering if I should keep walking. I wanted to go back to that feeling in the lake, when I was about to float away. Sad that everything was gone, but content that I wouldn't have to worry about things anymore. Happy that I wouldn't be a liability anymore.

It would be better if I were gone.

The car got closer and I saw headlights beginning to round the corner. It was now or never. If I stayed, I'd almost definitely mess up again, and someone had already died because of me. If I left, Tripp wouldn't have to look after me and he'd be able to carry on without the burden of my stupidity. Yes, this would be better for everyone in the long-run.

In a haze of dying eyes, screaming voices and pain all over, I took a step into the road.

No one else will die because of me.

The car got closer, it came around the corner at a speed that would've caused Tripp to swear about it if we were both witnessing it. Breathing quickly and not fully sure what was happening, I took another step as the car came at me and finally, I was able to scream.

My legs locked in place as instinct told me to run but intention made me stay in place.
Tripp won't have to worry about me anymore.
I braced for impact, but it never came.
The car swerved around me at the last second, knocking me over in a gust of wind as it rushed on by. The driver yelled something at me through the open window, but I didn't hear what.
I lay there in the road like a beetle that had just been stepped on, taking quick, short breaths while my heart ran a million miles-per-minute, staring up at where the stars would be seen, if there wasn't so much light pollution round here.
I blinked several times, replaying what had just happened, wondering if it was real or if this was a dream. I couldn't hear any cars anymore.
Every part of my body was shaking and jellified. Half of me wanted to get up and move away from this terrible spot, half wanted to stay here forever. All of me could not move. Against my will, I imagined what would've happened if the car hadn't swerved.
The thought made me scream and cry up to the stars, not caring if anyone heard me. Here, hearing screams and cries wouldn't set off alarm bells for anyone. They were practically a lullaby.
I screamed for Gideon, for Sandrine, for Zen, for Delta, and most of all for Tripp, like I'd been stabbed as horrifying images and memories span through my head

and made me feel sick. I didn't feel so cold now, but the shivering wouldn't stop.

Lying there, pathetic and paralysed, I once again saw the disturbing visions from the lake, but this time one stood out to me - Delta's eye, crying tears of gold.

The vision turned from a vision to a memory and I once again saw Delta sobbing over my dead body. I remembered how much he'd tried to bring me back, how heartbroken he seemed that I was gone. Seeing him like that hurt my chest, and I knew he'd be doing the same thing if he were here now. If the car hadn't swerved.

He didn't hurt himself and cry all over me so that I could throw it all away.

"I'm sorry, Delta." I whispered up to the sky, wondering if he would hear it. I'd let him down again now.

Another memory swam through my mind, back in the old office where we'd been held. The memory of a promise, not to die if I could help it. Would he have still meant it? After what I did?

Shivering and sobbing, I managed to sit myself up and held onto my head to stop the spinning.

I looked back behind me at Tripp, who was still fast asleep on the bench. We'd grown up hearing cars and screams during the night, I didn't expect him to wake up when he was so tired. If he'd had another hour or so of sleep, and if he wasn't mad at me, I think he would've woken, but he didn't and I decided that I wouldn't tell him about this.

I was ridiculous and stupid, he already knew that and I didn't need to prove it to him further.

Slowly, I crawled back to the pavement, letting out little cries of pain every time my hands touched the floor. I had gloves on but any amount of pressure on the acid burns hurt like hell.

I tried moving with fists, then with my hands turned sideways or on their back, but it didn't make any difference. My hands were ruined all over and I didn't have the strength to walk. My knee hurt too, every time I moved my right leg. I'd forgotten about how it had been oozing and suddenly gagged when I remembered, wondering if it would heal of it's own accord if I stopped putting pressure on it.

When I got to the curb, I sat up on it with my feet still on the road. I put my head between my knees and just sat there for a few minutes, trying to slow my breathing and stop my quivering. I clenched my eyes shut and tried to pretend I hadn't just done what I did.

Gideon's eyes flashed before me.

When the buzzing in my head finally stopped, I turned around again and started my way up the three steps to the station bench where Tripp slept, blissfully unaware of me.

I pulled myself up onto the bench slowly, like how you move when you're ill and don't have any energy and just want to lie down and sleep.

I layered both our blankets on top of each other and lay them across the two of us, gently leaning my head on Tripp's shoulder, being careful not to wake him as I wiped away my tears. It was no use, they kept coming back.

My back and shoulders hurt where I'd fallen on them and my knee and hands gently throbbed.

I shut my eyes again, hoping I could forget about everything for a couple of hours of sleep.

I absolutely could not forget about everything. The images still burned through my brain and the voices kept telling me that it was my fault, I doubted that would ever stop, but I managed to keep the one telling me to get rid of myself at bay. For Delta.

"What is wrong with you?" I whispered quietly, as I tried to cry myself to sleep.

Chapter 40

Finally, the doors of the train station opened and my eyes flicked wide awake after so much almost-sleep. They stung horrifically and my face felt wet, but in grave need of moisturiser at the same time. My head hurt, but not much physically. More like my mind hurt.

I kept my head down and looked out of the corner of my eye at the man opening the doors. He didn't pay us attention, probably assumed we were a pair of drugged-up homeless kids who made a habit of loitering anywhere that we could.

I waited a minute after the man disappeared back inside the station so that he didn't think we were too eager and insane, before rolling up blankets and replacing them in their respective holders. It took a lot of will power to actually remove the blankets, they were the only things making the cold even close to bearable.

I felt strange in my own skin as I began to move, like when I'd looked in the mirror at home. I was an imposter in my own body.

Still struggling to keep awake myself, I gently started shaking Tripp awake, trying to normalise things. He was unresponsive for about ten seconds, so deeply asleep, but he eventually started to stir. Shivering and rubbing his eyes, he sat up groggily and looked around.

"We can go in." I said, hoisting my backpack and helping him stand. It was still a bit dark, but the blackness of the sky was now dark blue; it would be fully light soon. Around us, the day was just beginning to come to life. A few cars passing in front of us that made me uneasy to look at, a couple of dog walkers and a very brave jogger getting out early, still so cold and darkish. The whole scene reminded me of one time at the beginning of summer, when our parents were away for a weekend so on the Saturday night we decided to pull an all-nighter, just for the hell of it. We built a blanket-nest in the living room and spent the whole night eating flapjacks, playing board games and watching movies. It was really fun through the night, but at around half past six on the Sunday morning, the lack of sleep was starting to hit us so we decided to go to the park on the seafront in an attempt to wake ourselves up.

I had never felt more tired than I did on that day. We'd never walked around town at that time either, when it was eerily empty and things were only just starting to get going. We ended up coming home after about five minutes of depressingly trying to have fun on the swings and went to sleep for several hours in our blanket-nest.

I felt more tired than that now, but this time I was unable to sleep, rather than reluctant.

While Tripp got his bearings, I stared at the spot where I lay and screamed, only about three hours ago.

Where I tried to remove myself from the equation.

I shuddered as I thought about how close I'd gotten, how convinced I was that it was the right thing to do.

Thinking about that and the wisp incident, it scared me how easily I got manipulated into self-destruction. What was worse was that the second time, there was no evil little spirit doing it, I convinced myself to do that all on my own. I'd done something terrible and unforgivable, and I would live with the irrepressible guilt for the rest of my life, but that shouldn't have meant me cutting my life short. There was still that tiny little nag though, that maybe Tripp would be better off if he didn't have to deal with me.

What was wrong with me?

Tripp was still half- asleep, and I didn't try to get him more conscious as we walked into the station, we both needed all the rest we could get and I didn't want to disturb him too much. Plus, in this state, he wasn't too pissed off with me.

I wrapped both the blankets around his shoulders like a king of some fictional, frozen land, and sat him on a seat inside. It wasn't much warmer in here, but at least it wasn't completely frozen. He avoided my gaze and studied the flyers across the room, still pretty much ignoring me. Regretfully, I left him to it and went to the ticket desk. Walking was harder than I expected while I was this exhausted. Everything felt not quite real and I was so unstable. If a strong gust of wind were to come past, I would go down.

The handcuffs felt heavy on me, dragging me down and irritating my burned skin.

The guy who'd opened the door was now behind the glass divider of the desk, slumped over and writing something on a form in front of him.

He ignored me for a few seconds. That wouldn't usually have bothered me, but when he finally acknowledged me, he did it by keeping his head down and staring up at me with just his eyes, raised an eyebrow as if he couldn't believe I'd dared to tarnish this train station with my presence, then sighed and looked up properly, glaring at me. He thought I was gutter scum.

"What time is the first train to Dawlish Warren, please?" I asked, trying to talk politely and not be what he expected of me. He stared at his computer and lazily clicked on a few things before turning back to me, still glaring.

I suddenly got a bolt of lightning fear through me as I realised he may not be glaring out of annoyance, it could be out of recognition. I dropped my head so that he couldn't see my face as well and hoped that the hat was enough. Theoretically I'd be okay, people thought that we were currently in Meaden so he shouldn't be looking out for us.

"Half-eight." He said, my heart thumped as he continued to look at me.

"Thank you, can I please have two singles?" I kept looking downwards and took my backpack off to retrieve some cash.

"Got a railcard?" He asked, more absent-minded now.

"Y- No." My brain wasn't fully functioning and I suddenly swerved my words and changed my answer, remembering that 1) I didn't have it with me and 2) If I did, handing it over would be suicidal, as it had my name and photo on it. I looked up a bit as I spoke, and was able to see the man look back to the computer but glare at me with an annoyed side-eye. I smiled nervously and waited.

"Thirteen-fifty." He said. I pulled one of the wads of cash out of my bag, cursing myself for not having anything smaller, even if it wasn't my fault, and put a singular fifty in the little dip below the glass divider. Removing it would've been hard with gloves alone, but it was embarrassing trying to get it with my pained, partially immobilised fingers as well.

The man looked at me aghast and suddenly his demeanor changed when he saw the money.

He was surprised and no longer judgemental, his posture straightened slightly and he started moving quicker. I just hoped that he didn't think I'd stolen the money, it didn't exactly make sense for someone who looked like me to have that much money just lying around in a backpack. He took my note and hastily got my change out from the till as the tickets printed. As he handed the money and tickets through the divider, he spoke to me as if I was a princess.

"Here you go Miss, have a lovely day."

I was a bit taken aback and couldn't help but smile a little.

"Thank you, you too." I said gleefully as I gathered everything up and put the money in my bag. As I turned and walked back to Tripp, I wondered if I should feel more pleased about the power I had briefly held, or insulted that he was only respectful to me when he saw my money. I decided to go with pleased, I didn't need any more sadness or insult to dwell on right now.

"Here you go." I handed Tripp a ticket as he stood up.

"Thanks." He said, a little less cold than he had been. Slowly, exhausted and in pain, we walked past the desk and out onto the platform. As we passed the ticket man he smiled and nodded at us.

It was cold on the platform, but there were walls of buildings on either side and a half-roof covering the top, so we were at least shielded from the wind. It was so absolutely deserted, it felt like a scene from a zombie-apocalypse movie. I'd been expecting to see commuters, but then remembered it was Sunday and wondered when people would start turning up.

"What time is it now?" I asked as we sat on a bench and leant against the wall behind.

"Seven." Tripp said, looking at his watch with a hint of exasperation. I felt bad constantly having to ask him for the time and cursed myself for forgetting to get a new watch after mine broke a few months ago.

"Thanks." I muttered. He looked away and stared along the track into the distance. He was clearly still shunning me, and the knot of guilt in my stomach just tightened as he kept his eyes away from me.

I looked down at my knee and wondered how concerned I should be. It didn't hurt right now while I was sitting down, but it felt like it was slightly swollen. Maybe that was just because of the bandage. I knew I should ask Tripp about it, he might be able to do something to make it better, but I couldn't face asking him for a favour right now. Besides, it had only been kicked. And maybe slightly cut. In two places. Very deep cuts. Nothing life threatening, I told myself, nothing worth getting worried about.

My eyelids got heavy again and tried to go down, but anytime my eyes were shut, I saw Gideon's. It wouldn't stop, the image was relentless and unforgiving, so I just had to sit there, continually trying to get some sleep but unable to keep my eyes shut for more than a second. The handcuffs kept echoing his final, desperate grip on my wrists.

After a little while people started arriving onto the platform, so I adjusted my hat to make sure my hair was fully covered, and pulled up the hood of my coat, keeping my head down so that no one could see my face.

Once our train finally arrived onto the platform, we went right to the back carriage where no one else was getting on. Like before, we got a table and sat opposite each other in the window seats. We both put our backpacks on the table, but I kept Gideon's bag over my shoulder, I really didn't want there to be any risk of it getting lost or separated from us. I leaned my head against the window and tried to shut my eyes again and get some rest, but it was no good. The haunting would not stop.

As the train began moving, I stared out the window and once again, said goodbye to the home I'd lived in my whole life and wondered what horrors lay ahead.

"Are you okay? You look terrible." Tripp broke the silence. His gaze was intense, and the scar on his cheek seemed to have grown. Smaller parts had gotten more visible, so it looked like his face was about to crack open. I stared at him, shocked that he'd actually spoken to me without me first saying something to him. Even more than that, he'd shown concern for me. He cared about me, and for a moment, didn't seem to hate me.

His face was still frowning and somewhat glaring at me, but his eyes were warm and worried. Not nearly as much as usual, but it was progress.

"Yeah, just...can't sleep." I said, trying not to let on that there was anything more. That I'd almost died again a few hours ago.

"How are your leg and ankle?" I asked, hoping that he wouldn't go any further with questioning me.

His eyes lingered on me for a second - he knew I wasn't telling the whole truth - then looked down at his injuries.

"Painful. But I put some burn cream on it last night so it's not as bad as it was." He said. There was still a tension between us, but the way he was talking, things felt almost back to normal. "Do you want some for your hands?" He asked, unzipping his backpack.

I didn't answer for a second, still in disbelief that he was being so nice to me. He handed me the half-full tube and I hastily removed my gloves.

"Thank you." I said as I stared down at my hands. They were red and covered in sore blisters and scabs, like I'd stuck them in a furnace. They got a lot more painful and sensitive without the gloves, but the cream was easy to get out of the tube. As I rubbed it in, the burning sensation got worse and I actually saw steam rise up from my flesh. I winced as I stared at it, but like when I plunged my hands into the water, the pain wore off quickly.

"I think there's something wrong with my knee." I said grimly, taking the chance while I had it, while he didn't seem to completely hate me. I put my gloves back on and handed Tripp the burn cream. He looked at me curiously and I continued. "There are cuts in the front and back, where James kicked me, I think he might've had a blade in his shoe." As I spoke I realised something I hadn't thought of before. "And...I think the blade might have had some kind of poison or venom on it. The whole knee is bruised and the cuts were oozing some kind of pus." I said quickly. Tripp sat forward, looking really worried now. Seeing my brother who was going to be a doctor look so uneasy made me feel anxious about it again, having been able to talk myself into not worrying about it.

"Does it hurt?" He asked.

I shook my head. "Not at the moment, but it was hurting a lot when you were asleep, while I was-" I caught myself, remembering how much pain I'd been in as I crawled back to the pavement. "-trying to get to sleep too. I think the cold was getting to it a lot. It aches when I walk, and I think it's quite swollen today."

Tripp nodded, listening intently. He was worried about me and still annoyed with me, but as I spoke I saw the excitement in his eyes that he got when hearing about weird or gruesome medical stories. The excitement that was the reason he wanted to be a doctor.

"It could just be the fact that it was an untreated wound, the blade might not have had anything on it. If you've kept moving on it, it hasn't really had a chance to rest so it'll do weird stuff." I could tell his mind was racing with infections and disease. In other circumstances I'd have laughed at his childlike glee, but this wasn't really the time.

"I put some tea tree oil on it and a bandage at the house." I said, hoping that I'd done the right thing.

"Good." Tripp nodded again, then looked around. "Someone might come in here, but I'll have a look later."

Chapter 41

The next forty or so minutes passed like the time on the
bench. With Tripp managing to sleep and me limply
trying to, but my mind simply would not allow it.
I felt like crying but I had no tears left, I felt like being
sick but nothing would come up, I felt like screaming
again but this really wasn't the place.
I wondered what Delta was up to. I hoped he was safe,
staying out of the way and hadn't seen what I did outside
the station. It was highly unlikely, but I wouldn't have
been at all surprised if he spent the night flying high
above me and Tripp, watching and trying to make sure we
were okay.
When the train came to a stop, I jolted upright as I
realised we were at Dawlish Warren. Again, no one had
come through to check the tickets that I had paid for.
I was exhausted, but I gave Tripp a gentle kick on his
right foot under the table to get him up.

As quick as we could, we both stood and put our backpacks on, before we hopped off just before the doors shut behind us.

We shared a nervous glance, knowing that we were about to walk into the belly of the beast.

We kept our heads down and our hoods up as we left the station, avoiding eye contact with anyone.

As we walked, I looked out to the beach. A couple of months ago, our parents had taken us to this beach to observe a dead whale who'd washed up. It was both interesting and sad, and had the car-crash quality; didn't want to look but couldn't look away.

What I hated was how casual about it our parents had been, they treated it like a normal day out. They were enthusiastic about it, encouraging us to take photos because it was 'a great learning opportunity', even though it was cordoned off and we couldn't get closer than about eight feet.

Tripp and I walked on in silence, towards the building that we'd been made to visit several times in the last few years.

A walk that we knew well, that always felt like walking towards a funeral. Tripp leaned on me as we walked, but as we got closer, he got colder and more distant.

We both knew that it was because of me that we had to be coming here.

I stared down in shame, thinking about everything that had happened over the past week and sighing in resignation. If not for Zen, I'd be ready to give up again, but she needed help. We *had* to get to her.

Approaching the site of the SCREB base brought back awful memories and sent shivers and chills down my spine. Despite everything, Tripp and I clung to each other tightly, like a pair of magnets.

The site was located along the empty coastline, about fifty feet away from the main beach, but surrounded by trees, so it was on a terrain that was a peculiar cross between soil and sand. I always thought it was an odd place for something like this, but there were no houses or other buildings around, and the sea held some seriously weird creatures, so maybe it was the perfect place.

The wind whipped harder and the atmosphere changed as we got closer and closer. You could practically taste the pain and suffering.

Not to mention the death.

The sky and sea were ominous greys and the will to walk got more and more faint.

The building itself - The Imposter - didn't look like anything special, just a huge brown-brick building that looked like a prison, with evenly spaced windows and a glass door that had a silver letter sign above it.

Ama and Co. Pharmaceuticals

What a sham. What an insult. This building was masquerading as a place where medicines were made, where healing was supposed to be the driving force, but below lurked a living hell.

The walls were tall and beige, the cobblestone courtyard was suspiciously clean, and nothing had any personality.

I looked up at the grey sky, and the few birds that were in the air were making an active effort to fly around the building.

The wiry fence surrounding the courtyard was high and had barbed wire topping it. As we got closer and closer, and our steps got smaller and smaller, my heart raced and my stomach turned and I felt a buzzing in my ears. The silence was eerie, and the smell was a sickening mix of sterile and industrial.

I was wide awake now, as if I'd taken fifteen shots of espresso. Or had enough sleep.

Sat on one of the benches outside was a guard wearing army fatigue style clothes. He held a huge gun down by his side carelessly as he smoked a cigarette, staring up at nothing in particular.

'Twas James.

As we both caught sight of him and realised who it was, we veered off to the right so that we would get out of his line of vision.

He was clearly bored and putting in no effort, but if he saw us, we were dead. I suspected he, of all people, had been placed on duty because they knew we were coming.

I looked at Tripp in panic, wondering what the hell we should do now. There was no way we'd be able to get as far as the door unnoticed, and that gun was huge.

Tripp looked around, then gestured with his head at a massive tree growing outside the fence, about twenty feet away from us. It had loads of twisty, climbable branches, some of which reached out over the fence, the perfect place to drop down onto the courtyard. Strangely enough, it still had lush green leaves. I looked around, and realised that all of the ones surrounding the outside were still in full bloom, as if it were the middle of summer.

I nodded and together we started towards the tree. We moved quietly and carefully, never taking our eyes off James.

I was both astonished and amused by how little he was paying attention, in this top-secret government building, and how much trust and faith had been placed in him. I knew his parents were very high up here, which was the only reason he was allowed to do anything, but clearly his heart was more in the secret missions rather than the sitting and waiting around. It was good for us though, it meant that we could get away with sneaking where probably no one else would let us.

The tree should've been easy to climb, with all the branches it had, but our tired bodies, Tripp's bad leg and ankle combined with my bad knee and hands made it quite an ordeal, but we helped each other and managed to make it to branches that we could sit on. It only took us about three times longer than it normally would've.

We crouched, hidden in amongst all the bright leaves, looking out between the branches at James. He flicked his cigarette and looked at his watch, then sighed and lay down on his back, still smoking and staring up at the clouds.

"We should put all the money together, then we can just hand it over in one." Tripp said, trying not to show the fear in his voice. I looked up at him to see that he was shivering and he'd gone all small and afraid again, like in the bathroom stall at the pub.

I swallowed nervously and unzipped my backpack. My change from the train tickets was tucked away in the inside pocket, I gathered it up and handed it to Tripp before digging out the bundles of fifties. With quivering hands, we counted them up again to make sure none were missing, and put them all in Tripp's backpack. He zipped it shut and put it back on his back slowly, trying not to get psyched out.

A sense of dread hung in the tree like a cloud. There was nothing left to do, no more ways to procrastinate or put it off any longer. We had to go in.

"Sorry I yelled at you." Tripp said. He sounded like a child again, scared and anxious. I felt so bad and remorseful seeing him so upset and afraid, knowing it was my fault.

"Sorry I fucked up." I said weakly. There was nothing I could do to change what I'd done, and the shame of it felt like it was choking me every time I thought about it.

Tripp smiled sadly, sadder than I'd ever seen, and hugged me. He held onto me tightly, like it might be the very last time he got to. I held on tightly too and never wanted to let go, so happy that he was willing to hug me again, but so sad about what it symbolised.

He let go and quickly wiped his eyes, before turning around so begin the climb across the branch and into enemy lines.

Chapter 42

While I didn't know why they were still there in the dead of winter, I was so glad to have the leaves shielding us from the wind and unwanted eyes.

We moved slowly across the branch, keeping watch on James as he continued to lie down on his bench and stare up at the sky.

He didn't seem so far away anymore.

The fear inside me grew as I realised just how dangerously close he was - his bench was about ten feet from where we would drop to the ground.

We were gonna have to be impossibly quiet and careful.

Now, I fully realised; this was suicidal.

Tripp stopped just before he would've emerged from the leaves and I came to a halt behind him.

He took a few deep breaths and I felt a chill through to my bones.

He was lopsided, all his weight on the right leg with his left drooping limply behind him on the branch. I think the nerves were getting to him too much, his foot and ankle started to go into spasm.

He started to move forward again, but the shaking of his leg got worse. The quivering spread to all his limbs, more like a nervous tick than a result of wounds now, making him unstable.

"Tripp?" I moved forward and put a hand on his back to try and stabilise him. He took a few more deep breaths, shivering like mad, and reached out an arm to keep going. His fatal mistake.

His hand was so wobbly, it slipped and completely threw off his balance. He tried to grab onto the branch and I tried to grab onto him, but it was no use. He went crashing down through the leaves with a shriek and fell to the ground. I leaped forward ready to go down after him, but my limbs locked as I heard James yell something nondescript. There came the sound of the cocking of a gun and footsteps towards Tripp. My protect-Tripp-instincts kicked in and overrode the fear that kept me paralysed, and I quickly crawled right to the end of the branch, about to drop down.

"Where's your sister?" James asked, not yelling anymore, but still loud and commanding.

I braced myself to make my entrance.

"She's not here!" Tripp cried. I had begun to throw myself down but managed to stop my momentum and pause just as he said that.

"Really?" James sounded skeptical. I peered through the branches to see him take another step towards Tripp. He looked up into the tree and I backed away a little, so he didn't see me. Just looked back to Tripp and pointed the gun at him. Tripp was sprawled out on the ground where he fell, shaking and and holding his hands up in fear.

"No, we got separated." He said. "And if she *was* here," His voice got louder and I think anyone - literally *anyone* - who wasn't James would've twigged what he was doing. "I'd tell her to *stay away.*"

My ears pricked up and I stared down, blood pumping and heart racing.

"Why's that?" James asked suspiciously.

"B-because there would be no use in the both of us being stuck here!" Tripp spluttered out. "At least if...if she was out, maybe- maybe she could get help from the...the outside." He finished, the nervous stutter creeping back in.

I sat, holding my breath so that I didn't make a sound. Was he serious? Did he really mean that? After what I'd done, he was telling me to run away and leave him here? Maybe he was right though. If we were both trapped here, we'd have little to no hope of finding Zen and getting out, and Delta would have no idea what had happened to us. If I got away and regrouped with Delta, there was a slim chance I could do something.

Since Tripp was usually the brains behind our operations, I listened to him. I didn't like it, but I could hear in his voice that he meant what he said. It was quivering and weak, but definite. He wanted me on the outside.

There were a few seconds of silence where I swallowed, James tried to calculate if Tripp was up to something in saying that, and Tripp waited to see if I would heed his words.

"And why have you come?" James asked, as if he didn't already know.

I'm fairly sure I heard Tripp's heartbeat hammering away and threatening to go into cardiac arrest as he spoke.

"I-I have a load of money. I...I want my...my dragon back." He sounded so small and afraid, so desperate and hurt. As he spoke, it was clear that he realised how ridiculous the request was. He was one of the company's most-wanted, he'd just waltzed on in and was asking to take one of the rarest animals they'd been able to get their hands on so that he could disappear with her. Of course it wasn't going to happen. The idea was laughable.

Literally, it turned out, James started laughing slightly maniacally when Tripp said it. I shrank down in the shame of how it sounded, neither of us had thought it would sound so ridiculous before.

"Fuck me, do you know the pay rise I'm gonna get when I bring you in?" James said euphorically. He walked towards Tripp, still pointing the gun at him, as Tripp hastily fiddled with something in his bag, but I couldn't see what.

A balloon of panic inflated inside me as somehow, only now, the gravity and reality of the situation hit me.

Tripp, my twin brother, Tristan, was being held at gunpoint and made to go into the building filled with the people who most wanted him dead.

I wanted to scream, or jump down and punch James before grabbing his gun and shooting him in the face, but I was held in place by fear and Tripp's words. He wanted me- *needed* me to stay and go in from the outside. I had to help him and this was probably the only way I'd be able to.

No more words were spoken, but through my obscured view I could make out Tripp being forced to stand and wincing as he put weight on his left leg. The enormous gun was pressed into his back and he was marched towards the building.

He looked up at me as he walked away, with more fear in his eyes than I had ever seen in a living creature.

We made eye contact for a microsecond but in that time, he used his eyes to confirm what he'd said - he told me to go. To get Delta and figure out a way to get him and Zen out.

Then just like that, he was gone. He was the property of our greatest enemies and walking straight into a terrible fate.

I sat in shock over what had just happened. Finally, I took a breath and tried to process what I just witnessed.

I was alone.

My brother was gone.

SO WHAT THE HELL HAPPENS NOW?

Chapter 43

My train journey back home was uneventful, just me
keeping my hat on, my hood up and - somehow - my head
from exploding.
The whole way I felt like curling up into a ball and crying
myself to death, I had to work hard to breathe evenly and
not have a panic attack.
No one seemed to recognise me. No one seemed to care
about the girl in the corner who was just on the brink of
having a mental breakdown.
I tried not to let my thoughts spiral out of control, but it
was almost impossible. Tripp was gone. Another item on
the list of terrible things that were my fault.
I stared down at my scorched wrist, at his watch that he'd
dropped on the ground for me while he was fumbling in
his bag, along with a single wad of fifties, that James -
bless his poor, simple mind - hadn't noticed..

Once I got to Paignton station, I rushed off the platform and ran back home, down the filthy, questionably-smelling street.

I had a half-clear plan in my head, amongst the panicking and screaming tiny Irises that were already having mental breakdowns.

I would go into the house, get more medical supplies and matches and socks, and anything else I might need, then sleep as much as I could make myself, to get my energy back. Then tonight I would call Delta back.

We'd go back to the building and get a good look in order to figure out a plan to get our brother and sister out.

Yes, that would work.

TRIPP'S GONE!

I fought to keep myself from going into a meltdown. I could get to that once I was inside.

I had to be careful as I approached home - if anyone saw me entering, even if they didn't know who I was, I would be going straight into the house of the family who died/mysteriously disappeared. That was sure to raise alarm bells.

I slowed down and looked around, but there was no one outside. As quickly and quietly as I could, I leaped over the shrine without stopping to examine anything, and got into the house.

I didn't like the fact that the door was being left unlocked. Next time I left I wouldn't be in such a hurry, so I'd dig up the spare key in it's plastic tub from under the bush and lock it.

As soon as I was in, I threw my backpack off, threw myself onto the settee, and threw my screams and sobs into a cushion. I knew I had to be quiet; the walls between neighbours were not thick and I couldn't have anyone know I was here.

I had to get up when I heard the phone ring in the kitchen. I knew I should ignore it, answering it would be an absolute confirmation that one of the missing kids was here, but I was drawn to it. I felt compelled to answer. Weak and trembling, I got up and went to the other end of the house. My knee was in agony and made me walk with a limp, but I got to the kitchen and leaned on the countertop while I looked at the ringing phone. It was literally calling to me.

I told myself I was being stupid, but I reached out a shaking and aching hand to answer.

"H-hello?" I asked quietly, regretting my decision to answer. Maybe if I hung up now, they wouldn't know it was me.

I was about to put it back down and flee, but the voice that spoke threw a rush of relief over me.

It was Tripp.

He spoke three simple sentences, quickly and urgently, before the line went dead.

"This phone call is being traced and they're coming for you. Get *far* away. Love you."

Thank Yous

Thank you so much to Minnie and Rosie, for the Barbie game that inspired SCREB; to Tabby, who gave me the book about mythical creatures that helped me for this book and the ones still to be written; to Hannah, who read the story before anyone else and gave me medical advice; to Issy, who introduced me to Riptide and helped me get into writing; to Bernie, who gave me the guitar after which Zen was named; to Uncle John, who gave me the wisest advice of all, "just don't make it shit."; to Nicholas, who didn't really believe in my plan, which just made me more determined; to Lottie, who supported me and got excited to read this which made me excited to write it, and is just lovely in general; to Sarah, who encouraged me while teaching me how to drive and said "I could be teaching the next JK Rowling"; to Cressida Cowell, who made me fall in love with dragons; to Rick Riordan, who made fall in love with books; to Connie Glynn, who encouraged me so much without even knowing it; to Fluffy, Jareth and Splodge, on whom Zen and Delta's personalities were based.

To Grandma and Grandad, who believe in me blindly; to Granny, who I know would've been one of the most excited people to read this.

To my dear readers, whom I so hope will like my story.

Most of all, to Mum and Dad, who raised me, homeschooled me, taught me how to swear, put up with me being stubborn and refusing to learn to read when I was a kid, a billion other things, and let me drop out of college to become a writer. Even when it seemed very much like my life was going nowhere. I love you.

About the Author

Gracie Carter was born & raised in Devon and home educated with her three sisters for almost all of her young life. She fell in love with books at the age of 9 after listening to the *Percy Jackson and the Olypmians* audio books, though the idea of actually writing only came about at around age 15.

The Lost Dragon is her first published book.

Printed in Great Britain
by Amazon